"There's no exi

In answer, Kessel's eye
communicate his unde ... of
having a tongue.

Annja studied the only thing in the room: a table with a book on it. "Somewhere here there's got to be a clue how we're supposed to get out of this place. I mean, we could take the crawl space and go backward through the maze—"

She heard a rumble and a cloud of dust poured into the room. The crawl space had caved in. Annja sighed. "All right, the only way out of here is to figure out a way forward."

There seemed nothing special about the table. And as far as she could tell, the book was a hardcover edition of the King James Bible. Overhead, a single light burned in the ceiling. It didn't appear as if some type of guillotine would drop on them if she picked the book up.

Before Annja could stop him, Kessel flipped open the cover. Nothing happened. But there was nothing written on the pages, either.

Annja tried to pick the book up, but it didn't budge. Flipping through it where it was, she found a small button at the back. Annja glanced at Kessel. "What do you think?"

He shook his head.

But Annja's finger was poised over it. "What have we got to lose?"

She pressed the button.

The lights went out, plunging the room into darkness. Annja heard a sudden movement and a grunt.

"Kessel?"

And then there was nothing but silence.

Titles in this series:

Destiny
Solomon's Jar
The Spider Stone
The Chosen
Forbidden City
The Lost Scrolls
God of Thunder
Secret of the Slaves
Warrior Spirit
Serpent's Kiss
Provenance
The Soul Stealer
Gabriel's Horn
The Golden Elephant
Swordsman's Legacy
Polar Quest
Eternal Journey
Sacrifice
Seeker's Curse
Footprints
Paradox
The Spirit Banner
Sacred Ground
The Bone Conjurer
Tribal Ways
The Dragon's Mark
Phantom Prospect
Restless Soul
False Horizon
The Other Crowd
Tear of the Gods
The Oracle's Message
Cradle of Solitude
Labyrinth

LABYRINTH

TORONTO • NEW YORK • LONDON
AMSTERDAM • PARIS • SYDNEY • HAMBURG
STOCKHOLM • ATHENS • TOKYO • MILAN
MADRID • WARSAW • BUDAPEST • AUCKLAND

If you purchased this book without a cover you should be aware that this book is stolen property. It was reported as "unsold and destroyed" to the publisher, and neither the author nor the publisher has received any payment for this "stripped book."

Recycling programs
for this product may
not exist in your area.

First edition January 2012

ISBN-13: 978-0-373-62154-5

LABYRINTH

Special thanks and acknowledgment to
Jon Merz for his contribution to this work.

Copyright © 2012 by Worldwide Library

All rights reserved. Except for use in any review, the reproduction or utilization of this work in whole or in part in any form by any electronic, mechanical or other means, now known or hereafter invented, including xerography, photocopying and recording, or in any information storage or retrieval system, is forbidden without the written permission of the publisher, Worldwide Library, 225 Duncan Mill Road, Don Mills, Ontario, Canada M3B 3K9.

This is a work of fiction. Names, characters, places and incidents are either the product of the author's imagination or are used fictitiously, and any resemblance to actual persons, living or dead, business establishments, events or locales is entirely coincidental.

® and TM are trademarks of Harlequin Enterprises Limited. Trademarks indicated with ® are registered in the United States Patent and Trademark Office, the Canadian Trade Marks Office and in other countries.

Printed in U.S.A.

THE LEGEND

...THE ENGLISH COMMANDER TOOK JOAN'S SWORD AND RAISED IT HIGH.

The broadsword, plain and unadorned, gleamed in the firelight. He put the tip against the ground and his foot at the center of the blade. The broadsword shattered, fragments falling into the mud. The crowd surged forward, peasant and soldier, and snatched the shards from the trampled mud. The commander tossed the hilt deep into the crowd.

Smoke almost obscured Joan, but she continued praying till the end, until finally the flames climbed her body and she sagged against the restraints.

Joan of Arc died that fateful day in France, but her legend and sword are reborn....

1

There's something about the fall, Annja Creed thought as she sat on the stoop of her building, watching leaves skitter across the pavement of the basketball courts on the other side of the street. A brilliant crystal-blue sky illuminated the day, and she breathed in the crisp air, filling her lungs and letting go a sigh. It felt good to be back home after months on the go.

I don't do this nearly enough, she thought. Chasing relics across the globe, fighting off the rogues and ne'er-do-wells that seemed to be reaching epidemic proportions… She nodded to herself after a sip of her mocha latte.

I need more downtime.

And that was the truth. As a breeze slinked its way under the T-shirt she wore with her jeans, Annja recognized that she actually hadn't stopped in a very long time.

The sword that only she could use—that of Joan of

Arc—had opened her life to so much, she barely had time to appreciate any of it. The bad, the good and the bizarre.

But at the moment, all she wanted to do was watch the rest of the world go by, sip her latte and give thanks for such a gorgeous autumn day.

Maybe I'll take a nap later. She smiled. A week's vacation and absolutely nothing scheduled.

There was that new exhibit at the MOMA she could take in. And after that, maybe some well-deserved bookstore browsing in the Village.

"Annja Creed?"

She frowned and turned to study the man who'd addressed her. He was well built, in his mid-thirties and had about two days' worth of growth on his face. But he didn't look all that bad, she decided.

"Yes."

He smiled. "I was wondering if we could talk for a moment?"

Annja's frown deepened. Despite his disarming manner, she sensed something dark in him. "Well, since you asked so nicely..."

He sat on the step below hers. He was careful, making sure she noticed that he was giving her the strategic advantage of the higher ground on the stoop. But why?

She took another sip of her mocha latte, but it didn't give her the same sense of soothing calm it had before.

"Damn."

He looked at her. "Something wrong?"

"I think it's entirely possible you just ruined my latte."

He raised a shoulder. "I apologize for intruding. It did indeed look as though you were having a moment."

"A moment?"

"Relaxing in this lovely weather."

It wasn't quite cool enough for a jacket, yet the man seated below her wore a navy windbreaker. There was something about him that seemed familiar. Not the man himself, but rather his manner.

Military?

Government spook?

Or just one of the countless enemies she'd come across during her travels?

"So, what can I do for you, Mr.…?"

He held out his hand. "Jackson. Mike Jackson."

"Mr. Jackson." Annja nodded. "Okay. So what's up? And how did you know where to find me?"

The smile he flashed told her that he knew plenty about her already. "It wasn't that difficult. I don't really think anyone's privacy is assured these days. Do you?"

"I do my damnedest to try," Annja said. "But apparently I'm not having all that much luck."

"If it's any consolation, you were tougher to run down than some of the other people I've been tasked with finding."

"And why would you be tasked with finding me, Jackson?"

"My client wishes to speak with you."

"Client."

He nodded, glancing around the neighborhood.

"Skip tracer?"

"I'm not a private investigator, if that's what you're asking."

Annja considered the latte again, giving it one final chance to woo her back. *Forget it.* "You're an information broker. Hired to get what clients need."

"That's more accurate."

"And who wanted you to find me?"

Jackson glanced at her. "The same people who would now like to have a word with you."

"They can make an appointment if it's that important. I'm on vacation, Jackson. If they want a meeting next week, then I'll be happy to talk to them. Until then, I'm not doing anything unless I distinctly feel like it."

Jackson took a deep breath through his nose. "Yeah, see, that's going to be sort of a problem."

"Not my problem," Annja said. "I don't need to see anyone."

"The truth of the matter is, they don't have all that much time to wait for you, Miss Creed. They're in something of a hurry."

"Look, Jackson—Mike, right?—I don't go a long way on passive-aggressive behavior. And I don't like being bullied, either."

Jackson seemed momentarily taken aback, but then cracked a grin. "If you don't agree to come with me, the people I work for are going to kill someone."

"Who?"

"Reginald Fairclough."

Annja shrugged. "Don't know him."

"But he apparently knows you. He's made his cooperation with my clients conditional on meeting with you."

"And where is he? In Manhattan?"

"Western Massachusetts."

Annja looked closely at Jackson. "Did you just hear me say not a minute ago that I am on vacation?"

"I did hear that, yes."

Annja stood. "I think this meeting is now at an end,

Mr. Jackson. When I come back down, I don't want to see you on my stoop or I'm going to get angry." She leaned over him. "I'm not sure how much you know about me, but you don't want to see me get angry."

Jackson stared at her. Annja finally turned and walked inside, taking the stairs up to her loft. She dumped the remains of the latte in the sink and let the faucet run for a few seconds to wash it down the drain.

Western Massachusetts. She shook her head. Like that was going to happen anytime soon.

"Miss Creed."

Annja turned. Jackson stood in her living room, with two other men behind him. If Jackson had a slight military bearing, Annja's instincts told her these two were total danger.

"I thought I told you I don't like being bullied."

Jackson nodded over his shoulder. "I apologize, but my clients are quite insistent."

One of the men stepped out from behind Jackson. "My name is Scott Greene. Have you ever heard of me?"

There was something familiar about that name. Annja racked her memory and then the face clicked. Greene was an environmentalist. But on the lunatic fringe.

Wonderful, she thought. What did he want with her?

"You're a militant environmentalist," Annja said. "You here to police my apartment and tell me how I'm destroying the planet?"

Greene sniffed. "I could spend hours yelling at you for using those crummy old-fashioned lightbulbs instead of CFLs."

Annja nodded. "Yeah, I haven't had much time lately to reduce my carbon footprint. Speaking of which, if you don't leave my place immediately, I'm giving serious thought to reducing yours—to nothing."

Greene didn't move. "Hear me out."

"I don't want to talk to you, Greene. This is me giving you one last chance to get the hell out of my place."

Greene looked at the third, yet unnamed man and nodded. The guy took out a silenced pistol and leveled it on Jackson's right temple. As Jackson's mouth dropped open, Greene said to Annja, "Cooperate, or I can have my associate blow a nice hole in the side of the good Mr. Jackson there."

Annja shrugged. "He works for you. I just met him. I don't care if you kill him or not."

Jackson's eyes bulged but he didn't move a muscle.

Greene smirked. "Ah, nice try, Annja. But we've done some research on you. And I know for a fact that seeing an innocent man killed—in your apartment, no less—would drive you insane."

Annja's heartbeat raced. She could draw the sword and be done with these three idiots before they could even react. She wondered how the cops would view it. Could she argue home invasion? That she'd felt threatened? They did have a silenced pistol, after all. And there were three of them.

But what if they didn't believe her?

Annja leaned against the sink. "Jackson already told me something about a Reginald Fairclough. I don't know the name."

"He's an antique book dealer. Quite a famous one," Greene said. "His collection of works is without peer."

"So, what's he want with me?"

Greene shook his head. "Old Reggie has something

I want—quite badly—and in order to retrieve it, I must first get you to his house. He wants to talk with you."

"About what?"

Greene looked pained. "I don't know."

Annja shrugged. "Listen, I can't help you. I'm dead tired. You tell Reggie to call me. That's about the best I'm going to be able to do for you."

"That's not good enough, Annja."

Before Annja could react, she heard the small pop, and Jackson crumpled to the floor beside her love seat.

Greene hadn't even hesitated. And Jackson was dead.

Annja watched a thin trail of smoke issue from the end of the suppressor on the pistol Greene had whipped out from his holster, beating his colleague to the punch.

"I think it was a good idea that you see how very serious I am about this, Annja. I don't like being told I can't do something."

"Apparently," she said.

"You'll come with us now," Greene said. "Otherwise I'll have my associate here shoot you."

"And how would that help you with Fairclough?"

Greene smirked. "I'd find another way. I always do."

And somehow Annja didn't doubt that.

2

The body of Jackson sprawled on her floor made Annja acutely aware of her predicament. Greene didn't need to shoot Annja, despite his threat to do just that. He'd already placed Annja in one hell of a pickle. How was she going to explain the corpse in her home?

The pair could leave her right now and all she'd be able to tell the police was that Greene had been here. But would they believe it?

Greene gave her a moment and then cleared his throat. "I take it you've run through all the alternatives before you?"

Annja glanced at him. "You didn't give me very many to choose from."

"Why would I? I need you, Annja." Greene scratched his goatee. "The sooner we're out of here, the better."

Annja shook her head. "We can't just leave Jackson. Eventually, he'll start to decompose and the smell will bring the cops."

Greene shrugged. "Don't worry so much, Annja. I've got that handled. I'm not a complete monster."

"I think I'll wait before I make up my own mind on that one," Annja said.

Greene's associate stepped up and produced what looked like a large garbage bag. He unrolled it and spread it around Jackson's body. Annja looked up at Greene.

"You knew this was going to happen."

Greene shrugged. "I believe in planning ahead. I wasn't sure how receptive you'd be to my request. Jackson was pretty much obsolete as soon as he agreed to track you down for us."

The other man rolled Jackson into the bag and then zipped it up.

"I'm amazed you're using a plastic bag for that. Doesn't that go against everything you stand for?"

"It's recycled plastic," Greene said. "And besides, it contains the effluence better than cloth."

Annja cocked an eyebrow. "You've done this before, I take it."

He laughed. "Many times. Where other environmentalists like to preach wholesome universe nonsense, I prefer to act. I'm not about to sit idly by and watch the planet ravaged by politicians and their corporate masters. Not a chance. I'll remove whatever threats are dangerous to Mother Earth."

"Results oriented," Annja said.

"Results, yes. I firebombed a cosmetics factory that had been testing its products on animals and flushing toxic waste into the drinking supply of a small village in Cambodia. And when that building was reduced to ashes, I went after—and got—the people who owned it."

"How?" Annja asked, buying time as she tried to think how to extricate herself from this situation.

"I made them drink the poison sludge they'd been spewing for decades into the drinking water. Unfortunately for them, the concentration was so much higher than the water normally held. I guess they came to see that the stuff they used to make cosmetics with wasn't healthy."

"And what happened to the people who were employed by the factory? How are they supposed to make a living now?"

Greene shrugged. "They'll find a way. Their welfare isn't my concern. If anything, they ought to be thankful to me for cleaning up their water. But they were secondary. The primary goal was to stop the factory from polluting the environment."

"So you're not a humanitarian at all."

Green laughed. "I make no pretense of being a humanitarian, Annja. My goals are simple—wipe the toxicity of the human stain from the planet. Help rebuild the wonder that once was nature."

Annja frowned as the other man finished hefting Jackson's body over his shoulder. "What now? Is he just going to walk out of here with the corpse?"

Greene smiled. "You really think anyone is going to ask him questions?"

Greene's associate must have stood more than six feet two inches and weighed about two hundred and sixty pounds. He was big and muscular. Annja didn't think any of her neighbors would bother him.

"No," she said simply.

Greene nodded. "Exactly. Now let's get going downstairs." He stopped. "Unless, of course, you'd prefer I let my associate leave the body here and then we call the police?"

Annja sighed. She could argue her way out of the murder; she felt confident of that. Plus, she knew a few of the cops at the local precinct. She'd be able to straighten it out, but was it worth the grief?

I need to install some serious surveillance on this place, she thought. Video cameras would forestall this type of bull.

"Annja?"

She stared at the floor. A tiny residue of blood remained on the hardwood. Greene followed her gaze and chuckled.

"We'll leave that here as a souvenir."

"Be hard to clean once I get back," Annja said. "I'd prefer to clean it up now, if you don't mind."

"We don't have time for this," Greene said. He studied her for a moment before relenting. "You've got thirty seconds to get it done."

Annja ran for the kitchen and grabbed a sheaf of paper towels, holding them under hot water. Through the window, she saw a cruiser parked on the curb across the street. If she could just get the two cops' attention…

"Annja."

She turned and saw Greene standing at the entry to the kitchen. Annja lifted the wet paper towels. "Got them."

She went back to the living room and knelt, mopping up the blood. Fortunately for her decor, the bullet had stayed inside Jackson's skull. A larger caliber bullet would have exited the skull and strewn brain matter.

Annja spent a few more seconds scrubbing the spot. While it looked clean, she knew that if a crime scene tech ran a UV light over it, there would be blood traces. She'd need to clean it better when she got back.

She stood. "Let me just throw these away and we can go."

Back in the kitchen, she ditched the ball of towels in the trash. A glance out of the window confirmed the cruiser was still there. Could she get their attention?

The window.

Annja looked over her shoulder and into the living room. Greene had his back to her and was talking to the other guy.

Now.

Annja pushed the window open, hopped up onto the counter and crept out onto the fire escape. Her loft was five stories up. She kicked at the fire escape. Speed was more important now than stealth.

A bullet splanged off the metal handrail in front of her.

"Annja!"

So much for surprise.

She kicked the fire escape down on the second attempt and dropped two stories before she even knew what she was doing.

Footfalls on the fire escape above her confirmed that Greene was in hot pursuit. Or his associate was.

Annja took the steep steps three at a time. She kicked at the release on the next level, watching the steel ratchet toward the street.

Another bullet hit the walkway ahead of her. They were still using a silenced pistol.

Annja's breathing was coming hard.

She was close to the ground now.

And the cruiser was still there, idling.

"Hey!" Annja waved her arms and then felt something hot bite into the side of her arm. She glanced down and saw blood.

She'd been shot?

Instantly, she felt woozy. She started to turn and was overwhelmed by dizziness.

Annja went over the railing of the fire escape.

And landed on the garbage cans below with a crash.

Dazed, she sat up and put a hand to her head. More blood.

Not good.

She stood and tried to claw her way out of the pile of trash. That's when she heard the sirens. And saw the cruiser's lights go on.

"Hey, you okay?"

Miraculously, one of the cops was heading toward her. He rushed to grab her as she fell. "Miss!"

He helped her down to the sidewalk.

Annja struggled to take a breath. "Men—armed. My…apartment."

Concern creased the face of the police officer. He started to reach for his radio as his partner approached them.

"She okay?"

"I don't know," the first officer said. He pushed a button on his radio and started to speak.

"Oh, my God, Annja!"

Annja could barely move her head. She recognized the onset of shock.

And then Greene's face swam into view overhead. "Thank God she's okay!"

The first cop looked at Greene. "You know her?"

Greene sighed. "She's my sister. She's been taking medication for depression and I was over to discuss some family issues. She got upset. I was in the bathroom, but when I came back out, she was gone. I thought she'd jumped."

"Damn near did," the second cop said. "She took a header off the fire escape. She's lucky to be alive."

Greene feigned a sigh. "Thank God you were here."

The first cop stood. "She's going to need a doctor. And we'll have to get some information from you."

Greene nodded. "Sure, sure. Whatever you guys need."

And then Annja saw Greene bring up his pistol almost in slow motion, extend his arm and shoot both police officers dead. The sound suppressor muffled the gunshots and, since they were in the alley behind Annja's apartment, no one even noticed the two cops go down.

Greene stepped over each of them and calmly shot them again in the head.

He looked back at Annja. "Just to be sure. These guys have a bad habit of wearing body armor these days. It's not as easy to kill them anymore."

Annja tried to talk but nothing came out of her mouth. Greene squatted next to her. "That's the drug we tagged you with. It's nice, isn't it? It's an ancient pharmacological specimen from the Amazon. Does the trick nicely and you don't have to listen to a twenty-minute lecture on side effects like you do with the shit the big pharma guys hawk on the evening news." He smiled. "You ought to thank me for not just killing you and being done with it."

Annja grabbed his arm and glared at him as best she could. But its effect only amused Greene. "I admire your spirit, Annja. I really do. I have to admit, I don't know all that much about you—but I intend to rectify that situation immediately."

He got his arms under her and Annja felt herself lifted to her feet. Greene's breathing seemed light and easy and she could feel the strength in his arms and core as he hauled her upright.

Somewhere in the distance, she heard an engine and guessed that Greene's associate had gone for some vehicle. Sure enough, seconds later, a dark van rounded the corner and drew to a stop next to them.

She heard the side panel door slide back on its rails. "All right, Annja, in we go."

Annja felt herself heaved into the back and then the door slid shut and darkness closed over her.

She took a deep breath. The pile of blankets beneath her felt soft. Warm.

Almost comfortable.

Western Massachusetts, she thought.

Well, maybe a little trip wouldn't be so bad.

Provided she didn't end up like the recently deceased Mike Jackson.

3

Annja tried to blink and realized something had been tied around her head, over her eyes. A blindfold. Had she passed out during the trip? She felt strangely rested, but she could also tell there were some lingering effects from the drug Greene had shot her with.

Her legs ached and Annja tried to stretch them out. She kicked something solid.

"So, you're awake."

Annja propped herself into a sitting position. "Can I take this off?"

"Your hands aren't tied. You can do whatever you like."

"In that case, I want to go home," Annja said. But she reached up and pulled the blindfold off. The interior of the van was still dark. Judging from the hum of the engine, Annja figured they must have been cruising along at about seventy miles per hour. Fast enough to get to their western Massachusetts destination within a few hours, but slow enough not to provoke any police they'd be passing on the highway.

Smart.

In the darkness, she saw a match flare followed by the red glow of what had to be a cigarette. Greene's face was briefly illuminated before it went dark again. He was sitting in the backseat with her.

Annja stared. "You smoke cigarettes?" Somehow that seemed directly contradictory to Greene's avowed mission of saving the planet.

Greene inhaled deeply. "This is not a cigarette."

And a second later, Annja caught a whiff of the smoke. Marijuana. "You smoke pot?"

"Yes. Is that a problem for you?"

Annja coughed. "Aside from suffocating on your passive smoke, no. I'm curious how you justify it, though."

Greene shrugged. "What's to justify? It's not like I'm buying into the massive health conspiracy that was covered up by the tobacco companies."

"Yeah, but you're still smoking."

Greene laughed. "I don't think your argument is going to prove convincing, Annja. I've been smoking pot for a number of years now. And I quite happen to appreciate the efficacy of the cannabis herb. It's wonderful stuff."

"I just wouldn't have expected that sort of thing from you. I mean, I imagine you're pretty healthy—what, a vegan?"

Greene shook his head. "Vegetarian, yes. Not vegan. That's too strict for me."

"And fit, too. You work out a lot. Someone trained you somewhere at some point in the past."

"Yes."

"And yet you put that carcinogenic substance in your lungs. I don't get it."

Greene leaned over and blew a puff of smoke into Annja's face. "Yes, well, perhaps you don't deserve to get it. Ever think of that, Annja? Or are you so presumptuous to believe that you have a lock on the workings of the universe?"

Annja waved the smoke away. "I'm not presumptuous."

Greene leaned back. "That remains to be seen."

Annja looked at the front windshield. The wipers flicked intermittently, scattering the small accumulation of drizzle. "Where are we headed?"

"Springer Falls. Have you ever heard of it?"

"No. I don't get up here all that much."

Greene nodded. "I've had a chance to read up on some of your exploits. You've been all over the world recently."

Annja sighed. "It feels like I've been away forever."

"But never to Springer Falls. Maybe this trip will be a departure—a chance for you to enjoy yourself," Greene said. "And maybe afterward we could find a way to work together, you and I."

Annja smirked. "I've seen how you work, Greene. You drop people without even thinking about it. Why in the world would I work with you? I'd never feel easy with you around."

Greene inhaled and let out another stream of marijuana smoke. "I'm decisive. Ask any successful person and they'll say attitude is absolutely necessary for achieving your goals."

"By decisive, they were probably talking about something a little less extreme than, say, murdering people."

"You interpret it your way," Greene said. "But I happen to believe I have a better handle on it than you."

Annja waved her hand again to dispel more of the smoke. "I hope we don't get stopped."

Greene hefted his pistol. "I hope so, too. For the trooper's sake."

Annja shook her head. "You planning on leaving a trail of bodies in your wake, Greene? Sooner or later they'll track you down and give you the death penalty for your crimes."

Greene sniffed. "If I was scared of dying, I wouldn't be the man I am today."

"A murderous, pot-smoking lunatic?" Annja sighed. "Some man. What sort of greatness have you achieved?"

"Greatness is measured in many ways. My exploits may not make sense in your limited world view, but some day, my supposed crimes will be seen for what they truly are—revolutionary."

"Ecoterrorism," said Annja. "You can phrase it however you'd like. It doesn't change the fact that you're a killer."

"Potato, potahto. Your judgment doesn't concern me in the slightest."

"Apparently."

Greene inhaled again. "Do you know what it's like to watch the planet being ravaged and destroyed right in front of your eyes?"

"I've been around the world," Annja said. "I've seen abject poverty, environmental disasters. And, usually, they're caused by people like you who con themselves into believing their cause is just. Except justice is a facade. You're all after power or money. Greed drives you and others like you. You can try to spin it, but it doesn't change that you're out for yourself."

Greene slapped her so suddenly that the shock of it sent Annja reeling. She tasted blood in her mouth and took a breath.

"You don't know me, Annja Creed. And you have no right to criticize the work I've done."

Annja wiped her mouth. "You were the one who kidnapped me, Greene. I don't want to be here. But you gave me no choice. So, as far as I'm concerned, I have every right to comment on your petty little world vision. Don't like it? Then you can drop me off here."

"Or I could just kill you."

"Nah, you need me. Reginald's waiting, remember?"

"I told you I could find another way if it became necessary."

Annja smirked. "Yeah, you said that. But I don't believe you. If there was another way, then you probably wouldn't have driven to Brooklyn to kidnap me. But the fact you drove down to New York tells me you've run out of options."

Greene sat smoking quietly for a few moments. "All right, I'll be honest. I do need you. But would you prefer to do this in relatively decent health or in a world of pain?"

"You're into torture, too? Well, there's another character trait to be proud of." Annja shook her head. "You're just full of greatness, aren't you?"

Grudgingly, Greene laughed. "Compliments will only get you so far, Annja."

She could, of course, use the sword to kill Greene and his associate behind the wheel. But what would that achieve, except her freedom? Annja would never find out what Reginald Fairclough wanted with her. Or how he even knew her.

She racked her brain but the name still didn't ring any bells. Of course, it was a little tough thinking when she was feeling the secondhand effects of Greene's marijuana.

Her head swam, but Annja blinked the dizziness away. "Tell me more about the book dealer."

Greene eyed her. "We have a detente?"

"We don't have anything, Greene. You've got a captive—for the moment—and my piqued curiosity. I don't think I know Fairclough, yet he wants to see me. That intrigues me."

"Lucky me," Greene said. "I've piqued your curiosity." He chuckled quietly and then coughed. "Fairclough is one of the most renowned experts in early history texts. I don't suppose you know much about that, do you?"

Annja shrugged. "You'd be surprised."

"I'm sure."

"Fairclough apparently thinks I've got some value."

Greene mercifully stubbed out his cigarette and regarded Annja. "He's bordering on insane."

"Well, good, then you two will have a lot to talk about."

"He's also dying right now. As we speak."

"From what?"

Greene smiled. "I've got him hooked up to a slow IV drip. It's currently leaking a motley assortment of narcotics into his bloodstream. I'd give him about thirty-six hours before he's dead."

Annja looked at Greene. "Why in the world are you killing him?"

"He's got something I want. I thought I told you that earlier."

"You mentioned that. But you didn't tell me what it was you're after."

"I want a certain book in his collection. It's very old. Ancient, in fact. Fairclough acquired it a few years ago. It's his most prized possession."

"Well, I don't blame him for not wanting to give it to you. A manmade book? You'd probably just burn it."

"I will do no such thing," Greene protested. "In fact, I want to study it and learn what it has to teach."

"What's so special about this book?"

"It's an ancient account of the history of the world. The tome used to be in the library at Alexandria. Of course, the history ends with the destruction of the library."

Annja narrowed her eyes. "I thought the texts in the library were incinerated during the fire."

"They were."

"But not all of them."

"Not all of them," Greene agreed. "And Fairclough got his hands on this text. Perhaps you've heard of it?"

"Maybe."

"*The Tome of Prossos,* the ascetic."

"What do you hope to learn from it?"

Greene shrugged. "It might tell me a lot about how the world used to be before we all got into the business of destroying our home."

Annja waited for him to continue. When he didn't she prodded, "Is that it?"

"Does there need to be more?"

"I guess not," Annja said. "But I don't think you're being honest with me. Whatever. I'll talk to Fairclough.

But don't think for a moment that I'll help you get it back from him."

"You might change your mind once you meet him. He can be quite persuasive."

"Does he kill people to get his point across?"

"Not that I know of."

Annja nodded. "Well, there's a big point in his favor already."

Greene leaned back and looked through the windshield. Annja felt the change in the engine's thrum. They were slowing down. Greene's associate took an exit off the highway, and she watched as they drew into what looked like a small town.

"We're almost there," Greene announced.

"Good," said Annja. "I'm dying to get out of this van. It reeks in here."

Greene eyed her. "I'd be very careful of judging what you don't fully comprehend, Annja."

"I don't know how much is left to comprehend," she said. "You want a book that Fairclough owns, and he doesn't want to give it to you. I don't blame him. And for some reason, he wants to talk to me. So fine, I'll talk to him."

Greene watched her for a moment and then looked down at his gun. "We'll be there in about fifteen minutes. Fairclough lives on the outskirts of town in a rather large estate."

"Is he retired or actively still in the business?"

Greene shrugged. "The internet allows him to work from the comfort of his home."

"Technology's not all bad."

"That remains to be seen. Maybe when this…meeting…is over you'll understand that."

"Or maybe not," Annja said.

Green hefted the pistol. "Maybe not. Indeed."

Annja leaned back and waited for them to arrive at Fairclough's mansion. She had her own ideas on how to resolve this situation.

4

Fifteen minutes later, the van rolled to a stop before turning left down a long winding gravel road—to Fairclough's estate, presumably. Annja tried her best to pick out details as the van rolled in, but the cloudy evening sky cast long shadows across much of the landscape. Still, Annja could see sprawling lawns, well manicured, and shrubs perfectly coifed, creating the idea of an English country estate. As they drew around the corner hedged in by a massive rhododendron, Annja could see Fairclough's house for the first time.

Floodlights aimed at an angle to the brick and stone exterior displayed the full magnificence of the mansion. Light poured out of the massive windows and ivy crawled over one entire side wall.

"Impressive," Annja said.

Greene sniffed. "It's horrendous. A grotesque stain upon what would otherwise be a beautiful landscape."

"You'd deny him his right to own a home like this?

It's not like he got his money from poisoning kids or burning down forests."

Greene shrugged. "Money is greed. Its only real value is in bringing our planet back closer to the purity of its origins. Does it look as if Fairclough cares about anything but his own personal pleasure?"

Annja shook her head. "His bank account is his own business. As far as I'm concerned, Fairclough got his money doing something good—promoting the value of books. I think a lot more people could use a reminder of how great books are. No one reads much these days unless it's an easy-to-digest sound bite. Just take a look at the last election cycle."

Greene cocked his head to study her. "I don't vote."

"Then you've got no right to complain."

He laughed. "You're pitifully naive, Annja. You think your vote matters?"

"I don't know. But it's a right and a responsibility, so I take it seriously. Not that I'm around much during elections."

"You're allowed to vote only because the corporations—those with the real power in the world—let you. This is how they manipulate you into thinking you have some measure of power, when you don't. None whatsoever."

"What paranoia."

Greene raised his eyebrows. "Think about it—what happens if one party gets too much power? Next election, the other party gains more power to balance it out. In recent years extremism has become mainstream with the advent of the Tea Party. I mean, really, look at that swath of candidates who came to power last year. Idiots, racists and people who wanted to destroy the Constitution they claimed they would die to protect. And you all fell for it. Pathetic."

"So, what would you do—kill them?"

Greene shrugged. "Well, it's not a perfect solution. But for the time being, it works pretty well."

"Can I get out of this van now and get some fresh air?"

Greene nodded.

Annja grabbed the side panel door release and jerked it back on the rails. As it slid open, a rush of fresh air greeted her and she breathed it in deeply. It felt good to flush her lungs.

The air outside was heavy with moisture and she could see droplets of water on the grass. She stepped out and felt the gravel beneath her shoes.

Greene emerged behind her and she heard the driver's door close with a slam. She glanced and saw Greene's associate come around the hood of the van.

Greene waved him over. "Annja, you haven't been properly introduced to Kessel yet."

Kessel stood in front of Annja and folded his arms. He said nothing.

Annja looked him up and down. "Does that pose go over well with the ladies?"

Kessel said nothing. Annja glanced at Greene. "Real conversationalist you got yourself here."

"His tongue was cut out during the first Gulf War by the Iraqis when he was captured and tortured for information."

"Why would they cut his tongue out if they wanted him to spill?"

"Kessel told them from the start that he wouldn't divulge any information that would compromise his unit.

They didn't like that response. So, instead of trying to break him, they simply sliced his tongue off like some piece of meat and fed it to a dog."

Annja shook her head. "Horrible."

"Effective," Greene said. "But it did have an effect on Kessel that led him eventually to me. He came to see that all the wars being fought were simply proxy battles engaged in by corporate masters. That soldiers like him were being manipulated as expendable pawns. He grew to despise the vast industrialism rampant in the world today."

"You really think that?"

Greene nodded. "Yes. I do."

Kessel nodded, as well. "All right," Annja said, "let's go see Fairclough and get this over with."

Greene stopped her. "Annja, I don't want you thinking this is going to be a quick job. If Fairclough is as I expect him to be, you may find yourself in for quite a challenge."

Annja frowned. "It wouldn't be the first time."

They walked up the footpath to the main house. As they approached, the door swung open and another gun-toting associate of Greene's waved them inside. "Welcome back," the man said.

Greene nodded at Annja. "This is Creed, the one Fairclough wants to see."

"Good stuff." He beamed at Annja while pushing his dreadlocks back with his free hand. "I'm Jonas. Nice to meet you."

Annja smirked. "Another true believer?"

Jonas smiled at Greene. "She didn't swallow the Kool-Aid, huh?"

"Hardly," said Greene. "I think we'd best treat Miss Creed as a hostile witness, if it pleases the court."

Jonas bowed low. "Well, there will be time enough for us to bring her around to our cause."

Annja shook her head. "You're wasting your time, Jonas. I don't go in for extremism. You guys might have some good ideas about cutting back on pollution and making sure corporations are responsible for taking care of the environments they operate in, but there's no way I can condone how you carry out your goals. Murder doesn't wash with me."

"Then you've obviously never been presented with some of the greedheads that we've met," Jonas said. "When you can't even get them to try to see your perspective, what choice is left?"

"I might hate them," Annja said. "And I could understand the frustration you feel, but I wouldn't resort to murder."

Jonas laughed. "Murder can never be justified—is that so? Well, we'll see how you feel about that later. Right now, I'm sure our leader wants to get back to see his patient."

"Indeed I do," Greene said. "Let's go."

Jonas led them down a carpeted hallway lined with huge mahogany doors and beautiful landscape paintings. Annja pointed at one as they passed. "Seems like Fairclough has an appreciation for nature, as well."

"Paintings hardly express a passion for saving the world." Greene sneered. "Investments that will eventually yield him even more money and power. There's little to celebrate in such a collection."

Annja rolled her eyes. "Good God, man, do you ever take a break from the self-righteousness?"

"The environment is my religion," Greene said. "And I take umbrage at your insulting tone."

"Yeah, well, I call it like I see it," Annja muttered.

Jonas paused at a set of double doors. "This is Fairclough's bedroom," he said to Annja. "We've had him cooped up in here since we arrived."

"And when was that?"

"Two days ago."

"Did you explain what it was you're looking for?" she asked Greene. "After all, if you asked nicely enough, he might give it to you."

Greene shook his head. "We asked him. Begged him, in fact, to release it to us. We told him we could keep it even safer than he could. But he refused to listen to us. Said something about us not understanding its nature and how we'd destroy it. Imagine the arrogance of the man."

Annja sniffed. "Yeah, I guess I can certainly relate to that." She eyed Greene. "So that's when you hooked him up to your poison drip?"

"Well, we needed to convince him," Jonas said. "No sense only taking a threat so far. You need to show people you mean business, after all."

Greene smiled. "Jonas is our medical professional. He did three years on an extended tour with a small missionary outfit down the Amazon. What he saw there propelled him to the realization that modern society is corrupt. That the only true way forward is to go backward."

"Back to what our ancestors practiced," Jonas added. "Their knowledge of nature and the universe was without peer. And yet we've gotten away from that with our machines and our supermarkets and shopping malls.

The whole thing is so ludicrous, it amazes me that more people don't see it."

"Yeah," said Annja, "I can't imagine why they wouldn't all flock to the notion that killing people and engaging in terrorism is a viable means of helping the planet. Crazy."

Jonas frowned. "Your sarcasm is a real downer, Annja. I hope that before this is over you at least try to keep an open mind."

"I always have an open mind," she said. "But that doesn't mean I let my brain and common sense fall out."

Greene chuckled. "Good one."

Jonas nodded. "I like her."

"Look," she said, "enough with the brainwashing, okay? Let's see Fairclough and be done with this. My head still hurts from force-smoking your blunt in the van."

"Fair enough," Greene said, nodding to Jonas. "Let's get inside."

Jonas pushed the doors open and they filed in. As Annja stepped into the bedroom, she was amazed at the opulence. She'd never known the antique book market to pay so handsomely. But Fairclough had either invested wisely over his career or he had money coming in from other sources.

Fairclough's bed was a towering four-poster surrounded by several modern paintings that looked familiar, as if she'd seen them in exhibitions.

She saw the array of medical equipment next. Machines buzzed and beeped and hummed while digital readouts kept chirping out updates and monitoring the health of the man they were hooked up to: Reginald Fairclough.

For his part, Fairclough looked tiny in such a huge bed. His frame was thin and wiry and his face appeared gaunt. A mop of white hair topped his head, which seemed almost unnaturally large for his body.

Annja saw the IV drip stand next to the bed and watched as the clear liquid in the plastic squeeze bags dripped down the tube and into the old man's arm. *God knows what they're pumping into his bloodstream,* she thought. No matter who he was, Fairclough didn't deserve to be treated this way.

No one did.

"What are you poisoning him with?"

"I told you," Greene said. "It's a little concoction we came up with based on Jonas's experience in the rain forest. It's quite a compelling cocktail of native herbals."

"And the great thing is," said Jonas, "if he helps us, we can reverse the effects almost immediately."

"You can?"

"Well." Jonas hesitated. "If he tells us soon. Otherwise, it will get progressively worse until it's irreversible."

"What happens then?"

"He'll lapse into a vegetative state."

"And then he'll die," Greene said. "So I suggest we get started."

5

Reginald Fairclough, Annja decided, looked exactly the way she thought an antique bookseller ought to look. With his oversize head and white hair, he had the appearance of being highly intelligent. His thin frame indicated that he probably spent a lot more time thinking than engaging in physical activity.

"Is he in a coma?"

"I think he's asleep," Jonas said. "Let me see if I can do something to bring him around."

Annja watched as Jonas leaned in and adjusted one of the taps on the IV bag. The drip slowed and then Jonas tapped Fairclough on the shoulder. "Wake up, old man. Got someone here to see you."

"Quite the wake-up call," said Annja with a frown. "Your bedside manner is horrible."

"I didn't hire him for his bedside manner," Greene snapped. "His skill with toxins is incredible."

"Should I call him Dr. Poison?"

"Jonas is fine," Jonas said. He tapped Fairclough again. "Can you hear me?"

Fairclough shifted under the blankets and his eyelids fluttered slightly. A croak escaped his mouth.

"Does the poison make him sick?" Annja asked.

"It's actually a stronger version of what I shot you with," Greene explained. "It's a bit like being very drunk without the nausea and vomiting."

Jonas blanched. "I'm not good with vomit."

Annja cocked an eyebrow. "You're a medical doctor and you can't stand the sight of vomit?"

"Never could," said Jonas. "And anything to do with urine or feces is out, too. Just freaks me out, man."

Annja filed that nugget away. Knowing that Jonas had weaknesses could come in handy. In the meantime, she looked at Fairclough as he started moving. His eyes rolled open and he squinted in the bright light.

Greene nudged the bed. "Come on, Reggie. Wakey-wakey. You see who we went and found for you?"

Annja leaned closer. "Mr. Fairclough? I'm Annja Creed."

Fairclough's eyes rolled to Annja and he seemed to focus on her for a moment. Annja watched a glint appear in his eyes. He seemed to recognize her. But for the life of her, Annja couldn't figure out where she might have known him from.

"Annja Creed." Fairclough's voice rasped as if he hadn't had a drink in days.

Annja looked at Greene. "Can you at least get him some water?"

"Sure, we're not complete savages here." He nodded to Jonas, who reached for a glass of what appeared to be water on the bedside table. He put the straw up to Fairclough's lips.

Annja watched as Fairclough drank and then sputtered some of it back out with a sharp cough. He looked like hell and, even if she didn't know he was being poisoned, she would have thought he had some serious health issues.

Fairclough managed to take in some more water and then pushed Jonas away with one of his hands. There was anger in his eyes as he recognized Jonas and Greene.

But he smiled at Annja. "You don't remember me, do you?"

Annja felt embarrassed. "I'm sorry, but I really don't. I wish I did, but I just can't place you. Have we met before?"

"Indeed," Fairclough said. He looked at Jonas. "Help me sit up, you ignorant errand boy."

Jonas glanced at Greene, who nodded. Jonas helped Fairclough into a better position, at which point Fairclough backhanded Jonas across the mouth. It was a sudden flash of Fairclough's character, and it caught both Jonas and Greene completely by surprise.

Jonas reeled away, clutching his face. Annja saw a line of blood start to trickle down and grinned. "Looks like he hasn't quite been neutralized just yet, huh?"

Jonas looked at Greene. "That bastard hit me!"

Fairclough looked quite pleased with himself, but Annja saw that the exertion had cost him a lot of his strength. She might not have remembered him, but she admired his resolve.

Greene nodded at the door to Jonas. "Go get that cleaned up."

"You want me to leave you here alone?"

"Kessel's out front. And I don't think Annja's going to try anything right now. She's too interested in what our host has to say."

Jonas left and Greene added, "I should remind you that if you try anything, it won't go down well for you."

"No need to repeat yourself," Annja said. "I'm well aware of what you're capable of. After all, I've already seen you kill three innocent people today. I'd say that qualifies you for scumbag of the month."

Greene smiled. "Talk to him. Convince him to give me the book and you might just go home alive."

Fat chance of that, Annja thought. There was no way in hell Greene would let her walk out of here. But she put that concern out of her mind for the time being. She'd deal with that eventuality when she had to. Worrying about it now was a waste of time and energy.

Fairclough reached out for her hand and she let him take it. "Come closer, Annja."

She sat on the edge of the bed, careful not to disturb the IV dip. She wondered what would happen if she ripped the thing out. Would it somehow injure Fairclough more? Would it kill him?

She couldn't risk doing anything just yet. "I'm here," she said.

"A few years ago at a history conference on the Egyptian influence on world history, you gave a talk on the Late Period's Thirtieth Dynasty that was truly compelling."

Annja squeezed his hand. "I'm glad you enjoyed it."

"Egypt is one of my passions, you see. And it was thrilling to hear such a talk coming from someone like you. I mean, I've seen that dreadful TV show—"

Annja held up her free hand. "I'm nothing like the other host, I assure you."

"And I realized that, after you gave your presentation. I actually tried to say thanks, but you were whisked away immediately after your talk. I thought you might have had a family emergency or something so I didn't pursue you."

"No family emergency," Annja said. "Just another relic that someone wanted me to chase down for them."

"And now you're here."

"Because you sent them to bring me here."

The old man bit his lip and looked away from her. "I'm sorry," he said quietly. "I shouldn't have put you in danger." He began to cough weakly, and Annja brought the glass with the straw back to his mouth. He drank, but didn't say anything more.

Annja looked around, giving him time to compose himself. "You have a lovely home."

"I wish you were seeing it under better circumstances. Unfortunately, one never knows what sort of riffraff will drop by unexpectedly."

She smiled. "I had that same thing riffraff drop by on me earlier today. Rather rude of them."

"Indeed," Fairclough said. "But we are where we are and must endeavor to make the best of a bad situation. These lads want something of mine very badly, as I understand it."

"A book. Greene said it was called the *Tome of Prossos?*"

Fairclough nodded and another short cough escaped him. "An early record of human history up until the great conflagration at Alexandria."

"How is it that you have a copy? It was my understanding that all the books in the library were incinerated beyond retrieval."

"They were," he confirmed. "But there was also a movement afoot to make copies of all the texts in the library in case the unfortunate happened. Foresight that proved to be too late to save most of the texts. However, the *Tome of Prossos* was already copied."

"And you have this copy?"

Fairclough inclined his head. "I have the only copy in existence. And I hope to have it in my possession awhile longer, mind you."

Greene chuckled. "You don't know what to do with it. The knowledge in that book shouldn't belong to only one man. You've got to let the world have it. It belongs to the planet."

Fairclough looked at him. "You're a hypocrite on top of everything else. As if my releasing it would signal the great reformation you so fervently wish. You'd hoard the book yourself, using what its pages speak of to further your own ends."

"My own ends are to benefit the planet," Greene said.

"Are they?"

"Of course."

"Then why don't I simply release the book to the public over the internet? Would you have a problem with that?"

Greene shifted. "Well, yes, I would. But not because I wouldn't have control of the book, but because its power would be usurped by corporations and other greedheads."

Fairclough waved him away. "Bah! You don't know half of what the book contains."

"Well, neither do I," Annja said. "Is this why you

asked to see me? Because of the book? If that's the case, would you mind filling me in on the details?"

Fairclough smiled at her. "It's quite simple. As you know, the tome contains a written account of the history of the world, from its creation—according to Prossos—to mankind's ascent through the Egyptian dynastic ages. It's a marvelous read, provided you understand it."

He glanced at Greene. "And let me just say for the record—you will not understand it."

"I'll take that chance," Greene replied.

Fairclough looked back at Annja. "The real treat about the tome is that it also contains within its pages a codex that reveals a method for healing the planet in times of duress."

"Meaning what, exactly? You can cure the planet?"

Fairclough's smile grew. "Imagine knowing how to reduce the toxicity in the environment. That is what the book contains, and that is what I believe our good friend Greene here really wants it for. He doesn't want to learn from the lessons of history so much as be the savior of the world."

Greene shrugged. "Sure, I could stand with being called a savior. Who wouldn't enjoy that?"

"You could be so much more than just a savior," Fairclough said. "Provided you knew what to do."

Annja cleared her throat. "How do you solve the codex?"

Fairclough shrugged. "I haven't been able to crack that yet. It's one reason I opted for retirement, so I could work on just that. It would have been nice to give the secret back to the world."

Greene sighed. "All right, enough of this. Tell her where the book is so we can get it and leave this place. It makes me sick just thinking how much money it must've taken to buy this joint."

Fairclough gripped Annja's hand tighter. "You know as well as I do that he'll never let either one of us out of here alive."

"I was thinking about that."

Greene frowned.

"Having seen what I saw today," Annja continued, "I don't doubt you'd kill us as soon as you could."

Greene did his best to hide a smirk. But he failed and looked away. Annja frowned. She looked back at Fairclough. "I think we can take that as an indicator of what we're in for."

Fairclough nodded. "Exactly. So you can see that I really have no reason to reveal the book's hiding place."

"I'm still not sure why you asked to see me, but—" Annja lowered her voice "—I might be able to do something about this situation. However, I'd need to get to the book first if we have any hope of nullifying the poison in your veins."

Fairclough looked at her hard. "Are you sure?"

Annja nodded. "Yes."

"It won't be easy. I took steps to protect the book and make sure it wouldn't ever be stolen from me."

"A security system?"

"Something like that," Fairclough said. "I'd rather hoped never to have to use it, but when they broke into my house the other day, I had no choice. I was barely able to get it protected before they took me hostage."

"All right," said Annja. "So how do I disarm it?"

Fairclough waggled his eyebrows. "It's not really something you can decode. You have to find your way through the maze."

"Maze?"

"Yes," he said. "The book is hidden at the center of a maze I designed under my estate."

6

Greene started laughing. "You've got to be kidding me."

Fairclough looked at him and sighed. "I'd expect nothing less from someone like you. It always amazes me how little those who claim to stand for ideals actually think."

"You're telling me there's a maze underneath this house?" Greene shook his head. "How in the world did you manage to construct that?"

"I hired people to excavate the area and build it to my precise specifications."

"But what's the point?" Annja asked. "I mean, no offense, but if you wanted some elaborate security system, there are plenty to choose from. You could hire someone to design you a completely unique system."

"I'll tell you why," Greene said. "Because he's gotten too much into the pages of some of his books apparently."

Fairclough regarded him. "I had the maze built because I didn't trust the security systems everyone else uses. Electronics can be defeated. Ciphers and codes don't matter a whit to me. But genuine ingenuity is a prize I value above all else. Needless to say, most of the ruffians who would steal the book don't possess even a fraction of it."

Greene started forward. "Keep the insults up, old man, and I'll—"

"Kill me?" Fairclough laughed. "Seems to me you're already doing that, you ignorant pup. Now be quiet while I talk to this wonderful woman here."

Greene looked as if he might be tempted to hit Fairclough.

Annja held up her hand. "All right, so what's the deal with the maze? Do I just go down there and find my way to the center of it to retrieve the book?"

"That would be too easy," Fairclough said. "I had to make it difficult to discover and even tougher to get through."

"So, what happens when I get in there?"

Fairclough looked pained and glanced at the IV drip as if aware his time was very possibly fleeting. "There are puzzles you'll need to figure out."

"Puzzles?"

"Challenges," Fairclough clarified. "Think of them that way. They're tests, of course, and unfortunately the penalties for failing them are rather…absolute."

"Absolute? What does that mean? Deadly?"

Fairclough nodded. A wave of pain washed over his face. "I'm sorry for putting you through this, Annja. You don't deserve it.

"I had wanted to warn you that the copy of this book

exists—because of your understanding of Egyptian history—but I never expected..."

"I won't argue that point," Annja said. "Can't you just shut the thing down?" she asked.

"No." Fairclough's voice sounded weaker. "For reasons that will become obvious once you enter the maze."

Annja looked skeptical. "You're not giving me much to go on here."

"I know, and I'm sorry."

"How do I get into the maze?"

Fairclough coughed. "There is an entrance in the barn behind the third horse stall. I don't have horses any longer, but I've kept the barn there. I don't think you'll have any trouble finding your way in."

"All right." Annja sighed. "But listen, couldn't you just give me the answers to the challenges?"

But Fairclough's eyes rolled back in his head. Greene felt his neck for a pulse. "He's passed out. Probably from the pain."

"Can't you reduce it?" She chafed the old man's hand.

Greene shrugged. "Well, yeah, I could. But why would I?"

"So I can get more answers out of him. So I can have a better shot at finding your precious book."

Greene smiled. "He told you what you needed to know."

"Hardly. I've got a really bad feeling about this thing. 'Reasons that will become obvious once you're in the maze'? I mean, what's that about?"

Greene shook his head. "I don't know and I don't really care. But you'd better get going."

Jonas came back into the room. He glanced at Fairclough. "He pass out from the pain again?"

"Seems to have," Greene said. "You know the old coot has himself a maze underneath this place?"

Jonas stepped back. "For real? That's pretty wild."

"You two should come with me," she said. "That way, when the maze kills you, I'll only have to deal with Kessel when I come back up with the book."

Jonas laughed. "Man, you're funny, Annja. I like the way you unload those barbed comments like that. It's kinda hot."

"You're a buffoon." She looked at Greene. "Let me guess—you're going to stay up here while I do all the work, right?"

"Well, I need to be here and so does Jonas so he can monitor our patient." He smirked. "However, since you seem to have developed a liking for Kessel, you'll be glad to know he's going with you."

Annja's brows furrowed. "He'll get in my way."

"I doubt it. I think you might find him useful."

"How so?"

"I suppose it depends on what sort of challenges Fairclough has put into the maze, but Kessel is incredibly strong and adept at killing things. If you come across guard dogs for example, he can dispatch them quickly."

"You know this for a fact?"

"It wouldn't be the first time we've come across attack dogs, if that's what you're asking."

"Fine," Annja said. "The sooner I get down there, the better. I want to go home and forget this day ever happened."

Greene smiled. "And I want that book. You'd do well to remember that when you start thinking about getting the better of Kessel. I've already instructed him to simply kill you if you give him reason to suspect anything is amiss, and try to get the book himself."

"He wouldn't find it without me."

Greene shrugged. "I wouldn't be so cavalier. Kessel is remarkably intelligent. Just because he doesn't have a tongue doesn't mean he can't read. And he reads a lot. Last year he read several hundred books on a wide range of topics."

"So, what you're saying is he's not just a mean-looking killer. There's a real intellect behind all that brawn."

"Exactly."

Annja smirked. "Yeah, well, we'll see if you're right."

"Yes, we will."

Annja studied Fairclough in the bed. He hadn't shown signs of coming back around. Jonas followed her gaze and sighed.

"The pain takes him after a while. One of the symptoms of this particular toxin. He'll be out for a good long time."

Greene smiled. "Unless, of course, we increase the dosage of the poison into his bloodstream."

"Why would you do that?" Annja asked.

"Because you're not moving fast enough," he said. "You're on the clock here, Annja."

Jonas checked his watch. "As I said, I can monitor the flow of toxin into his body. But after a certain time, we won't be able to undo the damage."

Green glanced at Jonas. "How much longer does our antiquated bookseller have to live?"

Jonas looked at his watch. "I'd estimate no more than twelve hours. That's the maximum time I can reverse the damage."

"What's happening to him now?" Annja asked.

"His neurological system is being ravaged but the effects at this point are temporary. An increase in the dosage will accelerate the damage and make it irreversible."

"And if you stop the flow into him?"

Jonas smiled. "It's not that easy, Annja. It's not as though you can simply rip the IV out and expect a full recovery."

Damn, Annja thought.

"He needs to receive the counterdrug to this one to make a full recovery."

"You have it?"

"Of course we have it." Greene nodded to Jonas. "Show her."

Jonas brought out a small black doctor's bag and unzipped it. Reaching in, he pulled out a different IV bag. "This is the drip that will reverse the effects of the drug on Fairclough." He eyed Annja. "You don't know how to administer an IV, do you?"

"I can't stand needles."

"Ah, good," Jonas said. "Then you will obviously need to keep me around after you get the book."

Annja smiled at Greene. "How about that? Your doctor just sold you out."

"He did no such thing."

"Sure sounded like it." Annja glanced around. "Where's the automaton you call Kessel?"

"Waiting outside the door," Greene said, "although if I were you, I wouldn't be so quick to dismiss him that way. He's very touchy about his condition."

"I'll keep it in mind. Are we done here?"

Greene nodded. "Twelve hours. You have a watch?"

"Must have forgotten it back when you kidnapped me."

Greene unstrapped his and tossed it to Annja. She turned it over and looked at it closely. "A fake Rolex?"

"What about it? Keeps good time."

Annja held it up. "Another hypocrisy. You like the way it looks."

"I like the way it keeps time."

"I'll bet you have a few real ones back home in your underwear drawer."

Jonas shook his head. "We both got one when we were in Hong Kong to protest the environmental impact of recycled computer parts. There's nothing special about them, but they do keep decent time." He rolled up his sleeve and Annja saw he wore one, as well.

Annja checked Greene's watch and made a note of the time. "Fine, but when I come back, you'd better have that bag rigged and ready to go."

"We will."

Annja fixed them both with a long, hard glare. "One more thing—this isn't over. When I return, we're going to have a serious discussion about your little organization and its stated goals for killing innocent people."

Greene waved her off. "Whatever makes you feel good, Annja, that's fine. Now run along. Kessel is waiting."

Jonas grinned. "Have fun."

Annja frowned and walked out of the room. Kessel stood just outside, as Greene had promised.

"You coming with me?" she asked.

Kessel nodded.

"All right, then. Let's get to it."

7

Kessel led Annja back down the carpeted corridor and broke left near the entrance, taking her through a massive kitchen that could have easily handled the workload of two restaurants. Annja marveled at the shining cookware and six-burner cooktops with names she recognized from the fanciest restaurants. She whistled quietly. Fairclough certainly knew how to live.

A single heavy door led from the kitchen out to the backyard. But *yard* wasn't quite the appropriate name for the sprawling lawn that greeted them. Floodlights illuminated a pair of tennis courts in the distance, an Olympic-size swimming pool and a beautiful flagstone patio area complete with its own outdoor kitchen and bar area.

Annja frowned. Fairclough didn't seem like the type to do much entertaining and yet this home seemed custom-made for it. Then again, it would provide interesting cover for his underground maze. Perhaps he'd invested in this elaborate setup to simply help hide the book he sought to protect.

Either way, the place was luxurious and amazing. Annja found herself staring in wonder at the carefully trimmed plants and bushes they passed.

Kessel, for his part, seemed unmoved. He simply kept striding ahead toward a distant spot concealed behind a low rise in the yard. As they crested the grassy slope, Annja saw the outline of a large building and assumed this was the barn.

It looked old, in stark contrast to the rest of the estate. She could tell by the clapboard weathered to a fine slate gray that it had been built more than a hundred years ago.

Kessel stopped in front of the main door and pointed. Annja glanced at him. "You're not going to get the door?"

He just stared at her.

Annja sighed. "Look, if you're coming into the maze with me, we need to get some basic communication down. I take it you're familiar with hand signals?"

Kessel didn't respond for a moment but then finally nodded once.

"All right, then, we'll go with those. And improvise if something comes up we can't describe, okay?"

Kessel nodded again, this time a little faster. Annja grunted and pulled on the massive wooden door.

It creaked and then swung open. The smell of horses and hay enveloped her and she sneezed twice. So did Kessel, and it was the first time Annja heard him make any sort of noise.

"I'll walk out of here with a massive allergy attack if I'm not careful," Annja said. Kessel grunted behind her and she turned. "See? That's not too much to ask, is it? We might even get along, you and I."

Kessel raised an eyebrow.

Annja smiled. "Maybe not."

She found a switch on the wall and threw it on. Instantly, light flooded the stalls and she saw the one marked number three. Annja pointed. "I think that's our destination."

She led him over to the stall and looked inside. Nothing but hay and dust. A giant spiderweb hung in the upper corner, carefully crafted by a master weaver who was apparently hiding. Annja shook her head. "Don't care for spiders much."

Kessel nudged her into the stall. Annja looked around. "What do you think? Trapdoor? Would it be that easy?" She knelt and hauled back a whole pile of hay. But all she saw was a dirt-covered wooden floor.

Annja stood back up. "Guess not."

She backed out of the stall and examined the entry. But the simple latch over the gate didn't seem out of place at all.

Kessel, for his part, stood still, studying every inch of the stall with his eyes. Annja looked at him. "See something?"

Kessel shrugged, stepped forward and touched a single nail jutting out of the closest wall. Annja heard the click and then saw a portion of wall slide back and in, revealing a black crawlspace.

"Well, look at that. Your first contribution to the cause." She smiled at him. "It's a shame you're one of the bad guys. We might have gotten along well, you and I." She shrugged. "Oh, well. I'll take point. Don't let me catch you staring at my ass."

She thought she saw a glint of amusement in Kessel's eyes. Good, she thought. If she could reach him somehow, it wasn't out of the question to try to turn him against Greene.

Maybe.

The crawlspace was dark and dank. Annja sneezed again as she entered, aware of the moist earth smell. How had Fairclough constructed this thing without his neighbors knowing about it? Surely they would have had to haul away tons of dirt and stone to make this.

Given how utterly massive the estate was, he could pretty much be assured of privacy. Unless, of course, his neighbors could task satellites to fly overhead and spy on him.

Highly unlikely, in other words.

The crawlspace led down at a slight angle for twenty feet. Annja felt her knees bruising against the cold stones beneath them. She shifted her weight and kept moving. Behind her, Kessel made very little noise.

If he was that stealthy just crawling, then what was he like when he wanted to kill someone? She didn't intend to find out.

The crawlspace turned at a sharp left and she saw ambient light coming from somewhere. She glanced back at Kessel. "Got light up ahead here."

He nodded, and Annja turned back to the crawlspace. Her head kept bumping the top of it, dislodging dirt on her head. As long as it didn't get in her eyes. She'd need a nice long hot soak when this was all over, she decided.

Annja followed the crawlspace until it opened up at last and she could stand. Kessel drew himself out of the crawlspace like some winter bear just awakened from hibernation. His massive girth filled the architecturally complete room they found themselves in as he stood and stretched his limbs.

"Glad we're out of there," said Annja. "Not crazy about having to find my way through dark small spaces."

Kessel nodded.

The room was approximately eleven feet by eleven feet with a simple table in the center. In the middle of the table sat a book.

Kessel headed right for it.

Annja stopped him. "Hold it, slick."

He paused and looked at her. "You really think that's all there is to this?" she asked.

Kessel shrugged.

Annja shook her head. "You're smarter than that, Kessel. And there's no way Fairclough would put the book he's trying to protect right here. There's no challenge in this. And he did warn me of puzzles. I'm guessing this must be one of them."

She looked around the room again. Something seemed odd about it and the third time she looked she finally understood. "There's no exit."

Kessel's eyes blazed. And then he nodded understanding.

Annja studied the table. "So, somewhere, there's got to be a clue how we're supposed to free ourselves from this place. I mean, we could go back through the crawlspace—"

But at that moment, she heard a rumble and a cloud of dust poured into the room. The crawlspace had caved in.

Annja sighed. "All right, so much for that. Looks like the only way out of here is to figure out how to move ahead."

She examined the table again. There seemed nothing special about it. It was made of wood with four simple straight legs jutting down toward the stone floor.

"Nothing there," she muttered.

But what about the book?

Annja peered at it from all angles but could detect nothing special about it, either. As far as she could tell, it was a hardcover edition of the King James Bible. Fairclough didn't strike her as religious, but then again, she'd only just met him. He could have been a zealot for all she knew.

But maybe he simply had an appreciation for the book and what it had done for the English language, rather than its content.

Annja glanced at Kessel. "What do you think?"

He shrugged.

Annja agreed. "Yeah, we don't have much choice, do we?"

Kessel shook his head.

Annja looked at the book again. She could, of course, pick it up and see what happened. But was that the wisest move?

Overhead, a single lightbulb burned in the ceiling. It didn't appear that some type of guillotine would drop on them if she picked up the book.

She pointed to Kessel. "Do me a favor—check those walls for any hidden firing ports, would you? The last thing I want is to find myself impaled by a spear or projectile I can't see."

Together, they ran their hands over every inch of the walls they could reach. But try as she might, Annja couldn't find anything to suggest something lethal awaited them if they opened the book.

At last, she sighed. “All right, let’s try it.”

Kessel flipped open the cover before Annja could stop him.

“Hey…”

He stared at the book. There was nothing on the pages. Annja leafed through it but found nothing at all written in it. She glanced at the spine just to make sure she hadn’t missed something.

“Well, that’s weird.”

Kessel frowned.

Annja tried to pick the book up off the table, but it didn’t budge. “Is it stuck?”

Kessel tried, too, but it wouldn’t give. Annja nudged him out of the way and started leafing through the pages again. “There’s got to be something in here we’re missing.”

On the fourth time through, she finally found it at the back of the book. The last page covered a small button in the upper corner. Annja glanced at Kessel. “What do you think?”

Kessel shook his head.

But Annja poised her finger over it. “What have we got to lose? If we don’t press it, I don’t see anything else in here we could try. We either stay here and starve or press this and take our chances.”

Kessel nodded.

Annja pressed the button.

Several things happened in the next instant. First, the lights went out, plunging the entire room into total darkness. Annja heard sudden movement and a grunt.

“Kessel?”

And then there was nothing but silence.

“Kessel?”

No response.

Wonderful, she thought. Now she truly was alone. Villain though he might have been, Annja had felt at least some small measure of comfort knowing he was with her in the maze.

Now she was alone.

Then the floor gave way underneath her. Annja felt herself falling past the table, past the King James Bible trap that she'd triggered. She plunged down, unaware of how far she was falling until at last she fell into water. Annja dunked under and came up sputtering, gasping for air. The sudden cold shock had stunned her almost senseless.

She guessed that she'd fallen at least twenty feet but couldn't be sure. It was still completely dark in the… pool she found herself in, adding to her insecurity about her position. After all, Fairclough had warned her that it would become obvious there were challenges within the maze itself. And Annja had the distinct impression that meant Fairclough might have stocked the maze with a few living surprises.

There might even be piranha in the water with her right now.

She wiped her eyes and tried to focus.

In any event, she was out of the room with no exit. Now she just had to figure out where she was.

And what had become of Kessel.

8

The first thing she did was determine the size of the pool she'd dropped into. Annja swam in one direction until she bumped into stone. A wall. There, she thought, that tells me there's at least some end to this.

She swam back the way she'd come but grew tired partway across. It wasn't a small pool.

Annja took a deep breath and dove down, but again, she couldn't find the bottom before her lungs threatened to burst. She surfaced and gasped for air.

Not good, she decided. Better to stay close to the stone wall she'd felt. So she paddled back over and felt the cool, slimy stones, covered in mossy algae. And Annja hadn't detected any chlorine, so this was a natural body of water.

And that meant there might be other things living in it besides the algae.

Almost as soon as she came to that realization, Annja felt something brush against her legs. She jerked them up and away. She wasn't in salt water, so that ruled out sharks. And while she didn't relish the thought of facing anything in the dark, she could control her panic.

Now might be the time to see what it is I'm up against here, she thought. Annja visualized the sword waiting for her in the otherwhere. Instantly, the sword was in her hands, forcing her to tread water with her legs only. But the dull gray light the sword cast provided much-needed illumination.

Annja held the blade high overhead and attempted to see where she was. She glanced up at the ceiling and saw she'd misjudged the distance she'd fallen by perhaps a dozen feet. She could see the hole in the ceiling where she'd come plummeting through.

Any higher and I would have broken my back when I landed, she thought. Fairclough must have worked it out that way on purpose.

The stone wall at the one end gleamed in the light. Annja could see that the stones reached all the way to the ceiling, but looked impossible to climb. Then she slowly traced the wall. It went all the way around the water. She estimated that the pool was the length of a football field. Completely enclosed by the stone wall.

Again, she was in a room with no apparent exit.

She'd already tried to dive and hadn't reached the bottom. So how deep was it? And did the exit lie somewhere beneath the surface?

One way to find out.

Annja took a deep breath and dove, holding the sword out in front of her while she kicked through the water. Just having the sword gave her a lot more strength and her system felt flush with energy. Her lungs didn't protest so much as she swam deeper.

She could make out all sorts of plants and a sandy bottom roughly thirty feet below her.

She marveled at Fairclough's construction of this maze. It wasn't the type of maze she'd expected. This wasn't a series of corridors and dead ends; it was a complex series of rooms, each with its own unique set of conditions. In order to get through this, Annja was going to need all of her wits about her.

A school of small fish swam away from the light of the sword, and Annja saw their large white eyes, more accustomed to the darkness than the light. What else lived down here?

She got her answer a second later as she spotted what looked like a bull shark. It cruised lazily some distance away from her. Annja felt her heartbeat kick up a notch as she remembered that bull sharks could live in fresh water. They'd been found up rivers hundreds of miles away from the ocean.

The shark suddenly seemed to notice her and altered its course. It wasn't huge. But at roughly six feet long, it was still large enough to give Annja some problems.

If she'd been unarmed in the dark, it would have made short work of her.

But with the light and the sword, Annja felt ready for anything.

She hoped she wouldn't have to kill it. It was simply doing what it was supposed to do. As an apex predator, its job was to hunt and eat. But when it swam suddenly closer with its pectoral fins jutting downward, Annja could see that its attitude had changed from mild curiosity to anger. It seemed to view Annja as an intruder.

I don't blame it, she thought. If I ruled this place and someone threatening showed up, I'd be pretty pissed, too.

She flicked the sword blade up and aimed it at the shark's snout. It brushed against the steel and Annja felt the blade cut into the nostrils. The shark bucked and jumped away.

Annja watched it retreat into deeper water trailing a thin line of blood in its wake. She hoped that would be the last of interest it expressed in her.

She turned her attention back to surveying the area beneath her. Unfortunately, she ran out of air, so she had to surface and take several deep breaths.

There was no doubt the sword helped her stay underwater longer. But there were limits to what it could do. And if Annja was going to figure out how to get out of here, she'd have to be sure she could reach the exit in one breath; otherwise, she'd drown.

Annja waited until her heartbeat had calmed down and then took another deep breath and dove.

She barely missed the set of teeth that flashed past her head.

The bull shark was back.

Annja kicked hard to put distance between them and then floated in the water with the sword in front of her.

The bull shark came at her hard. Annja knew this was no time for indecision. She cut fast, slashing across the water in front of her, severing part of the bull shark's snout with a single swipe.

Blood flooded the water and the shark reeled away. Annja cut it again, a killing thrust to the underbelly.

I hope there's only one of them, she thought. Otherwise, the mess in the water would draw others in no time.

She surfaced, took another breath and then swam

deeper, beneath the blood cloud that hung suspended in the water.

The sword lit her way and Annja swam for the reeds growing down near the bottom of the pool. An underground pool stocked with a bull shark? Annja shook her head and kicked on.

The sword's light illuminated more of the bottom. Annja spotted more fish and a few turtles. There must have been a way to keep the shark fed, aside from the fish population contained in the pool.

Would have been nice if Fairclough had given me a warning, Annja thought. *I could have been killed back there.* And he didn't even know about the sword she carried. His only reason for getting her here was to warn her about the existence of that precious history book.

Annja made it to the other end of the pool and surfaced once more. With one hand on the stone wall, she held out the sword. She hadn't seen any other sharks and she doubted there'd be more than one. It would be too difficult to keep two of them fed properly.

Still, she didn't doubt that Fairclough could spring other surprises on her. She had to find her way out of the pool. While the sword would keep her healthy for some time, she could tell that the temperature of the water would eventually drop her core temperature and bring on hypothermia.

And that would kill her just as easily as a bull shark.

Annja waited again and then took a series of shallow breaths followed by one deep breath. Then she plunged beneath the surface again, kicking stronger than she had previously.

I've got to find a way out of here quickly, she thought.

She traced her way down the wall toward the bottom.

A mass of boulders sat near the wall itself. Was the exit there?

Annja floated in the water and tried to reason out what Fairclough would have planned for this room. Obviously, the real challenge would have been the shark. Once that was dispatched, though, was there a secondary puzzle?

Annja swam toward the boulders. Small crabs scurried away from her as she approached. Annja thought the topmost boulder looked unusual and she pushed against it.

It moved suddenly, almost causing Annja to lose her balance. As it rolled away, it revealed a long black tunnel.

Annja frowned.

That was the last thing she wanted to see. She jabbed the sword into the opening, but the blade's light faded about ten feet from the entrance.

Wonderful, she thought. There's no way of telling how far it goes. She could run out of breath and find herself drowning inside.

Not exactly the way she'd envisioned herself dying.

Annja surfaced and looked around, trying to see if she'd missed anything. But as far as she could tell, there was no choice. The stone walls of the pool ran right up to the ceiling high overhead. There was no way to climb the walls. And Annja doubted the exit would have been up there. Fairclough might have been devious, but he would have also planned for someone to find a way out, provided they got past his pet shark.

No, the more Annja thought about it, the more she suspected the exit really was the tunnel beneath the surface. She'd just have to take a chance that she could swim it in one breath.

Here goes nothing, she thought. Annja took another breath and plunged straight down toward the tunnel, pulling herself through it as she kicked harder than she thought possible.

The darkness seemed to stretch before her, yawning like some great black maw. Annja drove the sword out ahead of her, willing it to carry her forward, to lend her its strength.

Her legs ached from kicking. And she kept bumping her head against the tunnel itself, which was only about six feet in diameter.

I've got to keep going, she thought. *Come on, Annja, keep swimming!*

Annja didn't dare stop and look back. She had a gut feeling that she'd already passed the point of no return.

Her lungs started to crave oxygen more than they ever had before.

Keep going.

Annja closed her eyes and imagined the sword in her mind's eye. A new wave of strength surged through her body and it felt as if her muscles had more oxygen now. Annja's lungs still hurt from holding her breath, but she kept her eyes shut and kept plowing forward.

Just a little bit more.

The tunnel couldn't go on forever. At some point, Fairclough would have to end it and bring the person into another room so the fun could continue.

Right?

She prayed she was right.

Her legs ached now and Annja knew that this was the final energy she could pull from the sword. Eventually, it would need to be put back into the otherwhere. Annja didn't think it had an inexhaustible supply of energy to give her.

Nothing did.

I'm almost there, Annja told herself. A few seconds more.

And then she had the sensation of light ahead. Annja opened her eyes and saw that the tunnel had already started to open up. She could see the lighter water in front of her. The tunnel must have opened into a different room.

She kicked with every last ounce of strength she possessed and was rewarded by finally clearing the tunnel.

Air.

Annja shot for the surface.

Broke it.

And sucked deep lungfuls of air.

Finally.

Water dripped off her and her entire body felt cold. She needed to get out of the water and find a way to warm herself. Otherwise, she was done for.

She turned in the water and saw a sandy beach ahead.

Annja swam for the shore.

Grateful to be through the tunnel.

And still alive.

9

Annja waded out of the water and fell face-first into the sugar-soft sand. Her teeth chattered and her entire body felt chilled to the core. Annja briefly managed to put the sword back and then exhaustion washed over her. She closed her eyes and just wanted to fall asleep.

But she knew she couldn't. The watch on her wrist already showed her that one hour had passed since Greene had delivered his ultimatum to find the book or Fairclough would die.

Annja groaned and hauled herself into a sitting position. The sand was mercifully warm and her clothes already seemed to be drying, as if they'd been exposed to a fire. Annja lay back down on the sand and let the warmth, which seemed to be radiating up from under it, bleed into her and restore her core temperature.

Fairclough had planned for this, she guessed. After that swim, people would need to be able to warm themselves. Somewhere beneath her, there was no doubt an industrial heater.

Annja frowned. The heater probably wasn't left on twenty-four hours a day… Had it been activated when she reached the sand? In that case, there would have to be sensors embedded somewhere in the walls that would track her progress. Either that or cameras, with people watching her. If she could figure out a way to get to some sort of control room, there might be a way to bypass the maze itself and head right to the book.

Of course, in order to do that, Annja would need a more intimate knowledge of the maze. And that was something she didn't have.

She sighed and sat back up.

Kessel was still nowhere to be seen. Annja wondered if he'd fallen into some other pool somewhere else in the maze and if he'd had his own run-in with a shark.

Maybe he hadn't made it.

Annja smiled. She doubted it. Kessel was very strong…and smarter than she'd first thought. Maybe she could find an unexpected ally in the man—if she *could* find him again. He'd already shown a willingness to communicate with her. And Greene had sent him into the maze with Annja without consulting with the guy first. That had to have shown Kessel he was expendable.

"I'd be furious if Greene did that to me." Annja glanced around, suddenly sheepish that she'd spoken to herself.

A couple close calls and she was already cracking up.

She hauled herself to her feet and stomped around, feeling her muscles come back to life. A few deep breaths, knee bends and waving her arms around helped flush blood through her body.

Now, where do I go from here?

She took a look around this new room and saw that the sandy beach ended almost as soon as she got away from the water. Obviously, the beach was only there to serve the purpose of reinvigorating the person in the maze.

But beyond that, it was back to business.

The maze.

Annja padded out of the sand and paused only to shake some of it from her shoes. Then she put her shoes back on and turned around.

A wide corridor stretched out in front of her. Lights ran along the length of it, illuminating different-shaped stones that paved the floor.

She pulled the sword out again and knelt close to the edge where the stones started. Some of them were shaped like squares, some like rectangles and some triangles.

Annja tapped the point of her sword on one of the square tiles.

And threw herself down as a whisper of air breezed past her head. She heard a splash behind her and knew that whatever trip wire she'd triggered had fired its dart or spear into the water.

Good range, she thought.

She sat back up and tapped the edge of the sword on the triangular tiles. She heard the same punctured sound of air breaking overhead and watched this time as a small dart zipped past her and also landed in the water.

Last time, she thought, and touched the tip of the sword to the rectangle.

Nothing happened.

Annja nodded, stood and set off down the corridor, making sure to keep to the rectangular tiles.

The corridor went on for another fifty feet before ending abruptly. Annja stood on the brink of a pit that stretched fifteen feet before the corridor continued on the other side of it for another fifty feet or so.

The distance was too far to jump, and trying to get a running start would prove difficult relying only on the rectangular stones.

So how would she get across?

And if she did manage to span the gap, she'd have to make sure that she landed on the rectangles on the other side, as well.

Annja shook her head. Damn, Fairclough, you didn't make this easy, did you?

She glanced overhead, wondering if perhaps he'd left a rope hanging down that she could use to swing across the divide.

No such luck.

She sighed. This was getting tiresome. Annja would have preferred a simpler maze.

Hell, she thought, even facing a minotaur would have been preferable.

She knelt at the lip of the gap and peered into the chasm. The sword cast light only so far, but Annja thought she could see what looked like tips of spears jutting up at an angle, ready to impale those unlucky enough to fail the jump.

Punji sticks, she thought. Just like she'd seen in the jungles of Southeast Asia before.

But there had to be a way across. There had to be. Fairclough wouldn't have made it impossible.

At least, not yet.

Annja wondered what he might have lying in wait farther on in the maze. But for now, her task was relatively straightforward. Just get across.

Easier said than done.

She glanced over her shoulder at the placement of the rectangular tiles. They'd been spaced just far enough that she was confident there was no way she could get any type of running start.

No, there had to be another way.

Fifteen feet was too far to jump from standing at the ledge. And worse, Annja could see that the first rectangle was situated just out of reach, so that once she got to the other side, she'd have to immediately vault herself forward from the edge of the pit.

Annja looked beyond the chasm. Was there a way to run and jump and avoid the darts when she hit the other rigged tiles?

She could keep the sword up in front of her, of course, but would the blade be enough to deflect the darts? And if one of them hit her, did it have a toxin on it? Or were they simply darts with sharp points?

Too many variables, she decided. Too many unknowns that she couldn't risk without fear of losing her life.

But what choice did she have?

There was nothing on the walls that surrounded her except a series of holes where she assumed darts would fire out of. No hints about how to get across, no clues as to how to solve this puzzle.

Annja sighed. She wished she could have a few words

with Fairclough. Just to get a hint of how he had imagined this maze.

There didn't seem to be an rhyme or reason to it. Each room she'd been in so far hadn't behaved the way she'd imagined it would. The table room had held a hidden switch that then plunged her into a pool with a shark in it, followed by a long tunnel swim that left her nearly dead.

And now this.

She shook her head.

What am I missing?

Still kneeling at the edge of the pit, Annja slashed the air with her sword again. The gray light illuminated the tips of the punji sticks. But something seemed strange.

Annja looked again. And then she checked above the chasm.

There.

She stabbed up into the roof directly above the chasm and felt the blade pass seemingly right into the stone ceiling.

Except it wasn't stone.

It was a painted canvas designed to look like the rest of the ceiling. Annja's blade cut a swath through it and it dropped down to her. She tested its strength. Would it be strong enough to take her weight?

It was risky.

Annja pulled harder and felt some more of the material rip away from the ceiling. No, it wouldn't hold her.

No way.

But as she pulled the material she saw something white drop down.

A rope.

Annja smiled. So, Fairclough had given her a way

out. But even if intruders figured out the ceiling was a painted canvas, how would they have been able to get to the rope? Annja had the sword, luckily.

But other people?

She shook her head and grabbed the rope. When she put her full body weight on it, it held, and Annja swung across the divide easily.

She still had to be careful when she touched down on the lip of the divide on the other side. And as it was, she had to jump in order to land neatly on one of the rectangular stones.

But she did, aware that a line of sweat had broken out along her hairline.

Annja had little doubt that there'd be even more demanding tasks ahead of her.

She checked her watch before setting off down the corridor again. Twenty minutes had passed. The increments seemed small, but they added up. And somewhere far above her, Fairclough was getting closer to the irreversible effects of that toxin Jonas had pumped him full of.

I'd better get moving, she thought.

Annja stepped gingerly down the corridor and then saw the turn ahead of her to the right. She knelt at the corner and stuck her head out just enough to get a glimpse of what would be waiting.

Instinct caused her to jerk back as another dart zipped past where her head had been a second before.

More darts?

Annja waited and then stuck the sword back around first. This time, nothing shot out of the far wall.

So it had been only one?

Annja took a chance and stepped around the corner.

And felt nothing pierce her skin.

She exhaled and wiped the sweat from her brow. The corridor was dimmer than the one she'd just left. That made her suspicious.

If she couldn't see too far ahead, there was no telling what might be waiting farther along the corridor.

And she had no doubt there'd be more danger.

Annja kept her steps light, ready to either jump out of the way or drop to the floor if she thought she needed to.

But as the corridor continued, she started to think that this might simply be a passage to lead her to her next challenge.

Maybe I've passed this challenge already, she thought.

Maybe.

She heard a rumbling thunder then and forgot the need to stay on the rectangles. Annja let her body guide her and broke into a sprint forward. As the first stones rained down from above, she put her hands overhead to ward off what she could. As it was, she caught a few of them on her hands.

Praying that there were no more darts, she bent her knees, diving into a roll that brought her ten feet ahead of where the roof collapse had started.

The thundering stopped.

Annja got to her feet and looked back. The corridor was completely blocked.

There was no way back now.

Annja had no choice but to proceed.

10

The floor switched from the stone tiles to rock.

Annja stopped, aware of the change and wondering what might have triggered it. Had she passed into yet another level? The slope of the floor also flowed down at a slight angle. As she moved slowly ahead, the air grew cooler.

I feel like I'm in a live-action Dungeons & Dragons game, she thought. She wondered if there'd be an ogre around the corner.

Luckily, I have my sword, she thought with a grin.

But there wasn't an ogre waiting around the corner. And as Annja progressed, the light dimmed even more, making it difficult to see what lay ahead. She squatted, trying to see if she could make out any details of the landscape.

She heard vague noises.

A shuffling sound.

Was someone walking?

But if they were, they didn't seem to be getting any closer or farther away.

Annja kept moving. She used the sword to light the way ahead, and its gray illumination enabled her to see that she was approaching another corner.

The volume of the sound increased, but Annja wasn't so sure that she was hearing footsteps now.

But there was definitely something moving back and forth.

When she rounded the corner, she saw what it was.

A large scythe blade swung back and forth over the corridor, its steel edge looking incredibly menacing. Annja would need to pass through it to continue on.

The shaft that held the blade disappeared into a gap in the ceiling almost twenty feet overhead. Annja tried to get a look at the mechanism controlling it, but it was dark and tough to see. Plus, if she got too close, the blade would cut her open. And the size of the blade suggested that even a minor cut would be fatal.

Annja sighed. Fairclough must have had a thing for recreating old Indiana Jones movies. Some of these "props" looked like he'd lifted them right off the set.

Still, it wasn't much of a deterrent. Annja drew as close as she could to the blade and felt the breeze as it swung back and forth. There was a momentary gap as the blade passed her. If she timed it right, she could leap across and be on her way on the other side before it had a chance to cut her up.

But if she misjudged, that wouldn't be good at all.

Annja shook her head. It wasn't worth taking the chance.

So instead, she jumped onto the back of the blade itself, close by the shaft, and squatted there as it swung back and forth. Then she simply leaped off to the other side, rolled and came up in a crouch.

And immediately had to leap to avoid a slashing blade that cut at her exposed legs. Annja went high, looked down and saw that the blade cut in a circular arc. She came down, leaped forward again and landed in a squat, breathing hard, but having escaped injury.

That was a little too close for comfort. Fairclough was stacking his challenges now. Lulling people into assuming there was only one main task to deal with and then nailing them when they got lazy.

Like I did, she thought with a frown.

Well, never again.

Annja followed the corridor down another slope and then found herself facing a simple wooden door. Her first instinct was to check for trip wires, but a quick search revealed nothing out of the ordinary.

Annja opened the door and, after a quick visual once-over, walked inside.

She stood in a ten-by-ten room, brightly lit by fluorescent bulbs in the ceiling. But what made the room so interesting were the three doors set into the wall opposite the one she'd come through.

Annja closed the door behind her and heard a click.

She ducked, expectantly, but nothing happened.

Three doors, she thought. Three ways to leave the room?

She approached the door directly in front of her and turned the doorknob and pulled, but nothing happened.

Locked?

She tried pulling again, but couldn't get it to open.

All right, let's try the other two, she thought. She went left first, pulled on the door and it opened easily.

The problem was that she now faced a brick wall. Annja closed the door.

Right?

But when she opened that door, she faced a similar brick wall.

Apparently, she mused, the middle door would be the one she'd need to get open in order to proceed. But it was locked.

So what was the puzzle here? How to get the center door open.

Annja stood in the middle of the room and faced the three doors. There had to be a formula, she figured. If one of the doors was open, perhaps that would unlock the center door?

She kept the left door open and then went back to the center door. But it didn't budge.

Annja tried her luck with the door on the right, leaving it open while she tried the center door again. Still no luck.

This time, Annja left both doors standing wide open and again tried the center door.

But it still didn't open.

Annja considered hacking her way through the door with the sword, but judging by how the maze had treated her so far, she might end up tripping something particularly nasty if she didn't figure this out the right way.

Annja stood there with her hands on her hips and took a few deep breaths. She was rapidly losing any and all interest in the maze. Why couldn't Fairclough have just gotten himself a floor safe?

But Fairclough had enjoyed this. Even if he liked Annja, he was no doubt relishing the thought of her facing the challenges in the maze he'd created. Somewhere in his vegetative state, he was excited about what she'd be discovering down here.

She wondered briefly if Kessel had already met his end. Maybe there'd been another giant fish tank with something even nastier than the bull shark waiting for him. Annja didn't know. What she did know was she needed to figure out how to get through the door in front of her.

She glanced over her shoulder at the door she'd come through. Then she shrugged and walked back to it.

It wouldn't open.

"For crying out loud."

Annja looked around the rest of the room, but there wasn't much to see. White alabaster walls surrounded her except for the four doors the room contained. The three in front of her and the one behind her.

Annja tried the right door this time. But the center door didn't open. Then she opened the left door and tried again.

Nothing.

Annja closed the right door and kept the left one standing open. Then she went to the door she'd come through and tried it.

It didn't budge.

She closed the left door and opened the right door. Then she tried the door she'd come through originally.

This time, it opened.

Annja breathed a sigh of relief. Well, at least I got that far, she thought. There had to be a system here, and somehow, she'd get through it.

She walked back to the center door and tried it, but it was still locked. So Annja went to the left door and opened that one. Then she went back to the center door and tried opening it again.

And this time, it opened.

"Finally," said Annja. She checked the door frame and then stepped into another corridor. This one was pretty dark, so she pulled her sword out.

As the sword cast a glow down the hallway, Annja moved slowly, trying to figure out what Fairclough would spring on her next. So far, she reasoned, the puzzles hadn't been that difficult. If anything, they were more like delaying tactics than anything else. Annja hadn't found them to be too taxing mentally—more bothersome, really, than anything else.

But that could change quickly.

And, frankly, she expected Fairclough to be especially tough on her sometime soon.

But when?

She glanced at her watch. Two hours had passed. Annja blinked. When had that happened?

The floor changed back to stone tiles and Annja froze. She used the tip of the sword and probed each tile as she proceeded slowly. But nothing happened. Annja looked up and checked her surroundings.

The corridor was the length of a football field and Annja realized that she was tired. The stress of forever being alert was starting to take a toll on her. Plus, it didn't help that she'd burned herself out during the swim through the tunnel. What she really wanted to do was sit down somewhere and take a nap.

A nap.

She frowned. There was no way she could afford to do that. If she fell asleep now, she might not wake up in time to save Fairclough from the toxin Jonas was forcing into his body.

He didn't deserve to die, Annja thought. Although she might like to give him some hell for putting her through the maze.

Then she heard the hissing sound.

Snakes?

Her heartbeat increased. But no, the hissing sound wasn't natural. There was no rise and fall to it, just a steady low hiss that grew louder with every step forward.

Annja peered into the darkness, trying to use the sword to make out any details she might have missed.

There.

She spotted a piece of dust coming away from the wall. Annja moved toward it and examined the wall.

There was a round hole in the masonry. And something was blowing out of it. Annja sniffed it.

Gas.

Annja moved away from the nozzle and tried to estimate how long it would take for her to be rendered unconscious from the stuff spraying into the corridor. The answer didn't make her feel any better.

She had to get out of there fast.

With fifty feet of the corridor remaining, Annja had a choice to make. She could continue on, probing each tile for hidden trip wires and booby traps, or she could simply take her chances and run for it. There was a door at the end of the corridor, and if she could make that, she might have a chance.

But what if running meant she tripped a booby trap?

Annja took a deep breath, aware of the powerful effect of the gas on her already. Her eyelids felt heavy. If she stopped now, she'd fall asleep and possibly never wake up.

No, it was time to go.

Annja ran hard and heard the pops as several darts fired at her. Somehow, she managed to avoid them, aware that she was getting drowsier and drowsier all the time.

And then she was at the door.

Grabbing at the doorknob, she turned and fell into the next room.

Kessel.

11

He was surrounded by three large and angry-looking Doberman pinschers, their sleek black fur ruffled and bunched as their muscles shifted. A fourth dog lay dead near Kessel, its neck at an abrupt angle.

Annja frowned. How had he gotten this far into the maze? Was there another way through it?

"Kessel!"

He glanced up even as one of the dogs made a lunge at him. Kessel batted it away with a huge paw of his own. The dog scampered away, but not far. They thought they had Kessel cornered, and while he might have killed one of their own, there were still three of them to tear him apart.

Annja could work her way past Kessel and the dogs. They'd shown no interest in her so far, after all. Once she got past them, she'd be free to continue on. And that would mean she wouldn't have to deal with Kessel when this was over. She didn't relish the thought of having to fight him.

But Kessel didn't necessarily deserve to die being ripped apart by wild dogs. He hadn't actually killed anyone today. Greene had. As far as Annja was concerned, Kessel just might be the best of the three villains holding Fairclough.

Only just.

Annja started forward as she heard a low growl from behind her and turned.

Another dog squatted in the corner. And this one was bigger than any of the others. Judging by his girth, he ate better than the other dogs. He was probably the alpha male of the pack, which is why he'd sent his soldiers in first—before he moved in for the kill.

But now Annja was here and he was reacting to the threat she posed.

Or the threat she posed as soon as she yanked her sword out.

If the dog was concerned about the blade, it showed no sign of fear. How could it? Annja reasoned. There was no way such a dog would have ever risen to power in the pack if he'd shown the slightest hint of emotion.

Even in the face of staring down an armed human, the dog menaced Annja. It began to growl, a lower vibration from deep within its belly, moving up through its throat.

Annja didn't want to have to kill the dog, but neither did she intend to end up being mauled and eaten by it, either. Had Fairclough stocked the maze with these beasts and kept them underfed for just this purpose?

She was rapidly growing weary of Fairclough's mechanisms for keeping his old book safe and secure.

There were so many better ways he could have done this, she thought.

When the alpha dog attacked, there was no hesitation. It simply shifted and shot at her, fully committed and without any pause. One moment, it had been standing completely still. In the next, it was charging Annja faster than she could draw a breath.

Annja pivoted as the dog sailed past her.

Dammit, she thought, he's not giving me much of a choice here.

The dog came at her again and, this time, Annja tried to smack it with the flat of her blade. She caught him on his flanks, but the dog barely whimpered at the hit. He landed, skittered away from Annja, then turned and came racing right back at her.

Annja shook her head. Don't do this, she wanted to yell.

Ravenous as it appeared to be, despite its girth, the alpha dog would need to provide for its soldiers or risk being unseated from his position of power. And that meant that it would attack any viable target.

And Annja was viable.

So was Kessel.

The alpha dog rounded on her again, intent on snapping for her neck.

Annja had no choice.

She backpedaled and then cut quickly, severing the dog's head and just barely sidestepping a gush of blood that erupted from the stump. The dog's body crashed to the floor and lay still. Its head landed across the room, closer to Kessel.

There was a moment of stillness. The three dogs snarling at Kessel stopped. One of them nosed the decapitated head, sniffing around it. Annja heard a curious sound that was a combination whimper and growl.

They'll either break for it here, she thought, or another dog will try to take the alpha's place.

She hoped it would be the latter.

Kessel glanced at Annja and his eyes widened when he saw the sword. So much for keeping that a surprise, she thought. Oh, well, she'd deal with it when she had to and not before.

Another dog nosed the alpha's head, then sniffed the first dog that had nosed it. There were more growls. A whimper.

And then all three ran down the corridor away from Annja and Kessel.

Annja let out a pent-up breath. She didn't want to have to kill any more dogs today.

"That was close," Kessel said.

She whipped her head up. "Uh, I thought you didn't have a tongue."

Kessel grinned. "Yeah, well, that's not exactly accurate."

"No shit." Annja kept the sword handy. "You feel like explaining that one to me?"

Kessel shrugged. "Not much to explain. It was necessary to make it appear as if I didn't have a tongue. Greene's much more trusting when he thinks there's no fear of anyone letting his secrets out."

"And who would want to do that?"

Kessel smiled. "Oh, I don't know. Maybe a special agent with the FBI."

Annja eyed him. "You're with the Bureau?"

"I am."

"Prove it."

Kessel laughed. "As if. I don't carry a badge around with me, Annja. I'm deep undercover. Something like that would get me killed. Greene wouldn't even hesitate if he suspected me."

"How long have you been under?"

"Two years."

Annja shook her head. "That's a hell of a long time."

"Tell me about it. I almost forget what it's like to have a conversation sometimes. My throat gets all raspy, too." Kessel rubbed his throat and looked at Annja. "You don't seem as surprised as I thought you'd be."

Annja shrugged. "I've known my fair share of Feds."

Kessel smiled. "Well, at least that charade is over. I'm glad you know I'm one of the good guys." He hesitated.

"What's the matter?" Annja asked.

Kessel pointed. "So, where'd you get that sword?"

"We can talk about that later." Annja looked around, but the dogs didn't seem to be coming back anytime soon. "What happened to you after the floor gave way in the table room?"

"I fell," said Kessel. "Landed in some murky pool filled with nasty biting fish of some sort. I had to swim through a long tunnel to get out of it, but fortunately, I'm used to doing things like that blindfolded."

"You are?"

"I was a Navy SEAL before I joined the Bureau."

Annja nodded. "That accounts for the size of your upper body. All the swimming. You're not the first SEAL I've known before."

"You must run in some pretty strange circles, Annja."

She laughed. "I sometimes think I don't have any friends who would even know what normal is."

"So, what now?"

Annja pointed down the corridor. "We go on, obviously. Fairclough's running out of time. We're three hours in and I have no clue if we're anywhere near the center of the maze."

"That book could be anywhere," Kessel said. "Did Fairclough give you any indication whatsoever about its location?"

"Said I'd understand the maze better when I got in here. But damned if I can figure it out. I expected something a lot more mentally taxing. But so far, it's just been about physically being able to handle the challenges he's thrown at me."

Kessel laid a hand on her shoulder. "Well, he wasn't throwing them at you, per se. He designed this in case thieves broke in and wanted the book."

"Yeah, but I have to think of it as being aimed at me so I can try to figure it out better. If I just view it as a security system, then it doesn't make much sense. Fairclough wanted me for some reason—almost as if he knew I'd be the only person who might have a shot at getting the book." She frowned. "That sounds awfully pretentious."

"Kinda does," Kessel said. "But it also makes sense." He sighed. "I know Greene was pretty upset when Fairclough demanded he get you to come here."

"You've been undercover for two years and you still don't have enough to arrest Greene?"

"Well, not until today. Him murdering that guy Jackson was enough, obviously."

"So how come you didn't?"

"Because you decided to imitate a bird," Kessel said. "I was just about to reveal myself when you took off. I couldn't let Greene chase after you."

“You got the getaway van, though.”

“Yeah, better to help him than risk him putting a hole in your head like he did with Jackson. Besides, I still had Fairclough to worry about.”

Annja wasn’t sure if that made a whole lot of sense. Two years was an extremely long time to be undercover. Maybe Kessel was having a harder time shaking it off than he thought he would.

She’d have to watch him to be sure he really was what he claimed.

Otherwise…

She blinked, realizing again how exhausted she was. Kessel eyed her.

“You okay?”

“I’m tired as hell,” Annja said. “Traipsing through some weird underground maze isn’t exactly how I saw my vacation playing out.”

“Sorry you got wrapped up in this. Fairclough’s insistence that you be brought to his home set Greene back on his heels, but he’s determined to get at that book.”

“Why is it so important to him?”

“You heard what Fairclough said. Supposedly there’s some hidden code within its pages. That’s what Greene wants. He’s convinced that possessing the book will enable his plans for future terrorism.”

“Well, he’s already ruined my vacation,” Annja said. “So I guess the least I can do is make sure he never gets his hands on the book, huh?”

“I like the way you think.”

“You don’t know me well enough to say that,” Annja said. “And you might just change your mind before this is all over.”

"As long as you don't run me through with that giant sword you've got somewhere."

Annja stopped him. "Let's pretend that doesn't exist, okay?"

"Little late for that, don't you think?"

"Maybe it was just an optical illusion." Annja winked. "After all, I don't think anyone in the Bureau would believe you if you mentioned it to them."

Kessel looked shocked. "You think I'd be that dumb? I like my job. I mention something like your sword and they'll send me packing with a side trip to the shrink's couch."

Annja smiled. "As long as we understand each other."

"Absolutely."

Annja nodded and they set off down the corridor. Annja was still concerned about the presence of the dogs somewhere up ahead. They had to have some place they called home. And if that was in the maze itself, then there was a very good chance they would attack Annja and Kessel when they broached their territory.

The fight wasn't over yet.

Not by a long shot.

12

Annja and Kessel moved farther down the corridor. Kessel volunteered to take point, which was fine with Annja. She'd been on high alert ever since they'd been split up, and the strain of being so careful was tiresome.

"After I got out of the pool, I found my way into another corridor. That one had a whole bunch of spears that rained down on me as I ran through it."

"You're lucky you weren't impaled," Annja said.

Kessel laughed. "I don't know if luck has anything to do with it. I was just so scared, I ran faster than humanly possible."

Annja smiled. She liked that he was self-effacing. It was hard to imagine someone as large as Kessel being afraid of much, but here he was freely admitting to it. It was refreshing to hear. Most of the time, Annja found herself surrounded by guys who liked to talk the talk, but could never walk the walk.

The corridor opened up and started to climb at a

shallow angle. Kessel glanced at Annja. "What do you think?"

"We keep going. Somewhere up ahead, there's got to be an indicator of where the book is."

"It just feels like we're being funneled along," Kessel said. "As if we're being set up for an ambush of some sort."

Annja nodded. "That occurred to me, as well."

"It's like when I was on the Teams," Kessel said. "We'd plan an ambush by funneling the enemy into a kill zone. Get them moving into a space that we would totally dominate with explosives and gunfire. That would be the end of them."

"How long were you with the SEALs?"

"Ten years. Saw action in Iraq and Afghanistan. Saw a lot of shit. Lost some good friends, as well." Kessel went quiet, and Annja knew he was probably remembering the friends he'd seen killed.

After a moment, he took a breath. "When I got out, I floated around for a while. I wasn't sure what I wanted to do. But once you've been in combat, there's always that need to challenge yourself. I could have gone and worked for private security companies and pulled down a crapload of money."

"Why didn't you?"

Kessel shrugged. "I guess I thought I wasn't done serving my country yet. I was done with the wars, but I still had something to give back. So I joined the Bureau."

"Did you get a law degree first?"

Kessel chuckled. "Yeah, they used to really like having lawyers as their special agents. Still do. But they also know they need people with proven combat experience.

My jacket was fairly impressive. I had what they were looking for. And the training was pretty easy, at least on the physical side."

"And once you graduated from Quantico?"

"Right into operations. I worked a human trafficking rig out of New York's Chinatown. Seriously bad stuff. Talk about busting my cherry on some real scumbags. The stuff they did..." His voice trailed off again.

Annja kept her eyes peeled even though Kessel was still on point. She didn't think it was likely that he'd miss much. But Annja also knew that memories could derail an otherwise alert individual, so she kept herself tuned in.

"Once I was done destroying that ring, I wanted to do something a little different. Something about seeing ten-year-old girls pressed into prostitution rattled me. I needed something else."

"So you got Greene."

Kessel nodded. "Yeah. Ecoterrorism is one of the concerns at the Bureau these days. And Greene was one of the biggest ones they wanted watched."

"How'd you get close to him?"

Kessel smiled back at her. "I hung my shingle out as a former operator. The best lies are based on truth, right? So the Bureau doctored my medical records and I sat around in a dingy office in Newark until one day he came to me."

"And what about the whole tongue thing?"

Kessel shrugged. "I used a prosthetic insert to make it look like I had a fake tongue at first. Then once Greene got comfortable around me, I tossed it. Now if he sees my tongue, he simply assumes it's the prosthetic. I've never actually spoken to him."

"I'm amazed it was that easy."

"You're not the only one," Kessel said. "But he fell for it and took me in. I had to prove myself, of course."

"How?"

Kessel stopped and shook his head. "It's probably best if you don't know. Not that it was horrible stuff or anything, but if you knew it could compromise me in court if you were called to testify. So we'll just gloss over that part, if you don't mind."

"No problem."

"My main concern has been what Greene is really up to. This book has been an obsession of his for almost a year now. He's been driven to find it and uncover its secrets."

"You think there's something to it?"

"Greene thinks there is and that's what counts right now," Kessel said. "It doesn't matter much what I think because I'm not the one I've got to take down. Greene's desperate to hurt the people who have harmed his vision of a utopian planet. That makes him a dangerous dude. And I've been after my superiors to treat him more as a viable threat. To date, it's been a challenge to do that."

"But they saw him as a threat initially."

Kessel shrugged. "We see a lot of threats. Sometimes, someone gets assigned to see what the deal is. I've kept a running tally of what Greene's been up to over the past few years—the stuff he's done, the people he's hurt. I haven't seen it all personally, though, which is why he hasn't been picked up yet."

"You need to document it firsthand?"

"Yep."

"And now you've seen him kill Jackson."

Kessel took a breath. "That's enough for me."

"Meaning what?"

"Not all justice runs through the courts." Kessel looked at her. "I'm sure that's something you're familiar with."

Annja sighed. "Yeah, I've had some experience with that sentiment."

"It's not that I disagree with the justice system, it's just that sometimes there comes a point where you need to ask yourself if the universe—God, whatever—has put you in a certain position for a reason. Maybe so that you might be the instrument of decision."

Annja glanced around. The air felt still. Kessel was eyeing her, trying to figure out if he'd gone too far with what he'd said.

Annja nodded solemnly. "There have been times when I was forced to do exactly that—be the instrument of decision. But I was coerced into it."

Kessel shrugged. "Things happen all the time. Sometimes there's just nothing you can do about it."

Annja pulled out the sword. The look of wonder on Kessel's mug was priceless.

"That's incredible."

Annja glanced around. "Something doesn't feel quite right."

Kessel frowned. "Yeah. The dogs?"

"Don't know. They looked like they had some internal business to sort out instead of dealing with us, though. I can't see them running back here to try to attack."

"Damn, I wish I had a piece," Kessel said. "But I lost mine when I fell into that damned pool. No way I could take forever searching for it in the dark while those fish nibbled on me."

"I don't blame you. I had to deal with a shark."

Kessel pointed. "I'm guessing the sword came in handy with that particular problem."

"Definitely did," Annja said. "But I don't like killing things that aren't at fault for being true to their nature. The shark wasn't malicious—it was just doing what millions of years of evolution have programmed it to do."

Kessel shook his head. "Has it occurred to you that Fairclough might have a few screws loose? I mean, this maze is weird. And then he goes and stocks it with sharks, biting fish, crazed dogs and a whole lot of other shit. That registers on my kook scale, for sure."

"I probably wouldn't have phrased it quite that way," Annja said. "But I have to agree. Some of this stuff just seems completely strange. He could have bought himself a giant vault and secured the book behind two feet of hardened steel. Instead, he goes and does this."

"The cost of this alone must have been somewhat staggering," Kessel said. "I didn't think book dealers made this kind of scratch."

"I'm guessing Fairclough has a pile of money. Whether from trust funds or an inheritance. But he's got it just the same."

"He could have used that money to do some real, lasting good in the world," Kessel said. "I guess I'm a little embarrassed that he wasted it the way he did. All of that money spent on this."

"It's not how I would have done it," Annja said. "But we also don't know what his motivation was. I know he's got this book, but what does it contain that he feels is worth undertaking such a grand venture as this to protect it? That's what has me wondering."

"Good point," Kessel said. "I guess there's only one way to find out, huh?"

Annja nodded. “We keep going.”

“With no clue of where we’re headed or what to expect when we get to wherever it is we’re going.”

“Exactly.”

Kessel winced. “If I was still on the Teams, this is where we’d probably say someone higher up screwed the pooch on the intel.”

“But you’d still carry out the mission, wouldn’t you?”

“Most likely.”

“Then let’s get going.” Annja shrugged. “Besides, it’s not like we can go back. The tunnel caved in after I came some way down it.”

“Same thing happened to me,” Kessel said. “Nearly got killed in a rock slide, of all things.”

“Fairclough took into account the human proclivity to want to flee when things start getting rough. Take that option away and you can keep moving people forward toward whatever the point of this is.”

“Funneled into a kill zone,” Kessel said. “And damned if I don’t feel the same way I used to on missions.”

“You’re not alone. There’s definitely been a change in the energy of this place. It almost feels like…” Annja’s voice trailed off. “Well, I’m not quite sure.”

“It feels,” Kessel said, his voice lower now than it had been, “as if we’re being stalked.”

“Yeah, but by what?”

Kessel pointed at Annja. “I don’t know, but you’ve got that sword, which is a good thing.”

“Do you think it’s something alive?”

“Yeah,” Kessel said. “And that’s exactly what’s got me concerned.”

13

If they were being stalked in Fairclough's maze, they didn't have time to worry about it for long. As they came around another bend in the corridor, a large door barred their way.

Kessel glanced at Annja. "The entrance to another room?"

She shrugged. "Could be." She ran her hands over the doorjamb. "I don't think it's rigged to explode or anything."

Kessel smiled. "Let's see what this is about, then." And he opened the door, studying the darkness that lay beyond before cautiously crossing the threshold.

When nothing happened, Annja stepped in and decided she might as well close the door behind them. There was never any going back in the maze. The light from her sword did little to illuminate their surroundings. Annja could see barely two feet in front of her, but she knew Kessel was close by.

"You think something's in here with us?" he whispered.

"No, but the room feels much larger than we can see."

"Wouldn't the dogs had to have come this way, too?" Kessel asked. "If so, then how did they manage to open the door? I get the feeling that there's a lot happening here that we're not entirely being made aware of."

"Like there's another route through this maze that we haven't seen?" Annja nodded. "I agree with you."

Kessel sighed. "Well, only one way to figure it out. Let's go—"

Annja stood there for a second, not entirely sure what had just happened. "Kessel?"

He didn't respond. Annja sank to her knees and felt the floor next to her. Solid. She used the tip of the sword to probe, and as she stabbed at the area ahead of where Kessel had been standing, the sword found empty air.

Annja peered closer and ran her free hand around the floor.

There.

A large hole in the floor.

Kessel must have stepped right into it. Annja peered into the hole. "Kessel!"

She got no response.

Dammit, they'd only just reconnected and now he'd gone missing again. Annja glanced around the room and wondered if there were other trapdoors lying in wait. And if so, where did they lead?

She could take her chances and try to find a way across the room, of course, but she might end up in another hole that brought her to someplace other than where Kessel went.

Annja felt sure that Kessel had stepped into this particular hole. That meant if she went down the same one, she ought to end up wherever he was.

In theory.

Of course, she thought with a frown, knowing Fairclough, he might have some sort of system whereby the tunnels could send people to other destinations.

This whole thing was getting too much for Annja. If there'd been a way out of here, she would gladly have left and deserted Fairclough. All right, maybe that was just wishful thinking. The old book dealer needed her. She couldn't very well abandon him to his death.

She had a choice to make. She could try to cross the room and risk falling down another rabbit hole. Or she could deliberately take the same one Kessel had.

She sighed. It was a pretty easy decision.

Annja sat and swung her legs over the edge of the hole. She took a deep breath and then pushed off, making sure to first put the sword away so she didn't risk impaling Kessel.

As the room disappeared behind her, Annja reflected on the possibility that this tunnel might lead to some insidious death trap and that she might very well have just committed suicide.

The tunnel reminded her of a water slide park. She twisted through a greased shaft and then shot along straightaways that accelerated her speed to a dizzying rate.

It was also completely dark in the tunnel. Annja lost her bearings and even her sense of which way was up.

When the tunnel finally ejected her into brilliant white light, she almost screamed at the sudden shock. But then she dropped into a huge pile of pillows that cushioned her fall. And she began to breathe again.

Annja blinked and rapidly crawled off the pillows. As she landed on the stone floor, she glanced around.

There was no sign of Kessel.

She groaned. Where had he disappeared to?

The room she stood in was large, and filled with a dizzying array of doors. *Wonderful. More choices to make.*

Kessel had clearly made a decision to go it alone and not wait for her. That kind of pissed her off. But then again, he didn't know that Annja hadn't vanished down a different rabbit hole of her own. He wouldn't have known that she'd be coming down the same one. But why had he gone and shut the door behind him? Even if he'd thought the chance of her following was slim, he could've left her a clue. Just in case.

So, now what?

Pick a door.

She counted them. Twelve. Any one of the doors could be the one Kessel had chosen. Annja would have to hope that she chose the same one if she had any chance of catching up with him.

And if she chose wrong?

Nothing she could do about that, she decided.

She looked all of the doors over. Each one was different, either in color, shape or design. Annja recognized some of the designs as being of foreign origin. One wasn't a door at all, per se, but a shoji screen from Japan that would presumably slide back on rails.

Another was a heavy cherry-red wooden door carved with intricate Nordic runes. Scandinavian?

Annja smirked. What if each led to a different part of the world? How wild would that be?

Impossible. Unless Fairclough had also mastered teleportation.

Annja was rapidly reaching the point where she wasn't sure what to believe anymore. And Fairclough did seem capable of almost making magic. He'd already proven his capacity for building something truly unique in the maze itself.

She shook her head. Let's try to stay real here, Annja, she thought.

She took a breath.

If I was Kessel, which would I have chosen?

There was a simple but elegant white door that looked like something out of a mansion in the deep South. Another industrial steel one seemed to have been taken from a warehouse. Still another had a Victorian design that reminded Annja of a BBC production prop.

Which one?

In the end, she opted for the door that looked like it might lead into someone's garage. It was bruised and battered, with splinters of wood out of it, and smeared with grease.

Annja grasped the doorknob and turned.

The door clicked open and led to a new corridor in front of her. She stepped across the threshold but left the door open behind her. Just in case she somehow ended up in front of Kessel. It was a clue to her whereabouts.

Torches flickered from sconces positioned into the brick walls on either side. Ahead, she could make out a corner she'd have to turn into.

But otherwise, the corridor was empty.

Something was different here, though.

And she recognized it as a sense of foreboding. As if she was getting closer to something.

Could it be, she wondered, that Kessel was right and with each room and corridor she passed through she was being funneled into some ambush point?

Anything was possible. But right now, her priority was finding Kessel and making sure they managed to stay together from here on out.

She thought about calling his name, but then decided against it. No sense alerting a possible threat that she was nearby.

Annja drew her sword.

Its pale gray light failed to reveal any details she hadn't been able to make out already from the flickering torches, which sent shadows skittering down the corridor with each little shift in the air. Annja caught the scent of burning pitch.

How did Fairclough manage to keep this place functioning if he was lapsed into some state of toxic shock upstairs in his bed? It didn't make sense. Someone would have needed to light these torches, right? He must have designed a control room.

That meant Fairclough had help from someone. Someone he could trust.

A butler?

A manservant?

She'd seen neither upon entering the estate, but then again, she was in the midst of being kidnapped. And checking for the staff of a great mansion hadn't really occurred to her. And probably they had been held captive somewhere, too. Otherwise, they'd have alerted the police and freed their employer, surely.

Annja shook her head. Fairclough was more than she'd bargained for. She could remember the conference he'd heard her speak at, all right. And she'd had to leave early. But they'd never even met. Why had one lecture led to all this?

She had mounting concerns and no way to validate them with anyone. It was really frustrating.

She walked down the length of the corridor and, right before the corner, she stopped, sank to the stone floor and then poked her head around.

Another corridor exactly like the one she'd just walked down. Annja counted the number of torches and then looked behind her and counted again.

Same number, she concluded.

She glanced ahead and made a note of the color of some of the stones. Then she looked back.

The same.

Annja frowned. So now she was walking down corridors that were exactly alike? What was the point of that?

Disorientation.

Fairclough was deliberately attempting to disorient anyone who might have gotten into his maze.

But to what end? What would that prove?

Annja took a deep breath.

And then started down the new corridor.

14

If Fairclough's goal had been to disorient those in the maze by replicating the corridors, he was succeeding. As Annja stole down the second corridor, she couldn't help but feel overwhelmed by a sense of déjà vu. Her body wanted her to realize it was lost and she had to fight the instinct to stop and regroup.

Keep going. This is all part of Fairclough's plan to ensure his book was safe.

The torchlight flickered as she walked past. And then she thought she heard something farther ahead.

At another corner, Annja took time to stop and listen before peering around it. As she did this time, she saw a shadow disappear around yet another bend.

Should she yell out?

What if it wasn't Kessel?

True, she had the sword. She could probably easily dispatch anything that attacked her. But what sort of beast could Fairclough have kept down here that could survive for long periods of time? How was it fed and cared for? By whoever managed a control center? Wasn't that kind of employee a risk to the security of the maze—a vulnerable weakness that put the book at risk?

And why hadn't Annja seen or heard anything of the wild dogs in a while?

There's simply too much going on here that I don't have a clue about, she thought to herself.

She rounded the corner and then ducked back as her ears picked up the telltale twang of something being shot out of a hole. As Annja dropped to the floor, several metal star-shaped blades zipped over her head. They bounced off the rear wall and skittered away.

Annja picked up one of them. A senban shuriken, like the kind she'd once seen used in Japan. But that was years ago. And why would Fairclough have these in his possession? Yeah, he could get them anywhere, but the design seemed unique to the warrior family Annja had come to know well on her trip to the Land of the Rising Sun.

Weird.

She put one of the throwing stars in her pocket and kept walking. As she got to the end of the corridor, she peered down a new hallway.

And saw nothing but a brick wall.

Huh?

The corridor ended just as quickly as it began: a dead end.

But she'd seen a shadow pass down here. And more importantly, Kessel would have had to come this way. So where was he if he'd run into this same obstacle?

These puzzles were getting to be a pain in the ass

and she was ready for them to be over. A quick glance at her watch told her that five hours had now passed. She winced.

The longer she stayed underground, the easier it was to get so absorbed in the bizarre happenings down here that the real world seemed a distant memory.

And that was probably what Fairclough was counting on. If someone got trapped, they could wander for weeks and not find their way around or back to safety. They'd die of starvation.

Unless the dogs got to them first.

Or something else.

Annja approached the brick wall and pressed against it, but it was solid. There was even a torch in a sconce on the wall itself. Annja reached up and passed her hand over the flame, making sure it wasn't some high-tech illusion. But she felt the warmth of the fire and the bite of the flames. It was real enough.

And so was the wall, she decided.

She squatted on the ground. How would she get through this thing?

If Kessel had actually chosen the same door she had and had forced his way through, there would be obvious marks or signs of what he'd done. But there was nothing.

Annja got up and checked where the wall joined the sides of the tunnel. Was there a hidden spring that had caused the wall to block it? But all Annja could make out was a line of mortar. It looked like the wall had been deliberately positioned here a very long time ago.

What about the ceiling? Could this section of wall have dropped down?

But again, the mortar work suggested otherwise. The

door wasn't an illusion, nor did it appear to be something that she could release using some hidden switch.

Which meant there had to be another way past it.

Annja backtracked.

Aside from the flickering torches, she couldn't make anything out. And again, she had to fight an overwhelming sense of déjà vu which threatened to disrupt her perception of place and time.

Annja glanced back at the blocked corridor. No way past it. And turning the corner was the logical decision to make since there was a corner to turn.

But what if she should have simply stayed on a straight line?

Annja backtracked into the other corridor. This time, instead of turning at the corner, she kept going forward. As she got closer to the wall, the bricks loomed closer and closer.

And then she walked right through it.

She nearly fell over on the other side, amazed that she had managed to walk through a wall.

"Wow."

It had to be an illusion. Or some holographic generator. Annja wanted to check it out, but as she approached the fake wall, a giant sheet of steel dropped from the ceiling and cut her off. The message was clear: she could always go forward, but never back.

"All right," Annja said quietly. "I'll do it your way."

She turned and kept walking down the new corridor, which again was a perfect replica of the previous ones. Annja shook her head. The level of disorientation was difficult to combat. How much longer would this go on? Was she any closer to the center of the maze? Or Kessel? Or the dogs?

She had no clue as to her whereabouts. Fairclough hadn't been kind enough to provide a map. Or maybe there wasn't one. Maybe Fairclough didn't even know what lay ahead of Annja.

But somehow, she doubted it. The longer she stayed down here, the more she believed that Fairclough had designed this maze to be exactly what he wanted.

Which, as far as Annja could tell, was a complete and utter nightmare.

The dogs came at her so fast that she barely registered their sudden appearance as they rounded the corner.

In the blink of an eye, Annja's sword was out and a whir of flashing steel swung and hacked amid the yowls and cries of the dogs she was forced to cut down. The scent of blood hung in the air and Annja let the sword droop as she fought back her revulsion at the death she had caused and the adrenaline dump she'd been forced to deal with.

"What a waste of life," she said quietly. She didn't blame the dogs. To them, attacking her had meant survival.

Just as Annja had been forced to defend herself in the name of survival.

That didn't make their deaths any easier to stomach, however. And Annja found herself choking back the reflex to retch.

She'd need to have a few words with Fairclough when she got out of here. Stocking a maze with dogs wasn't humane. And she didn't think the animal rights activists would be too pleased with him.

She bent and wiped her blade on the fur of one of the dead dogs. She'd cut his throat and the stone floor ran slick with blood and effluence. Annja blanched. She'd been around death many times before, but this made her ill.

She rose quickly, put the sword away and then stalked down the corridor, aware of the sticky crimson footprints she was leaving in her wake.

I need to find Kessel, she thought. I don't like being alone in this madness. She came to appreciate the plan behind Fairclough's mission to secure the book. He wasn't just interested in keeping it safe; he also wanted to punish those who went after it.

Unfortunately, Annja was being forced to find it. She didn't want it for herself. But the maze didn't know that. As far as it was concerned, Annja was here to rob Fairclough. So it treated her like an enemy.

Almost exactly like how the human body would respond to a bacterial infection or virus, she supposed.

Interesting.

The blood trail she was leaving was fading into nothing. She heard noises up ahead and stopped suddenly.

Annja drew her sword.

And waited.

She heard grunts and obvious sounds of a scuffle. Was it the thing that had been stalking them? Had Kessel found it and were they now fighting?

Annja rushed around the corner of the next turn and then froze.

A boxing match was playing on flat-screen TV. Now what the hell was this?

Annja looked around but saw nothing else. The TV screen hung on the wall, and beyond that, there was nothing.

Unless.

Annja jerked around and as she started to head back

the way she'd come, a large section of wall dropped, once again, blocking her path. Annja had nowhere to go but forward.

But why distract her like this? Yes, the sound of boxing was effective at getting Annja to commit to coming around the corner faster than she probably would have.

She hesitated.

If there was a trip trigger that caused the wall to drop, and if she'd come around any slower, she might have been crushed by the sheer weight of the wall.

But she had come quicker than normal, clearing the falling wall.

She shook her head. The wall had only dropped once she'd started back. That couldn't be it.

The TV had another purpose. It had to have.

The boxing appeared to be on a video loop that ran for three minutes and then restarted itself. The sound effects were equally looped to give the impression of there being a fight in the corridor rather than a public ring match.

Annja looked around the TV screen but saw nothing out of the ordinary.

Someone had to have activated this, she thought. Or did she switch it on as she progressed through the maze?

Annja reached and punched the channel button. The boxing loop disappeared, replaced by a lot of white static. Annja kept flipping channels, aware of how silly it seemed to be doing this.

But then a different picture appeared on the screen. It looked like a different section of the maze. The stone walls were the same, but she could see a lot more details. It was almost as if she had a bird's eye view of the action.

Surveillance cameras, she realized.

They *were* being watched.

And what she saw on the TV didn't make her feel good at all.

Kessel.

He was making his way down another corridor.

And a shadow trailed behind him.

Big. Dark.

And ominous.

15

But where *was* Kessel?

That was the problem facing Annja. Judging by the television screen, Kessel was in a corridor exactly like the one Annja was in. The stone walls, the torches…all of it looked exactly the same.

It wasn't, though.

And the surveillance cameras showed that Kessel seemed to have no idea he was being stalked by a shadow. A large shadow. But what cast that shadow, Annja had no clue.

I've got to find a way to get to him, she thought.

But how?

She frowned. If this thing was stalking Kessel, then that might mean she could safely call Kessel's name without fear of it zeroing in on Annja's location. Unless there was more than one thing stalking them.

It was worth the risk.

"Kessel!"

Annja's voice seemed to echo up and down the corridor, bouncing back and forth off the stones and causing the torchlight to flicker in fiery spasms. She called again. And again.

On the television screen, Kessel seemed to pause. Had he heard her?

"Kessel!"

He had stopped now. His head was cocked to the side. Annja's heart jumped inside her chest. He must have heard me, she thought.

But then Kessel kept walking. And so did the shadow.

No!

Annja tried shouting several more times, but Kessel didn't seem to hear her. And with each step he took, the shadow behind him drew closer.

Always closer.

Annja tried to turn away from the television, but she was transfixed. Wouldn't Kessel have noticed by now? He'd been a Navy SEAL and was now an undercover FBI agent. His instincts should have been screaming at him by this time.

But he showed no sign of noticing.

None at all.

I've got to help him, Annja thought.

Somehow.

But then Kessel stopped short and cocked his head to the side again. Had he heard something?

He started to turn.

Annja saw his eyes widen.

And then saw the shadow block the camera view. Everything had been blotted out by the enormity of whatever Kessel was facing right then.

She saw fast movement on the television screen, as if Kessel was trying to fight.

Annja braced herself.

But when the shadow drew back, there was nothing in the corridor. Kessel was gone.

There wasn't even a trace of what had just transpired.

Nothing.

My God, Annja thought, what *is* that thing?

What had Fairclough put into his maze that could take down a trained SEAL so easily? Kessel might have tried to put up a fight, but it had been in vain. The shadowy figure had merely washed over him like a tidal wave, and drawn him back effortlessly into the sea.

Annja shook her head. If it had gotten to Kessel so easily, what could stop it from coming for her next?

She pulled out the sword.

This would stop it, she thought with a grim smile. But first she'd force it to take her to wherever Kessel was. Because Annja felt pretty sure that Kessel hadn't been killed. There was no blood. And no body. That meant there was hope.

She chose to believe the…thing…had simply knocked Kessel out and carried him off.

She hoped so, anyway.

The television screen went blank.

And then the screen came back again. And Kessel was again walking down the corridor. Annja frowned. And then she saw the shadow come back into the frame. The entire scene she'd just watched replayed itself again.

And again a minute later.

Another video loop. But had she seen it in real time the first go-round? There was no way to tell.

Annja's gut ached. If it had been pretaped video, then the shadow might not still be with Kessel.

And by shouting Kessel's name like that, she *had* given away her own location. Annja whirled around.

But the corridor seemed empty.

Still, gripping the sword, she felt a measure of confidence. Annja knew what she was capable of when she held the sword. And whatever this creature was, Annja felt sure she could take it on.

She just had to find it.

The video had been meant to get her to reveal herself to the creature. And Annja had fallen for it. Her voice had echoed all over the maze.

Even now the creature could be homing in on her.

Good, Annja thought, let it come for me. I won't be as easy to take down as Kessel was.

Hopefully.

Annja turned and started past the television screen. It seemed fairly certain that the creature couldn't get behind her since the wall had come down sealing off that direction. Annja couldn't go backward, but neither could someone sneak up behind her.

Unless there was a way to retract the wall and reopen the corridor. It was possible. Pretty much anything seemed possible after she had to battle a bull shark in an underground pool.

Her best option was to keep journeying ahead, rather than wait for the creature to come to her. It might not expect her to go on the offensive. It might expect her to hunker down and cower. Maybe that was the other point of showing Kessel being abducted like that. To produce terror.

But Annja wasn't just anyone.

And seeing Kessel taken so easily hadn't scared her as much as it had pissed her off.

A friend needed her.

And Annja was determined to help him.

She crept down the corridor, holding the sword out in front of her, almost as she held a gun. She was aware of the sound her shoes made on the stone floor and bent her knees more to help cushion the impact.

Annja approached a bend and steeled herself. But her instincts told her the creature wasn't waiting in ambush around the corner.

At least, not this one.

She crept on. The corridors never changed, each a direct copy of the previous one. And Annja found herself wondering where she could be heading. There were turns to the left and turns to the right. She seemed to be going around in circles, but she couldn't stop moving forward. What else could she do?

How had Kessel ended up in such a remote part of the maze? Annja had come down the same tunnel, and yet she seemed to be so far away from him.

Or was she? Maybe she *was* walking in circles… *around* him.

The constant replication of the corridors played hell with her senses. Each turn brought a new sense of déjà vu. Annja, who normally had a terrific sense of where she was going, found herself reduced to simply accepting the forward progress as a sign that she wasn't going backward.

As she came around another corner, the floor changed again. It went back to the rectangular, square and triangular tile patterns. Annja stopped.

Had she somehow gone all the way back to the start of the maze?

But how was that possible?

Or was this another section designed to look the same? Annja shook her head. A lesser-grounded individual might start flipping out if they'd been forced to go through this.

Not fun.

Annja squatted and looked at the tiles. Her memory of this part of the maze seemed sharp, and she wasn't sure if this was the earlier section or not.

One way to find out, she reasoned.

Using the tip of the sword, she poked the rectangular tiles.

Nothing happened.

Annja poked the triangular tile close by. And she heard the release of a dart that thudded into the wall behind her.

Okay, so that's the same.

She prodded a square tile.

Nothing.

Annja's frown deepened. So it wasn't the same place. It was different. This time she could safely traverse two different types of tiles, and as long as she avoided the triangular ones, she'd be fine.

Nice one, Fairclough, she thought.

Annja kept moving forward, slowing only when she came across an area of all triangular tiles. It spanned eight feet.

Another virtual chasm. She glanced up and jabbed at the ceiling, but this time, there was nothing fake about it. The tip of her sword clanged off the solid stone.

So much for that.

Annja backed up, aware that the safe tiles were fewer in number. Across the chasm, she saw more safe tiles to land on. Annja took a few running steps, leaped and then came down on the safe tiles on the other side.

Instantly, she heard the telltale release of darts. Not just one this time, but a whole bunch. She flattened herself on the tile floor and listened as the darts whistled overhead before slamming into the wall at the far end.

Annja examined the floor. She was on square and rectangular tiles. That shouldn't have tripped any darts.

But it had.

Ahead of her, she saw a triangular tile and tapped it with the tip of the sword.

Nothing.

She tapped a square tile and a dart released. Then she tapped a rectangular tile with the same result.

Fairclough had reversed the pattern.

Annja's heart thundered in her chest. He was taking advantage of false security whenever he could.

Fortunately, her agility had saved her life.

Again.

Annja stood on a triangular stone and kept moving, leaping from tile to tile until she could at last see the end of them. Beyond, the stone corridor resumed and she felt sure there'd be a moment when she could catch her breath.

Annja leaped onto the stone floor and sank to her knees, flushing her system with oxygen. Keeping her wits about her in this maze was damned hard. And tiring.

And the only thing she knew was that somewhere, possibly up ahead, the same creature that had so easily taken Kessel was coming for her.

16

Kessel awoke feeling like his limbs were being torn out from their sockets. As he blinked in the dim light, he began to process his surroundings. He was in a cavern with rough-hewn rock walls. Overhead, stalactites dripped down from the ceiling, pointed and deadly.

He was stretched akimbo on some sort of wooden rack or stretcher, his arms above his head and his legs splayed open, like some human *X*. The pain in his extremities was caused by a distinct lack of blood flow. His nerves screamed for release, but the rope binding his arms and legs was fastened well. And as much as he tried to pull and push against the knots, it was no use.

His mind clouded and he blinked again, trying to remember the incredible sight that had filled his vision in the middle of the corridor. A huge creature, which must have stood more than seven feet tall, covered entirely in fur. He'd had no warning of it aside from a vague feeling of unease.

Careless. That's the only way to describe how he'd been caught unawares. He'd grown weary wandering the maze, with every hallway exactly like the previous one. His mind had started to drift. He'd grown bored.

And that's when he got nailed.

His thoughts focused on Annja. What had happened to her? Had she been captured as well? Or had she not had the pleasure of coming across this creature yet?

When they'd been separated again, Kessel had found himself zipping down a long tunnel that had shot him into a room filled with sawdust. It had cushioned his fall, but not by much. Even now, his back still ached. But Kessel was used to bruises. They were part of his life.

What he wasn't used to was wandering through mazes that didn't seem to have an end.

Kessel frowned. Greene had sent him into the maze with Annja. Did Greene suspect that Kessel was with the FBI? Or was it just a matter of Kessel being the dumb grunt that got picked to go with Annja?

Again, Kessel had no idea.

What he did know was that he needed to get out of the bind he was in. He had to warn Annja about the creature.

A noise that sounded like shuffling caught his attention and Kessel clamped his eyes shut. It was better that the creature think he was still unconscious. But, it was tough keeping his eyes closed. What if the creature was coming to kill him now?

Kessel rejected that idea. He could have killed me plenty of times already, he thought. No, he was being kept alive. For a reason. But what?

He parted his eyelids ever so slightly and saw the

shambling movement of the furry creature. Kessel was immediately struck by the notion that Fairclough had managed to catch an actual bigfoot.

But that wasn't possible.

Bigfoot didn't exist....

The creature lumbered through the cavern, tending to the small fire in the corner, and then shuffled back out. Kessel let out the breath he'd been holding.

What the hell have I gotten myself into?

And where was Annja?

ANNJA WAS, AT THAT MOMENT, making her way down yet another corridor like the last one. *Where in the world is Kessel? And where is the thing that took him?*

She still had her sword out, but she had to admit that she was getting tired of carrying it. Fairclough's little maze had no rhyme or reason to it. Just more of the same monotonous scenery.

Over and over again.

Annja put the sword away. Her instincts would warn her if danger was close. After all, she'd been in plenty of scrapes before. Besides, she was still convinced she couldn't be snuck up on from behind.

Although...

The dogs had found other routes through the maze. So what was to stop the thing that had grabbed Kessel from using those routes, as well?

Nothing.

Annja stopped and sat on the floor. She needed a moment. A glance at her watch told her that seven hours had passed since she and Kessel had entered the maze. Time was ticking away faster than she had expected it would and she still had nothing to show for her hours inside.

It was the first time she'd been entrapped in something as elaborate as this maze. How had Fairclough managed to make this? What had driven him to build something so sprawling?

Annja eased some of the tension out of her stiff shoulders. This wasn't just about the book. It could have been the most amazing book in the world and it wouldn't have made sense to construct this maze. She was forced to consider that there was something else going on.

Something possibly more sinister than just the security of an ancient tome.

But what?

Fairclough couldn't have expected Greene to come for his book. And yet he'd said that he barely had time to get it into the maze. Did Fairclough have a direct line to the center of the maze? Was there some sort of hidden passageway in his house that would lead straight to the heart of it?

And if so, how come he hadn't told Annja about it?

Unless the old man had *wanted* to put her through the maze.

Her stomach hurt.

She had a small niggling doubt.

That perhaps she'd been brought here deliberately. That this maze wasn't about the book at all.

It was about her.

KESSEL STRAINED AGAINST the knots holding his hands, but with a sudden release of breath, he slumped back into the same position. There was no getting out of those bindings unless someone cut him free.

And the thought of waiting for the creature to do it didn't make him feel especially warm and fuzzy.

He tried to make out more details of the cavern he was in. The small fire in the corner gave off minimal heat, so he wasn't quite sure what its purpose could be. Cooking? He didn't see any utensils to cook with. Certainly there were no pots or pans or other implements that would lead him to think that the bigfoot—because that was what it resembled most—was a chef.

Was it for torture?

But again, Kessel saw nothing to indicate that a hot iron poker was being fired up to lay across his bare flesh and make him scream. It was simply a small fire in the corner of the cavern.

Across the cavern, he spotted the entrance. It was dark, as if a tunnel led into the place. But where did it connect with the maze itself? Or did it even connect at all?

Perhaps there were other routes through the maze as Annja had suggested. The dogs seemed to have no difficulty getting around. Were there extra tunnels or secret passageways for those who knew about them? Maybe the bigfoot had taken Kessel through one of them, which was why Annja hadn't seen him kidnapped.

I wish I could remember, Kessel thought. But the blow to his head had been a resounding shot that had dropped him in his tracks. He'd been knocked out before, but it was usually the result of a series of hits. This time, he'd taken the shot square on the button of his jaw and it was as if someone had flipped the light switch to Off.

Kessel was out before he even hit the floor.

Hell of a shot, he mused. The creature certainly knew

how to deliver a punch. But since when did bigfoot have a boxing career?

Kessel knew he had to free himself. Hanging around waiting for Annja to show up wasn't an option.

He glanced up at the ropes holding him in place. As far as he could see, it was nylon cord, not the PlastiCuffs they used instead of handcuffs these days. That was a positive sign. Getting out of the PlastiCuffs was almost impossible.

But rope could be cut.

He just had to find a way to cut it.

ANNJA STOOD BACK UP and resumed her walking patrol of the maze. She brought the sword out, noticing that its glow seemed diminished. It looks as tired as I feel, she thought.

Perhaps the sword's energy was a direct illustration of how Annja felt. She frowned. No, that wasn't true. There'd been times in the past when its strength had brought Annja back from the brink of death.

But what if something in the maze was draining its power?

How could that be? Annja's sword was known to exist to only very few people. True, she hadn't been able to conceal its existence as much as she would have liked, but it was hardly common knowledge that she was in possession of the legendary sword of Joan of Arc.

She turned another corner and saw the identical hallway that she'd just been traveling. She groaned. When was this going to end? The interminable walk was killing her.

But then she caught a glimpse of something at the other end.

Just a glimpse.

A shadow, really.

Was this the thing that had grabbed Kessel? And if so, could she engage it in combat? Or was it better to try to follow it back to Kessel?

Annja increased her pace. The shadow had a few seconds lead time on her. If she moved fast enough and was careful, she'd be able to catch up and not let it know she was behind it.

As she ran, Annja kept her knees bent and her body turned to minimize her profile.

Annja averted her eyes as well, allowing her peripheral vision to take in her surroundings.

The corner was coming up.

She brought the sword out in front of her, just in case she was about to walk into an ambush.

Annja flushed her lungs with oxygen. She could feel her heart thundering inside her chest. This was it, she felt sure.

Combat.

She was ready. The glow of the sword seemed to increase as well, almost as if the blade was hungry for action after so much inactivity.

Annja smiled. *I don't blame you one bit.*

Annja reached the corner.

Rounded it with the sword ready in front of her to confront the creature that had grabbed Kessel.

And she ran straight into a brick wall.

Annja's sword bounced off the wall, smacked her square in the face and then dropped.

Annja's vision swam and blackness reached for her.

A second later she dropped to the floor.

17

Kessel was still struggling with the rope bindings. With each exertion, his fatigue grew. The rope had cut the skin on the inside of both of his wrists, leading to bloody red abrasions. But Kessel had managed to eke out a small space within the binds themselves. The price for his hard work had been pain and a lot of sweat.

Kessel was used to both.

During Hell Week when he'd been trying to become a Navy SEAL, Kessel had gotten a total of four hours of sleep during the entire seven-day ordeal. He was pushed to his breaking point and then beyond. He learned to shut off the nerve impulses that screamed up and down his body, and discovered what it took to survive the rigors of combat when he was thousands of miles from home, and hundreds of miles behind enemy lines.

So the constant sawing of ropes on his skin as he worked to free himself would never stop him. He knew how to operate despite the pain; how to go beyond what his body, mind and spirit thought possible.

And he would succeed.

The gap in the bindings was growing larger in tiny increments. At this rate, he estimated it would take another couple of hours until he could get his hands free. Once they were, he could untie his feet and finally get out of the cavern.

Then he'd have to see about dealing with bigfoot.

He smirked. Kessel had killed plenty of people before. From Taliban fighters to Iraqi insurgents during black-bag operations that were still classified. Kessel had been the business end of antiterrorism for years before becoming a special agent with the FBI.

But he'd never had to deal with a creature that wasn't supposed to exist in the first place. At least this would be one for the guys back in Little Creek, the next time he got to Virginia for a few beers with the guys still on the Teams.

He could hear them now. "No shit, Kessel, you killed a bigfoot? That deserves another round."

He grinned. The brotherhood of warriors was something most civilians would never understand. Formed in the fires of harsh training and bonded in the crucible of real-world operations that tested their every limit, Kessel and his SEAL brethren would always be there for one another. Once in, never out.

Almost like the Mafia.

Except this Mafia shot a lot better than the criminals.

Kessel drew his attention back to the task at hand. He had to get out of these ropes. The bigfoot could come back at any time. And while Kessel thought he was being kept alive for a reason, he didn't kid himself that if he gave the creature enough reason, it *would* kill him.

And there wouldn't be much he could do about it if he was still strapped up as a prisoner.

He went back to working the binds, twisting the ropes and flexing his wrists over and over again.

And slowly, the ropes started to give way.

ANNJA'S HEAD SWAM. She felt a heavy weight crushing down on her like a suffocating blanket. Annja had suffered concussions before and several times she'd wondered if she was going to get to old age with as many brain injuries as a professional football player.

As consciousness gradually returned, she blinked her eyes. Winced. The corridor's light hurt her and she closed her eyes again, willing herself to take slow, deep breaths. Flush her blood with oxygen and then try to open her eyes again. See if that was any better.

It wasn't.

Annja opened and shut them again. But as she gradually started recognizing her surroundings the memory of the maze returned. So, too, did her instinct that she was in imminent danger.

She visualized the sword in her mind's eye and it appeared, hovering in front of her. Annja reached for it, felt her hands close about the hilt and an instant surge of power swept into her body, overwhelming the pain she felt and brushing it aside.

Her head cleared in a moment and Annja's eyes opened at the sound of something rushing down the corridor toward her.

She saw a shadowy form even as she tried to clear

her eyes and focus. But then she was knocked back onto her butt. Her sword skittered away, and vanished.

She rolled, coming up with the sword in her hands. She was tackled again and driven into the ground. An onslaught of punches and kicks thudded into her midsection. Even with the sword, her reflexes felt wobbly and slow.

Another hit took her straight in the mouth. Whoever was attacking, they knew how to hit.

Annja rose up again and drove her foot out at where she judged her attacker's midsection was. She scored, feeling her heel sink into his stomach. She blinked, saw the man stagger back.

Asian?

She readied herself for another attack, but instead of approaching her again, the Asian man turned and ran.

He was already drawing away fast.

"Wait!"

Annja tried to run after him, but she was no match for his speed. He rounded the corner. Annja stumbled after him, but when she turned the corner, he was gone.

And only another empty corridor stretched before her. An exact duplicate of the last few hallways.

Annja groaned and sank to her knees. It felt like she was living in hell.

KESSEL HEARD MOVEMENT and froze.

He shut his eyes and then cracked them just a little bit. He was close to freeing himself and he couldn't let the creature discover his efforts. If it came to it, Kessel would simply try to snap the rest of the bindings with sheer strength and go right at the bigfoot, hoping he could score on surprise alone.

The shuffling sounds grew louder. It was in the cavern. Kessel willed his heart to slow along with his breathing. That was critical to his deception. If the creature noticed his chest heaving, it would know something was going on. Kessel's bid for freedom would be over before it even began.

And he had to reach Annja somehow.

Figure out this damned maze, and then take Greene and the rest of his goon squad down.

Kessel saw a blur of fur pass in front of his eyes. It was close. And he could smell it now. It smelled disgusting—like a wet dog—and Kessel willed himself to remain still. He'd been subjected to far worse sensory overload than the smell of a wet dog.

Something light brushed over his face, almost like a feather. Kessel kept still. The creature was testing him, trying to see if he was truly still unconscious.

But Kessel was pretty good at deception. And he knew how to keep his body under absolute control.

He didn't even flinch.

The creature tried again, brushing something along his eyelids. But again, Kessel simply took his mind elsewhere, refusing to acknowledge the sensation.

No chance, he thought to himself.

Not now.

Not when he was so close to getting out of there.

A long tense moment passed and then Kessel saw another movement as the creature moved away from him. He was so relieved his discipline almost slipped—he almost released a long breath—but Kessel caught himself.

Let the creature think he was close to death and he'd never expect a surprise attack when Kessel finally freed himself.

If this truly was a bigfoot, then Kessel would need every advantage he could get. And surprise was sometimes one of the most potent weapons in a confrontation.

He just hoped it would be enough.

ANNJA FELT LIKE crying.

That was the truth of the situation.

She'd literally dragged her ass all over this crazy maze, dealt with a series of obstacles and challenges and animals. And yet, despite all of that, she felt no closer to her goal than she had at the beginning. As time kept ticking away, Fairclough drew closer to death.

And Annja's goal seemed to draw farther from her grasp.

Where was she supposed to go? Was this a never-ending series of hallways that she'd be trapped in forever? What had Fairclough actually designed here?

And God help her, but she was actually thinking that it might be better if he did die than subject anyone else to this cruel maze.

This wasn't a security system at all, she decided sitting there in the lonely corridor.

It was hell.

Her hell.

There wasn't a book in Fairclough's maze. There'd never been a book at all. Or if there was, it wasn't here. The realization didn't come as much of a surprise.

Fairclough had brought Annja here for the express purpose of putting her in the maze. Presumably to die.

But how did Greene figure into this? Was it just providence that had brought him to Fairclough's estate? And Fairclough, realizing that he might die without seeing his plan ever put into effect, demanded that Greene bring Annja here, in exchange for the book?

It was possible, she supposed. But it was tenuous.

And Greene had dispatched Kessel without blinking, so did he realize that Kessel was a plant?

Annja took a breath. What had she done to warrant this action by Fairclough? How did she know him?

But as much as she racked her brain, Annja couldn't figure it out. If Fairclough was out for revenge, Annja couldn't grasp what his reasoning might have been.

Of course, she made plenty of enemies around the world.

She glanced down at the sword. The truth is, she thought, this blade has brought me more grief than I care to admit.

Sure, she knew the sword had also saved lives, and helped her preserve good in the world. But was it worth the trade-off? Annja had people hunting her, stalking her and even trapping her now.

Where did it end? Where did her role as protector come to its conclusion?

She sighed and slowly got to her feet. If I don't keep moving, she thought with a small grimace, my end will come here.

And somehow, dying in the lonely corridors of this maze wasn't exactly how she wanted to go out of this world.

So she started walking.

Again.

18

Kessel waited until the creature appeared to have left again. Obviously, it hadn't gotten to Annja yet, unless it had killed her. But Kessel didn't think that was the case. And besides, knowing Annja and the fact that she had a sword she could pull out of nowhere, the creature would no doubt have been injured if they'd collided.

And what about that sword? Kessel had seen some strange stuff in his time, but he'd never seen anything as remarkable as what Annja could do. One moment, the sword wasn't there. The next, it was out and looking every bit as deadly as it seemed.

Incredible.

How she'd managed to come by a weapon like that, Kessel didn't know. And he wasn't sure Annja would ever let him in on her secret. But he felt fortunate just being in the know about the blade itself.

And he doubted many other people knew of it. Neither Greene nor Fairclough gave any indication that they knew it existed. And if Greene had suspected she was armed, he probably would have just killed her and been done with it.

No, the sword was a surprise. And Kessel looked forward to seeing the expression on Greene's face when Annja pulled it out and let him in on her deadly secret.

Kessel lifted his head and opened his eyes slowly. A quick scan of the cavern revealed the creature had left once again. Kessel returned to working on his binds with a renewed vigor. Like any other gambit, his bid for freedom wouldn't stay concealed for much longer. Eventually, the creature or someone else would notice that he'd been unconscious for too long, or they'd see the abrasions on his wrists, or some other indicator that he was anything but unconscious.

Back to work.

Kessel redoubled his efforts and wrenched his left wrist around and around. The gap within the ropes widened and Kessel maneuvered his fingers until he could slide them through the hole.

One hand free.

Time was of the essence. There would be no way he could hide one free hand if the creature came back. He had to get his other hand out.

Kessel stretched and brought his free hand over to the other one, ripping at the ropes and bindings until he tore open the knots.

His other hand was free.

Kessel bent over and began to untie his left foot first. It took far longer than he'd hoped it would, being tied with a number of cumbersome knots that required someone with longer fingernails than Kessel had to pry them open. But he kept at it, not knowing the meaning of the word *quit*.

And then he had one foot free.

Almost there. His senses were already screaming at him that danger was close by. His instincts, rivaled by paranoia at being discovered, hammered him to untie his other foot.

At least then he could face the creature with all of his skills at his disposal.

Kessel's foot finally came free and he stumbled down off the wooden stretcher that had held him in place for so long.

His joints screamed and he felt the rush of pain in his extremities as blood and feeling washed back into them. He flexed his hands and arms and then did a few deep knee bends to get his blood coursing to where he would need it to be in case of sudden combat.

What was his best move now?

He could make a run for it, of course, but where to? He didn't have any clue where he was. Running blindly, he was more likely to encounter the creature than avoid it.

So what was his next best option?

He nodded. Hide.

If the creature came in and saw he was gone, its instinct would be to head for the most likely escape route. And since Kessel had no idea where that was, he could, in effect, simply follow the creature out.

He'd have to deal with it eventually, of course. But he'd take it down when it came time to. First, he needed to get out of here.

He looked around the crevices and nooks and settled on one swallowed in shadow near the entrance to the cavern. Hopefully, the creature would rush right past it on its way out.

Perfect.

Kessel wedged his large body into the crevice, got his breathing under control and then let his consciousness expand, taking in all the natural sounds. He knew that the deep shadows would conceal him.

All he had to do was stay still and hope the creature reacted the way he expected it to.

Kessel got himself as comfortable as he could and then took several shallow breaths. He was ready.

And not a moment too soon.

Because not too far off, he heard something moving down the tunnel toward the cavern entrance.

The creature was coming back.

ANNJA TURNED DOWN another corridor and then stopped.

Had she just heard something?

She paused, listening to the crackling torches up in their sconces. But her ears were used to those sounds. This had been something else.

A lurching shuffle?

She frowned. I must be hearing things, she thought. *I've been in this damned maze for too long and now I'm starting to lose my mind.*

Wonderful.

But then she picked up the sound again. Annja narrowed her eyes. There was definitely something here.

Close.

But where?

The corridor had walls of stone just like every other corridor. It wasn't as though she was close to a door.

Or was she?

Annja eyed the surface of the walls. There'd been other instances where the walls had snapped open, locking parts of the hallways. And other sections had moved, as well. Was there another secret opening here somewhere?

Annja placed her hand on the section of wall closest to her.

Solid.

But she felt pretty sure she knew the direction of where the sound had come from. So she ran her hand down the part of the wall that she suspected. Pressed.

But it was still solid.

Annja shook her head. There had to be something she was missing. Some sort of latch or sign that there was a secret opening nearby.

She just had to find it.

She glanced back up to where the corridor started twenty feet away from where she stood. With a big sigh, Annja retraced her steps.

This was going to take a while.

THE SOUND OF THE approaching creature grew louder and Kessel stilled himself even further. With his blood flow restored to his arms and fingers, he felt primed and ready despite his exhaustion. Being knocked out had actually given him some rest, but he was used to going on fumes, anyway.

And then he heard the creature pass his hiding space, much sooner than he'd expected it would. It was mere inches away, but Kessel kept his cool.

And waited.

It didn't take long.

Kessel shuddered as a massive roar filled the cavern.

He'd never heard such a sound before. And then he heard the creature ripping the wood apart. It was strong, he realized.

And it would be much more of a challenge than he had reckoned.

So be it.

With another roar, the creature ravaged the cavern and then Kessel heard it approaching his hiding space.

It stopped.

Kessel heard it sniffing the air.

Shit, he thought, the bastard's going to smell me.

But instead, the creature raced off down the tunnel, out of the cavern.

Kessel rose from his hiding spot.

Time to go.

ANNJA WAS TEN FEET AWAY from where she'd started her examination of the wall when she heard a roar. She whirled around, the sword at the ready.

But there was nothing behind her.

What the hell?

It was loud and it was close by, but she still couldn't see where it was coming from.

Angry.

It sounded very angry.

KESSEL FOLLOWED at a distance, but close enough to watch the creature shambling at speed through the tunnel. The walls here were a stark contrast to the refinement of the corridors of the maze. Instead of being carefully masoned stonework, this looked like a system of caves.

It reminded him of Afghanistan.

He took a breath as the tunnel curved suddenly. The creature shifted and then roared again.

It was getting angrier.

In some situations, you could use that as a liability against the enemy. If you knew they had a bad temper, it was easier to get them to overcommit and then make a mistake.

But with a creature like this? Kessel didn't think its anger would be a weakness.

It would undoubtedly be a strength.

ANNJA GRIPPED THE SWORD tighter as another roar punctured the air. She felt sure she had identified the approximate location in the wall that concealed a secret opening of some kind.

But given the roar of the approaching…whatever…Annja decided to hang back and wait for it to open the portal, instead of trying to open it herself and risk blundering right into the unknown.

Was this the thing that had cast such a large shadow? That had so easily taken down Kessel?

Annja steeled herself.

Bring it on, she mused.

KESSEL SAW THE CREATURE stop and put one furry paw on a piece of rock on the wall. He heard a noise like shifting dirt and stone.

And then the tunnel swung inward to reveal a lit corridor beyond.

Kessel was almost back in the maze.

ANNJA HEARD THE SOUND of the wall swinging back.

And then saw the creature.

She froze as the mass of fur came lumbering through the opening.

For a moment, the creature halted, as if processing the sudden appearance of the woman standing before it. And the gleaming blade she held in her hands.

Whether it understood the potential of the weapon, Annja couldn't be sure. Because then it roared again and the air filled with the sound of its fury.

And the creature rushed out to attack her.

19

Annja saw the creature covered in fur coming for her, its paws—were they hands?—aimed at her face, and she dove to the right to evade its attack. She rolled, bringing the sword up in front of her.

Sasquatch?

On a trip, to the Pacific Northwest once she'd seen… something. Something that might have passed for Sasquatch.

She'd lost a good friend on that trip. And seeing the Sasquatch in front of her ripped the scab off that wound.

Sasquatch.

Was it possible? Was this real? Had Fairclough somehow found a way to capture one and place it here in the maze? And if so, how? The world had been searching for evidence of these creatures for years.

And yet, here it was.

There wasn't time to reflect on whether or not it existed. Something came at Annja. Intent on attacking her.

And if she didn't want to die, she'd have to do something about it.

Annja brought the sword up and cut from left to right as the creature lunged. The blade sliced air as it ducked and came low under her cut, its right hand slamming into her midsection.

Annja felt the wind gust out of her lungs and she fell back as another strike landed on her chin. Coming so soon after the attack by the mysterious Asian man, her head rolled and she felt sick to her stomach.

She almost missed the creature's next attack, but her instincts saved her again. As it swiped at her head with one massive claw, Annja's legs seemed to buckle on their own accord, dropping her out of the line of attack.

Blackness tickled the fringes of her consciousness. She blinked.

Can't black out now.

I'll die....

KESSEL CAUGHT A GLIMPSE of Annja from behind the creature, but then the attack happened so fast he barely had time to register what came next. It looked like a wave of fur simply rolled over Annja.

He saw something play out across Annja's face and Kessel recognized it as confusion. Was the appearance of the creature confusing her? That would be deadly.

Even as he watched, he saw the indecision cost Annja dearly. The beast caught her twice and nearly took her head off.

The blow the creature had landed on her jaw rocked her and she looked like she was going out on her feet.

If she loses consciousness, the creature will kill her, Kessel thought.

He had no choice.

Kessel launched himself out of the cavern, into the air and aimed himself directly at the mass of fur before him.

ANNJA SAW THE MOTION out of the corner of her eye, heard what sounded like a bad karate kiai, and then saw Kessel land square on the creature's back. He clamped his arms around its neck and then took it down.

Together with the creature, Kessel rolled forward, bringing his hands up in a choke hold.

Annja saw the creature buck wildly, determined to throw Kessel off its back, but Kessel had probably used this technique a dozen times in his real-world combat operations. Once the choke was on, it wasn't coming off until Kessel had finished the enemy.

And if the enemy had been human, then Kessel's attack would most likely have resulted in an easy kill. But in this case, the creature only reached up and tore Kessel's hands from around its neck, then hurled him into a wall.

Kessel hit the stones and collapsed.

He tried to stand.

But sank back down.

The creature, now clearly enraged, stood and shook its head.

And roared defiantly.

KESSEL'S HEAD SWAM through molasses. That didn't go so well.

Ordinarily, that sentry removal technique worked perfectly. It was quick, silent and brought the sentry down off the line of vision in case anyone was watching. The roll usually broke their neck and then Kessel was free to get up and continue on.

Not this time.

He brought one of his hands up to his head and felt the back of it. A large welt was already growing like a melon. Great. This was probably worth a doctor's visit or three.

The problem now was the creature was totally pissed off.

Not good, Kessel, he thought with grim realization. What should have taken care of the enemy had only succeeded in angering it even more.

He wasn't having a great day out.

ANNJA WAS BACK on her feet. Kessel's intervention had enabled her to regain her senses. The idea of killing a Sasquatch didn't sit well with her, but the creature was hardly giving her a choice. She couldn't sit by and let it kill her and Kessel.

She brought the sword up as the creature stalked her from across the corridor. Its eyes burned red with rage. This wasn't what she had expected to have to deal with. Not here in the maze.

It didn't make any sense.

As the Sasquatch rushed her again, Annja raised her sword, feeling its power course through her arms and down into her body. The power that flowed from this ancient metal infused her body and Annja prayed that her cut would be mercifully quick and painless.

KESSEL SAW A CHANGE come over Annja.

The indecision was gone, replaced by the look he'd seen on the faces of men who knew they were about to take a life. It wasn't machismo or bravado or a superiority. It was the cold, hard realization that she was going to strike down dead something that had once been born an innocent child. Something that for some reason or influence had seen its path in the universe bring it into direct conflict with her.

There was no joy in killing. Only the sad finality of an act that demanded no hesitation to carry out.

As Annja's sword descended, Kessel knew the strike was true. And as the blade cut through fur, skin, blood and bone, the creature reared its head back and wailed one single howl that ended quickly.

Annja's blade cut quick and cut deep. The sudden violent explosion of blood and gristle splayed across the walls of the corridor before the creature slid away from her.

Dead.

Annja dropped to one knee.

And Kessel went to her.

ANNJA WATCHED THE CREATURE slump over, still. It showed no sign of life. She'd taken it down with one cut, thank God. There was no sense in prolonging its suffering and she felt glad that her skill had been enough to finish the job quickly.

She looked up and saw Kessel coming toward her. "Annja?"

But Annja slumped over.

This time, she let the blackness take her.

KESSEL CARRIED ANNJA back into the cavern. The small fire that the creature had been tending still smoldered, and after laying Annja close to it, Kessel brought the flames back to life by blowing on the embers. He added some of the wood that had been used to tie him up, and as the flames burned higher and warmer, he reflected on the woman lying there.

As he suspected, the hit to her jaw had done its damage. He reckoned she had a decent concussion. As it was, Kessel's own head ached like someone had been using it for kicking practice.

But his determination to make sure Annja was safe had driven out most of the pain, at least for the moment. She lay breathing quietly, and while Kessel wasn't thrilled that she was unconscious, given the knock she'd taken, there wasn't anything he could do but wait it out. With no medical facility nearby and them trapped in the maze, he could only ensure she didn't slip into shock.

He snuggled next to her, cradling her head as best he could. With his back against the rock wall, he wasn't exactly comfortable, but he was definitely warm. The creature had positioned the fire so it had a natural reflector throwing heat back at Kessel.

If they could hunker down here for a few hours, gather their strength and then make their way through the other tunnels that branched off this one, maybe they'd find their way out. Kessel had seen the tunnels as he followed the creature, but he hadn't risked going down them.

Good thing, he mused. If he had, then Annja might well have been killed.

He pulled her closer. It was a shame she'd had to kill it. He knew that there had to be a connection between the two he couldn't quite fathom yet. Indecision didn't come easily for someone like her.

No, there had to be something that had given her pause.

Had Annja interacted with bigfoot before? Kessel almost grinned. This was one incredible woman if she had.

But what else would explain the fact that she'd hesitated to kill it?

Kessel glanced down at her face. She looked so peaceful lying on his lap. This was about the best he could do for her right now and he hoped it was enough.

He brought a hand up to the swelling on his head and judged that he would have a tidy headache for a day or two. The pain he could deal with. He just had to make sure it didn't get progressively worse. If there was bleeding inside his skull, the pressure would increase until it proved fatal.

Kessel squinted into the fire.

Looks like Fairclough isn't the only one on the clock now, he thought.

If they didn't get out of this maze soon, then Kessel would probably die. And maybe Annja, as well.

But he'd do his best to make sure that didn't happen.

But Fairclough? Kessel wasn't so sure if he could help that. By his own internal clock, they had almost used up the twelve-hour allotment Greene had given them.

And they seemed no closer to the center of the maze than when they'd begun.

20

Annja's first sensation was of being too warm. And how had she managed to find a pillow in this crazy maze she'd been traipsing through?

But that couldn't be right.

Gradually, she saw the Sasquatch coming for her again. She felt the panic at its relentless attack. She knew the gravity of making that decision to kill. And the finality of her action.

She jerked upright.

And felt a hand holding her back down. Heard a voice speaking to her in soft tones. "Hold on, Annja. It's okay now. You're safe."

She blinked and looked up. Kessel stared down at her, his concern clearly evident, but also relief. "Nice to see you made it back to the land of the living. I was afraid I'd lost you for a while there."

Annja tried to move again, but a sharp pain brought

her hand up to her jaw. "Where's the truck that slammed into my chin?"

"You killed it," Kessel said. "Although I'm not exactly sure what it was, now that you mention it."

"Help me up," Annja said.

"You sure?"

"Yeah."

Kessel put his hand under her upper back and helped her into a sitting position. Annja looked at the fire and smiled. "So, it was warm in here."

"Had to make sure you didn't lapse into shock. It was pretty much all I could do for you. We're a little short on doctors around these parts."

"And everything else." Annja rubbed her chin. "The Sasquatch hit me hard, but I'd taken another shot earlier."

Kessel quickly looked her over. "You were attacked again? By what?"

"By whom," Annja said. "And it was so sudden and fleeting, all I know is he was Asian. That's it. As soon as he hit me, he turned and vanished down the corridor."

"Vanished?"

Annja shrugged. "Well, he probably used one of secret passages that crisscross this place. But at the time, I didn't know about them. And when I gave chase and turned a corner, he was gone."

Kessel brought his hand up to the back of his head. Annja saw a flicker of concern cross his face. Another memory came back to her. "Oh, my God, I forgot all about your injury. I saw you hit that stone wall damned hard."

Kessel grinned, but it was weak. "Yeah, that beast threw me pretty good. I've taken some shots before, but that was harsh." He lowered his hand. "I've got a bump. Not sure if there's internal swelling or not."

"Headache?"

"Terrible."

Annja's stomach turned over. Kessel was downplaying it, but she knew he was concerned. And she knew enough about brain injuries to understand that he might well be in trouble if they didn't get out of the maze and quick.

"We can't stay here," she said.

Kessel nodded. "Agreed, but I'm not sure how we find an exit when every few hallways we take, things collapse behind us. Like I said before, we're being funneled toward something."

"Maybe toward the Sasquatch?"

Kessel studied her. "Was that really a bigfoot?"

Annja sighed. "Sure as hell looked like one to me."

"Seems almost too extraordinary to believe, but I saw the thing with my own eyes."

"My question is this," Annja said. "How the hell did Fairclough get his hands on one of them?"

Kessel shrugged. "No clue. But then again, I'm still struggling with the notion that Fairclough is using this maze to protect one lousy book. I mean, I'm all for preserving ancient texts, and if this particular one can be useful to modern society, then cool. But really—he couldn't have put it in a safety deposit box somewhere? He really had to go and build something this massive to secure it?"

Annja smiled. "Yeah. I've been thinking about it, too. It doesn't make any sense, does it? All this effort for the book. But it doesn't explain what we've been running into."

"Well, he did say there would be challenges."

"Yes, he did," Annja agreed. "But here's the thing—has any of this seemed familiar to you?"

"To me?" Kessel thought for a moment. "Well, no, actually. I don't think any of it's familiar."

"Exactly."

"What are you driving at?"

"For you this is all new, but a lot of this *is* familiar to me."

"How so?"

"The very first thing we dropped into—I got an underground pool with a shark. Well, this wasn't the first time I've dealt with sharks."

"I haven't had the pleasure of dealing with piranha," Kessel said.

"Right, that's because this maze isn't about you."

"It's about you?"

Annja smirked. "Sounds pretty damned presumptuous, doesn't it? But hear me out. There've been other things along the way. Not everything, mind you. Fairclough didn't hit me over the head with it so I'd be tempted to wiggle my way out of here immediately. It was only later on that the suspicion grew stronger."

"When?"

"The Sasquatch is another memory of mine. Or the legend of the Sasquatch, anyway."

"I suppose," Kessel said, "you're going to tell me you've also had to deal with Asian men who can disappear."

"In a manner of speaking," Annja replied. "When I was in Japan, one of my friends introduced me to authentic ninjutsu."

"Ninja?" Kessel knitted his brow. "They exist, but

there are so many posers, it's tough knowing who's legit and who isn't."

"The family I got to train briefly with was as legitimate as they come. And the experiences I had there were conclusive."

Kessel appeared to mull this over. "You might be right."

"It seems bizarre, I'll grant you," Annja said. "But I can't help but think that somehow Fairclough has set up this entire thing to catch me out."

"But for what?" Kessel asked. "Did you screw him over? Is he out for some sort of vengeance?"

"Could be," Annja said. "I can't honestly remember him from anywhere. But then again, I've interacted with a lot of people in my time. The TV series I host has me all over the world. And the people I've come up against with the sword aren't only the ones I leave dead. Fairclough could easily be one of them." Kessel whistled. "If you've got guys going to these lengths to harm you, I don't even want to know what guys who actually like you have to do to get a date."

Annja nudged him. "That hasn't exactly been a major problem for me, thanks."

Kessel nodded. "Well, sure. Considering most guys would shit themselves if they knew anything about you. How could they compete with the accomplished life you've led?"

"They don't have to compete with it. Besides, I don't really think of my life as having been one major accomplishment after another, anyway."

"You don't?" Kessel chuckled. "Seems to me you're being too humble there, Annja. As far as I can see, you've got plenty to be proud of. Hell, that sword you're carrying is more than most people could cope with."

Annja grinned. "Thanks."

"As long as it doesn't go to your head, then why not? The world needs more confident people like yourself." He smiled. "And me."

"And you," Annja said. "Let's not forget that."

Kessel laughed. "Oh, I won't. I've had to be my own cheerleader for years now."

"There's a visual." Annja was aware of the heat in the cavern. She needed to stand and get some blood moving. She glanced at Kessel. "How's your head? Can you keep going?"

Kessel nodded. "I'll be okay for now. I'm going to need a doctor, I can tell you that. Hurts like hell, but I can continue. Don't mind me if I happen to puke along the way."

"Just try to do it downwind." Annja pulled him up and he stumbled forward into her arms.

For a moment, neither of them moved. Annja looked up into his eyes and saw the embarrassed grin on his face. She smirked. "This how you do it?"

"Do what?"

"Pick up women." Annja gave him a squeeze. "You know, fight big burly monsters, knock your head on a bunch of rocks and then stumble into the arms of your chosen target when they try to help you to your feet."

Kessel's smile widened. "So, you've figured out my lone technique for seducing women. Now I'm in trouble."

"It was obvious," Annja said. "That whole head injury thing, it's kind of lame."

"Oh, totally," Kessel said. "And I was such a fool for thinking you'd actually fall for it."

Annja shrugged. "Well, nice try."

"Yeah."

Annja kept smiling at Kessel and he kept smiling down at her. Finally, Annja cleared her throat. "Are we going to stay like this? Because walking is going to be something of a challenge."

Kessel dropped his arms and backed away. "Good point."

"Not that that wasn't nice."

"Right."

Annja laughed lightly. "We're pathetic in the whole dating thing, aren't we?"

Kessel's laugh was hearty. "I think that might be a fair assessment. I'd never admit that outside of this maze, though."

"Your secret's safe with me."

"You sure? I don't have to bribe you to secure your silence?"

Annja glanced at him. "We get out of this place, we can resume our discussion of our bad dating habits… over dinner and drinks."

Kessel nodded. "That's the best thing I've heard all year."

"Just this year?"

Kessel eyed her. "Well, I'm not a monk, for crying out loud."

Annja stood and stretched, aware that her chin still felt as if she had a giant zit growing on it. "How do we get the hell out of here?"

Kessel pointed. "The way we came in. But there are

other tunnels that branch off it, not that I've explored any of them."

"And I'd be willing to bet that one of them will lead us out of this place."

"The sooner that happens," Kessel said, "the better. I'm going to need to relieve this pressure in my head. And short of doing it with a hammer and nail, that requires a real doctor."

21

They traversed the length of the cavern and then entered the same tunnel Kessel had taken to chase the Sasquatch. As he led them in, he reflected on the pain that enveloped his head. It came slicing across his temporal lobes like a circular saw cutting into brick.

But Kessel could contain it.

By separating himself from the pain, he could keep going for as long as it took to find their way out of the maze. It wouldn't be easy, but as they said when he went through BUD/S in Coronado, "The only easy day was yesterday."

It was a motto every SEAL knew by heart and, more importantly, lived by. It helped put things in perspective. This was the life he'd chosen.

But his head still hurt like hell.

And even as Kessel acknowledged the pain through a simple biofeedback exercise, and felt it lessen a little, he kept his legs driving forward down the tunnel, aware that Annja was behind him and anxious to keep moving.

So he did.

ANNJA GLANCED AT HER watch.

According to the hour, Fairclough's time on this planet had drawn to an end. Poisoned by the toxic sludge Jonas had let seep into his bloodstream.

But Annja wasn't so sure Fairclough was dead.

Whoever he is, she thought, he certainly knows a lot about my past and my previous adventures.

That was one of the things that concerned her. If Fairclough knew so much about her, then wasn't it reasonable to imagine that he also knew about her sword? And if he was still alive—and had the maze rigged with cameras—he surely must know about the sword now.

And if he had known about it before he brought her here, then she could extrapolate further that Fairclough would assume she'd use it to help her through the maze. If his plan was vengeance, then that would mean he'd have something somewhere in the maze that couldn't necessarily be bested by the sword.

Annja stilled.

She wasn't so sure she wanted to find out what that particular something or someone was.

The question was: Would she have any choice?

And the answer, she reckoned, was no.

THEY APPROACHED THE FIRST intersection. Kessel replayed the route in his mind. The bigfoot had opted to go straight but two other corridors branched off from here.

Which one should they take?

He glanced back at Annja. "I don't know. Without

a point of reference, I'm not sure what direction we'd want to travel."

Annja looked up and down both corridors and then closed her eyes. Kessel frowned. What was she doing?

When she opened her eyes again, she shrugged. "I guess one way's as good as the other. Why don't we head left."

Kessel nodded. "Left, it is."

They turned and walked down the secondary tunnel. The space was tighter, as if the tunnel had been constructed to keep the bigfoot out.

"What was that thing you did back there at the intersection?" Kessel called over his shoulder.

"What?"

"You closed your eyes for a moment. Are you okay?"

He saw Annja smile. "I'm fine. I just wanted to see if I could sense what direction we ought to go in."

"What—like a gut feeling?"

"Yes."

Kessel ducked at a low spot. "You ever get those before?"

"Sometimes they're pretty strong," Annja said. "But they can also be misleading. I think it depends on how much faith I have in my instincts."

"I never used to put a lot of trust in gut reactions," Kessel replied. "But then I had an experience in Afghanistan. I almost stepped on a land mine, but at the last second, I got this strong feeling—and put my foot down in a different place. I saw the mine just as I came over it. Couldn't believe it."

Annja steadied herself with a hand to the wall. "They're definitely real. Just depends on how much credence you give them. Some people live their lives by them, but I think they can be wrong, too. Just like anything else. Nothing is ever perfect one hundred percent of the time."

Kessel turned back and kept moving. More rocks hung from the roof of the tunnel, forcing them to duck their heads. Kessel winced. The last thing he needed was to add to his head injury.

It was bad enough already.

HE PROBABLY THINKS I'm a nut, Annja thought as she followed Kessel down the tunnel. Why did I close my eyes in front of him like that?

Because I wasn't thinking.

What difference did it make? Kessel already knew a lot about her. He'd seen the sword. He knew that she'd survived deadly adventures in her travels.

Why would he care if she took a moment to connect with her instincts before proceeding.

He wouldn't care, she decided. And she was frustrated with herself for thinking that she should somehow be embarrassed about it.

Not cool.

The tunnel they traveled through now was even a tighter fit than the last one. Annja found the going tough and she wondered about Kessel's head. She'd seen him put a hand to it twice so far and she figured that the pain was probably a lot worse than he would ever let on.

Special operators were a quiet breed, always humble about their accomplishments and always dismissive about anything painful or inconvenient.

Annja hoped he wasn't hurting too badly.

But she knew he was.

ANOTHER WAVE OF AGONIZING pain swept over Kessel.

It was getting worse. As much as he hated to admit it, the pain was increasing. Pressure was no doubt building in his skull. That meant there was bleeding on his brain.

Bad.

It didn't help that he had to keep his head stooped over to avoid the sharp rock hanging from the roof of the tunnel. That just caused more blood to head to his brain and to the injury.

His stomach rolled and he tasted bile in the back of his throat. Kessel bit down on his tongue and forced down the rising gorge. He had to get Annja out of here at all costs.

Whatever it took.

Which is why he was so incredibly relieved when he spotted a light farther up in the tunnel. An artificial light at that.

It had been placed there, no doubt, by someone who was used to traversing these tunnels. And while the maze itself might have had its own many dangers and pitfalls, Kessel doubted they'd run into very much opposition on the inside of the maze. This would be where they observed those who wandered the maze. Maybe they fed the animals from here.

Kessel didn't know.

And he didn't care.

All he wanted to do was get the hell out and make his head stop hurting.

WAS THAT A LIGHT?

Annja's heartbeat kicked up a notch. If there was a

light ahead, then that might mean they were close to getting out of the maze.

And that would be an amazing thing.

She quickened her pace to catch up to Kessel. "Do you see it?"

He grunted. "Yeah."

She frowned. Kessel's injury was getting worse by the minute. Annja had seen him stumble once or twice since they'd started walking again.

"You want a moment?"

He glanced back, and for a second, Annja thought she'd pissed him off. But then he only smiled meekly. "Yeah, if you don't mind."

"I don't mind at all. Take a break, get your breath back."

"Am I breathing hard?"

"Yes," she said. "You are." She came over and caught him as he nearly fell onto some of the rocks that jutted into the tunnel.

She lowered him, surprised at how heavy he was. "That better?"

He felt feverish and sweat rolled down his face. Kessel looked up at her. "I think I've got swelling in the brain. The pressure is building and needs to be released if I have any hope of surviving."

Annja stared at him. "You're not joking."

He tried to wipe away the sweat with the edge of his T-shirt. "Wish I was. But it feels like my skull is being used for a demolition derby."

"What can I do?"

Kessel pointed. "Scout ahead, find out what's up there. See if there's an exit. That's going to determine our next steps."

"Next steps?"

"We either find a way out of this forsaken place or else I'm going to ask a pretty big favor of you."

"What kind of favor?"

Kessel indicated his head. "You'll have to do it."

Annja's eyebrows shot up. "Are you crazy? I'll kill you."

"You might. But if you don't try, then I will most definitely die. I can't take too much more of this pressure."

Annja looked into his eyes. "Can you give me five minutes to see what's up in the tunnel there?"

Kessel grimaced. "Five minutes. No more. It's getting bad."

"Okay."

KESSEL WATCHED ANNJA skirt the rocks toward the light. He blinked. The pain was unbearable. Even looking at the light some distance away brought tears to his eyes.

He laid down on the rocks and tried to stretch out as best he could. It would be better if he was in the proper position before Annja came back. That way he could simply tell her what to do and hope she was able to deliver.

He knew she'd be frightened. Hell, he was scared of what might happen.

It'd be messy.

It would be scary.

But it had to be done.

And in another few minutes, Kessel would find out if Annja had what it took to do it.

He hoped she did.

22

Annja didn't like leaving Kessel. Cerebral edema wasn't anything to screw around with and the fact that Kessel had managed to go for so long without collapsing amazed her.

But he'd pushed himself as far as he could.

She crouched and moved down the tunnel toward the light ahead. It came from a single lightbulb.

Annja moved from rock to rock, straining to hear anything that might indicate the presence of someone. Or maybe even Fairclough himself.

She smirked. The more she thought about it, the more she'd come to realize that Fairclough probably wasn't dead.

That this whole thing was one big ruse to get Annja into the maze.

Yeah, well, it's time to change things around, she thought. *I'm not going to be a lab rat for anyone.*

She glanced over her shoulder at where Kessel lay. Stay alive, she thought. I'll bring back help.

She hoped.

HIS VISION WAS fading.

He could feel the pain starting to take its toll on other parts of his body.

Or was he simply losing consciousness?

It was weird, he mused. The pain that enveloped him was like a constant darkening of his mind. He took a deep breath, but wasn't sure if his brain registered any smell in the air.

He was thirsty, he realized. It had been hours since he'd had a drink. Same with Annja, he assumed. Sure, he'd gone without water before, but thirst might be another indicator of more physiological damage.

You're in a bad way, Kessel.

I hope Annja finds something helpful up ahead.

Because I could really use some good news.

ANNJA WASN'T SURE what she was looking at.

She'd come up ahead and found her way into what looked like a room rough hewn from the rock. A single lightbulb cast its light across the rock face, but aside from a plastic chair and a bottle of water, there was nothing else.

She grabbed the water bottle. At least there's this, she thought, quickly testing to make sure it was what it appeared to be. It might help comfort Kessel.

She turned and hurried back down the tunnel toward him.

Praying she'd been fast enough.

HE HEARD SCUFFLING.

Not another creature?

"Kessel."

That voice. Annja.

He cracked his eyes open and the pain of the dimly lit cave stung them badly. "Can't open my eyes."

"I found some water. Drink."

A moment later he felt a cool splash on his lips. The water flowed down his throat. He gulped and then retched slightly.

"Try to keep it down," Annja said quietly.

Blindly, he took her hand, a monumental effort that left him gasping for breath. "You've got to do it, Annja."

"It?"

"My head. Only you can relieve the pressure." Kessel forced himself to open his eyes. "You've got to punch a hole in my skull."

Annja blinked. "I don't think I can do that."

"You've got to. Or I'll die." Kessel's face contorted as another wave of pain swept over him. "Truth is, Annja, I'm going down here. If this doesn't happen soon, I'll be dead and it won't matter anymore."

Annja bit her lip. "But I don't have any tools and I've never done it before."

"People have been performing this procedure since prehistoric times, Annja. The technique is simple…."

"Easy for you to say."

"But it is. You only need to cut open the skin over the injury, punch the hole and the pressure should relieve itself very quickly. There will be a spout of blood from the hematoma, so be ready for it. But otherwise, once the pressure's relieved, I'll be a hell of a lot better than I am now."

"You'll still need a doctor."

"If we could find one, I'd be grateful, but there's no one around. Not even that quack Jonas up in Fairclough's place." He gripped her hand harder. "It has to be now."

"But I don't have a tool to cut with."

Kessel fixed his eyes on Annja. "But you do, Annja. You'll have to use the sword."

ANNJA LOOKED DOWN at Kessel. "Are you absolutely sure about this?"

Kessel managed a brief nod and then grimaced. "Yes. You have to help me. And now."

Annja's stomach churned at the thought of what she was about to do. She concentrated and quickly materialized the sword. Its gray glow illuminated the tunnel. Kessel smiled.

"It looks sharp."

"Never needs sharpening," Annja said. "But it's somewhat unwieldy for such a delicate operation."

Kessel brought her hand to the spot on his head. "Shave this area first using the blade. Once that is done, you'll need to cut the skin there."

"But how should I drill through the bone?"

Kessel took a breath. "That's the sticky part of this. You'll have to drive the point into the bone."

"Uh..."

Kessel nodded ever so slightly. "I know what you're thinking, Annja. You'll puncture it too hard and pierce my brain. I know the risks. But I'm certain to die unless you do this. So, as far as I'm concerned, the risk is worth it."

She hesitated before saying, "Okay."

Kessel smiled with his eyes shut. "Are you ready?"

"No. But I'll do it, anyway."

"Good. Because I'm going to pass out now. I'll see you on the other side."

"No, wait—"

But Kessel was already unconscious. It was hard to imagine how much pain he'd dealt with just so he could tell her what to do.

Now she had to deliver.

Annja took a breath to steady herself and then brought the sword up to Kessel's head. Using the edge of the blade, she worked it along his hairline as if it was a razor. It was tricky since the blade itself was long and unwieldy for such fine motor movement.

But she grew more confident with each swipe.

Finally, the scalp was exposed. Annja could see the discoloration of the injury. Kessel's skin was grayish blue, the result of bleeding. Annja repositioned the sword blade and made her first cut.

Blood pooled immediately, but it was mostly from the capillaries that fed his scalp. She hadn't yet relieved the pressure.

Speaking of pressure, she thought, this is about as weird a thing I've ever had to do with this sword.

She frowned. "Just get it done already."

Annja carefully folded the flap of scalp back to expose the skull bone underneath. It was tinged red from the surface bleeding, but Annja could see the indented part of the bone from where Kessel had impacted the wall. She grimaced as she peered closer. The injury was about the size of a half-dollar coin. And it was pressing into the surface of Kessel's brain itself.

Annja took another breath to steady her nerves. Her

heartbeat thundered as if she was getting ready to go into combat.

I need to calm down, she thought. If I screw this up, he dies.

She closed her eyes and imagined herself feeling calm and in control. As if she had just accomplished something and was already basking in the glow of success.

In her mind's eye, Annja went through the procedure Kessel had outlined. She visualized positioning the sword over his head and tapping it just enough to pierce the bone but not the brain matter beyond. She pictured just the right amount of force that would be needed.

Then she opened her eyes.

Steeled herself.

Okay, she thought. Here we go.

Standing over Kessel, Annja brought the sword up and turned its point so that it rested on Kessel's skull close to the injured area, but not on the indentation itself.

Annja took a final breath, held the sword with one hand and then positioned her other hand right over the pommel.

One hit, she thought. That should do it.

She exhaled, took another breath and then tapped the pommel with her hand.

The combined weight of the blade and the force of her hit made an audible crack.

She lifted the sword and saw the small hole she'd just made already pooling with blood. But it wasn't the great spurt Kessel had told her about.

I've got to remove that indented piece of bone, she thought with grim finality.

It's the only way.

She repositioned the sword and then began a series of delicate tapping all around the injured area. Annja was breathing fast and sweating by the time she was ready to tap the final hole.

With luck, this will be enough. There'd been a fair amount of blood already, and she felt sure that the pressure would be subsiding, but the only way to be sure was to get rid of the indented bone.

One more time.

Annja placed the sword over Kessel's head and prepared to make the final punch into his skull.

She took another breath.

Tapped the pommel of the sword again.

And heard a slight popping sound.

The indented piece of bone had come off and the blood that had been building up beneath it dispensed at last.

It was done.

Annja nearly collapsed from the stress of what she'd just done.

I'll need to bandage that, she thought. She used the sword to cut a swath from Kessel's shirt. Then she gingerly closed the flap of scalp and wrapped his head. He'd need to have something artificial implanted to protect his brain from any hits, but for the time being, Annja had done what she could.

Thank God, that was over.

Now only time would tell if she'd done it right or not.

And the only way she would know was if Kessel actually woke up again.

23

"Hey."

Hours had passed and Annja had fallen asleep with her hands still on the sword in case they were ambushed in the tunnel. She opened her eyes and saw Kessel looking at her.

"Hey, yourself." She sat up. "How are you feeling?"

"Ever have a migraine that just wouldn't quit?"

"Usually accompanied by nausea and vomiting."

"Yeah," Kessel said. "And you remember how it feels when that pain is finally gone?"

"Like a dull gnawing in your stomach. That hollow crappy feeling."

"Exactly." Kessel smiled. "That'd be about where I'm at right now. You did it, Annja. You did real good."

Annja shook her head. "That may go down as one of the most stressful things I've ever had to do. And I've been in plenty of stressful situations before."

"I know. And I hated like hell having to put that on

you. But I didn't have a choice. If I'd waited any longer, we wouldn't be having this conversation now. That's how close it was." Kessel looked around slowly. "You got any of that water left?"

Annja helped him sit up slowly and then gave him the bottle. He tilted it to his lips, but didn't bend his head back. "Still gotta move a little slow. I don't want to give you another reason to poke my skull."

"Yeah, thanks," Annja said. "How long until you think you can get up and walk?"

"Why? You in a rush?"

Annja smirked. "Nah, I love it here. Really. A new set of drapes and this is the perfect spot for me." She pointed at his head. "But you need professional medical attention, not the butchery of a swordswoman like myself."

"I'd say you didn't do anything close to butchering me," Kessel said after drinking.

"Just be glad you can't see the job I did. I had to connect the dots on your skull. I couldn't simply punch the hole and relieve the pressure. I had to remove the indented piece of skull that was pushing into your brain."

Kessel frowned. "That bad, huh?"

"Yeah. But you knew that, anyway."

He smiled. "You don't miss much, do you?"

"Not unless I'm really, really tired. I knew you had to suspect, judging by how you'd felt your skull. You would have known it was pressing in on your brain."

"I didn't want to worry you."

"Any more than absolutely necessary, given what I was going to do to your head." Annja smiled. "Well, the good news is it's done. And I certainly hope I never run across that again in my life."

"Makes two of us," Kessel said. "But we've got a bit of a problem ahead of us."

"What's that?"

Kessel frowned. "As much as it pains me to say it, I'm not going to be any good to you if we get into a fight. Any sort of injury to my head will probably kill me until something is put back over my brain to protect it."

Annja nodded. "I wish I could have replaced it somehow, but I had a hard enough time with the sword."

"Speaking of which." Kessel ran a hand over his head and felt the area she'd shaved. "How's the bald thing work for me?"

"I only shaved the area I needed to access. I didn't waste time turning you into Kojak."

"Hmm, I could use a lollipop right now," Kessel said. "Oh, well, I'll check it out when we get back. If it looks like crap, I'll just shave it all off and be done with it. At least that way it'll grow back in evenly instead of me looking like a walking lobotomy."

"Yes, that's what you should be worrying about right now—how pretty you look." Annja stood and stretched. "I wish we could find a way out of here."

Kessel pointed. "I still think we're headed in the right direction. Even if you didn't find anything down there except the water, that's still more than we've had to go on so far, right?"

"Yeah."

"So, we keep moving forward."

"The tunnel roof gets low up there, Kessel." Annja nodded toward his head. "You're going to have to be really careful."

"I'll be good. Just give me a few more minutes to clear my thoughts." He sighed. "But I gotta tell you, I feel a whole lot better than I did. Still a dull ache and all, but nothing like what I was going through before. I can't thank you enough."

"Help me get Greene and Fairclough and that will be more than enough," Annja said.

"No problem about Greene." Kessel slowly began to prepare to stand. "But are you so sure about Fairclough now?"

Annja shrugged. "On one hand, if I was neurotic and had enough money, could I see myself building something like this to protect a book? Maybe. But not likely. The more I think about it, the more I think he's someone out to exact revenge on me. Whether I deserve it or not."

"You been able to come up with anything that you might have done to get him so riled up?"

"Not a damned thing."

"I suppose you could always ask him the next time you see him."

"I intend to," Annja said. "It's just a matter of us finding our way out of this misbegotten hellhole."

"We will. Trust me."

"The sooner, the better," Annja growled. "I think I'm starting to really hate tunnels like this."

Kessel chuckled. "All right, slave driver. Give me a hand getting up."

Annja stopped him. "I didn't mean to say we should leave right away, it's just that I'm antsy."

Kessel held out his hand to her. "No, you're right. I'm out of immediate danger, but I do need to get a doctor to check this out. Make sure there aren't any other issues to deal with. Plus, there's the threat of infection.

The wound has to be cleaned and sorted out, properly bandaged."

"Yeah, sorry about your shirt." She carefully helped him to a standing position.

"Just glad it wasn't my Metallica T-shirt."

"Yeah, that would have been a shame." Annja rolled her eyes. "I suppose it's better than finding out you enjoy easy listening."

Kessel put his free hand to his heart. "And what's wrong with that? Some of my best friends are easy listeners."

"I guess I could get used to it. You know, if I needed to say—"

Kessel put a hand on the tunnel wall and bent over to kiss Annja. He held the kiss for a few seconds and then broke contact with a smile. "Just in case I don't get to say a proper thank-you."

"For what?"

"For everything." Kessel stared at her in admiration. "You're a hell of a woman, Annja. And I mean that."

Annja nudged him carefully. "All right, you big softie, let's get you out of this tunnel. Time's wasting and I'm looking forward to our sit-down with Fairclough."

"Sit down?"

"Beat down, more likely," Annja said. "Now come on."

AS THEY WALKED CAREFULLY through the tunnel system, Annja was mindful of the pace she set. Kessel nursed the bottle of water and she tried to help him as much as she could. But Kessel insisted on walking by himself. And she could see his determination to do as much as he could without her assistance. He'd accepted the help he truly needed, but now that the danger was past, he would only depend on himself.

Annja knew the feeling. She was fiercely independent, as well. And there was nothing worse than feeling so helpless that you had to hand over control of your life to someone else.

So she gave him his space and pressed on.

They'd long since passed the solitary lightbulb area where Annja had scavenged the water. Beyond it, they'd come to another intersection. Kessel opted for the left again. Annja agreed and they pressed on.

As they walked, the floor sloped upward at a shallow incline. Kessel cleared his throat after another sip of water. "This might be a good sign."

Annja looked at him. "You think?"

"We dropped a long way into the maze," Kessel said. "It stands to reason that in order to get out, we'd have to make our way back to the surface."

"I hope you're right," Annja said.

"Well, just so long as it's not like hiking Everest. In that case you may have to carry me."

"I don't think I could do that."

Kessel grinned. "Probably not. But you never know."

Annja pointed ahead of them. "There's another intersection coming up ahead, I think."

They slowed and Annja waited until Kessel had drawn even with her. The tunnel showed signs of being more refined and finished than it had down below. Annja looked at Kessel.

"What do you think?"

Kessel took the opportunity to rest against the wall. "It's really well lit up there."

"Is that a problem?"

"Concealment. We won't have any. If we get spotted, how do you want to play it? As far as they know, I'm still the mute that Greene hired to watch over you."

Annja raised her eyebrows. "You really think Greene doesn't suspect you of being a cop?"

"Why would he?"

Annja shook her head. "I don't know. It's just that he seemed pretty quick to send you into the maze. He was there when Fairclough gave me the rundown on what to expect. The idea that there was a lot of danger didn't even seem to faze Greene. He had no qualms about sending you along with me."

Concern creased Kessel's face. "I've had the same thought, but I've been damned careful. I don't even meet with my handler except maybe once every few months."

"Anyone else at the Bureau know about your work in Greene's organization?"

Kessel shrugged. "Well, I'm sure there are some. But my name wouldn't be on the operation report."

"Greene's organization is small, though," Annja said. "It wouldn't take a rocket scientist to figure out that if the Bureau says they've got a man inside, then there are only a handful of people who might be the mole."

"Yeah." Kessel sighed. "You make a good point."

"Just trying to head off any problems now," Annja said. "Besides—" she hesitated "—if there *are* cameras in this place, and a central control room, odds are pretty good they've at least seen us talking...even if they can't hear us. How do you think we should handle this?"

Kessel took a deep breath before saying quietly, "I suggest we take the chance and play it as if I was still Greene's man. Even if they know otherwise, they might play along. Buy us time. I've been wounded and you saved my life."

Annja grinned. "I saved your life? Why would I do a crazy thing like that? If you're Greene's man, why would I care about you? Wouldn't I be much more likely just to leave you to die alone in the tunnel somewhere?"

"You might be overcome with compassion."

"Well, if they know about the pressure I relieved, then they're going to ask how I did it. And if I tell them about the sword, the gig's pretty much up right then, isn't it? Even if they *haven't* seen it."

"Yeah," Kessel said. "Doesn't really look as if we're going to be a very convincing pair of liars, does it?"

"Nope."

Kessel nodded. "In that case, I suggest we change our plan. You know, go with our true nature and all."

"A convincing set of ass-kickers?"

"You got it." Kessel grinned. "It's a plan I can really get behind."

"Me, too," Annja said. "And I happen to think our return to the surface world is long overdue."

"Agreed."

Standing again, they continued up the slope. Toward the light.

And what lay beyond.

24

As they trudged up the slope, Annja saw movement. She waved Kessel down and he sank against the tunnel's wall as if he'd been nothing but a shadow. Annja brought out her sword and continued upward.

As she crested the incline, she made out the figure of a man bent over a console of television screens. Each one of the screens showed a different shot of the maze she and Kessel had just escaped from. She could see the time stamps on all the screens.

So this was where they watched all the action.

She gripped the sword tighter. It was time to set about destroying Fairclough's maze from the inside out.

The man turned.

It was the same Asian guy she'd seen down in the maze. The one who'd thrown the shuriken at her.

His eyes lit up with surprise, but his reactions were faster than Annja expected them to be. He vaulted over the desk and rolled, coming to his feet and flicking his hand at Annja.

She barely had time to jerk her sword up across her midline, deflecting the three shuriken he had sent zipping at her face. They skittered away, clanging off the metal video screen cabinet.

Annja tried to close the distance, but the Asian man turned and ran out of the room.

Annja gave chase.

Behind her, she heard Kessel shout, "Don't!"

But Annja was determined not to let the man get away from her this time. He obviously knew what was going on here.

However, as she raced down the corridor the Asian man had taken, she stopped short, realizing that she could be walking right into a trap.

Too late—another volley of shuriken came flying at her. Annja spun, twisted the sword up and around and felt the metal edge of one of the stars score a line across her face.

She dropped, rolled and came up ready to strike.

But the man was already gone.

Annja frowned. If this guy was really a ninja, then she was going to have a hard time dealing with him. The corridor she was in now was even darker than the tunnel she and Kessel had just been in. That meant her attacker had plenty of hiding spots. He could choose the precise moment to strike and Annja would never know what hit her.

Not good.

She started to back down the corridor to retreat to the control room. But as she did, her legs were swept out from under her.

Annja went down hard on her butt and barely had time to roll before a kick thundered into her midsection, causing her to suck fire.

He's talented, she thought.

Another shot to her chin threatened to drop her permanently. She recoiled, trying hard to keep her brain from becoming scrambled. It was the same spot she'd been hit twice before.

And they really knew how to hit.

I can't take that kind of damage again, Annja thought.

If she did, everything she'd done for Kessel would be for nothing. And she'd be dead, as well.

Annja drifted back toward the control room, each step carefully placed. And every shadow in the hallway seemed to move and melt away as if it had a life of its own.

Annja held the sword high in front of her.

Protecting her centerline from attack.

From the end of the corridor, one of the shadows seemed to bleed out into the center of the hallway. And then it drew itself up, becoming taller and taller.

What illusion was this? she wondered.

And then she recognized the form of the man she'd been chasing.

But now he wasn't running. Now he was coming for her.

She heard the sound of metal sliding from a sheath and saw the glint of steel in the dim light. The Asian man's katana.

Annja gripped the sword tighter. Her blood thundered through her body. She bent her knees and waited as the man advanced.

Unlike Annja, he seemed completely relaxed. His

eyes narrowed as he drew closer, seeming to glide toward her. Annja knew she was facing an extremely skilled swordsman.

But the frustration she'd felt at being run through the maze like a laboratory rat fueled her anger and she called out to him. "What is the point of all of this?" It felt good to hear her own voice and the power in it.

He smiled and she could see the whiteness of his teeth as he came even closer. Twenty feet separated them. Another step and they'd be in killing distance. Real sword fighting took place at much greater distances than commonly believed.

"You don't know what this is about?"

His voice was level and controlled and it sent a shiver running down Annja's spine. He sounded amused and simultaneously contemptuous of her. Frankly, Annja was surprised he'd even deigned to speak to her.

"I'm tired of running through this maze with no purpose to it."

"Oh, it has a purpose to it. Most assuredly."

"Then tell me what it is."

He grinned even wider. "You already know. You're just afraid to say it."

Annja gripped the sword even tighter. "Fairclough built this to trap me, hasn't he?"

"Has he?"

"He wants revenge."

"Is he the only one you've ever crossed? Is he the only one whose family you've destroyed?"

Annja frowned. What the hell did that mean? A family destroyed? And if not Fairclough, then who else could it be? Or was she understanding him properly?

But then the question flew from her mind. The Asian

man had achieved his goal: he'd confused Annja. And even as she recognized the tactic, he was already cutting down from high overhead, trying to cleave her body into two.

Annja barely had time to jerk her own sword against the katana and send it away from her. But then he was counterattacking, cutting back in a horizontal slash to her midsection.

Annja felt the laser sharpness of the katana slicing her belly and she gasped.

But the cut was only skin deep. And even as she caught the scent of her own blood, the Asian man was driving the pommel of his sword into her chest under her diaphragm.

Annja went down hard, clutching the sword against her in case he came down again.

He's so good, I don't have a chance here, she thought.

She kicked out at him, but he sidestepped her and used the tip of his katana to poke her thigh.

Again, the injury was minor. And the look on the man's face was full of contempt and superiority.

He doesn't think I can fight with my sword, she thought.

"Get up, Annja."

"How do you know my name?"

He smirked. "We all know your name here."

"We?"

He drove in with a sweeping, rising attack off his rear leg, looking to slice her from hip to shoulder. If he'd connected with the strike, Annja would have been dead on her feet.

But her instincts weren't entirely shot to hell. And as

he came on fast, Annja backpedaled so that the tip of the sword blade only cut the air a mere inch from her face.

Annja's breathing came in spurts. She had to get it under control. She had to mount an attack of her own.

But then she felt something sink into her shoulder and glanced down in time to see the metal spike embedded there.

Another shuriken, she realized. But this one was a throwing spike instead of the more common throwing star. It buried itself deep in the front deltoid and Annja knew that lifting her sword was going to be even tougher now.

"You are weak."

He'd said it in such a way that Annja had no doubt it was true. She was weak. She was battered. Tired. Confused. Hungry. Thirsty. And utterly without recourse against this man she didn't know or recognize, but who apparently knew all about her.

She sank to her knees.

Shattered.

And just like that, the corridor was empty.

The Asian man had vanished.

Again.

Annja glanced around, but even the shadows seemed to have retreated back into the walls. She frowned. Had she dreamed that encounter?

No.

The throwing spike was still buried in her shoulder. She looked down, grabbed the end of it and slid it out, gritting her teeth against the pain and nausea that accompanied the action.

She was covered in blood and sweat. Slowly, Annja

rose to her feet and walked back to the control room, slumping into one of the chairs.

Kessel entered the room a moment later. “Jesus, what the hell happened to you, Annja?”

“The Asian man I saw in the maze. I walked right into a trap.”

“I tried to stop you—”

She nodded. “I know, I know. It was my own stupidity that brought this upon me. I never should have given chase like that. Stupid rookie move. And he took advantage of it.”

“Who is he?”

Annja shook her head. “I don’t know.”

Kessel ripped another piece off his T-shirt, wadded it up and pressed it into the wound in her shoulder. “I may not have a shirt left by the time this is over.”

“Sorry about that.”

He smirked. “No matter. Let me see your stomach.”

Annja lifted her shirt and Kessel glanced at it. “You’re lucky. The cut’s only superficial.”

She shook her head. “No, luck had nothing to do with it. That was all skill. He could have killed me any time he wanted to. He played with me. All of this was just to warm me up for the final encounter. And it will happen when he wants it to.”

“Or maybe the person running this show doesn’t want it to happen yet.”

Annja nodded. “Fairclough.” She sighed. “I don’t know if I’m going to be able to handle this. I’m wasted beyond belief.”

“No choice,” Kessel said. “We either fight or we die.”

“You can’t fight,” Annja pointed out. “Your wound

is too delicate. You take another shot like the one that bounced you off the wall and you'll be done for."

Kessel sniffed. "I don't have the luxury of not fighting, Annja. If I leave it all to you, neither one of us will get out of this place alive. That's not to belittle you. On our own, I don't think either of us is enough."

"But together?"

"We just might have a shot," Kessel said. "But only if we go at them hard and fast."

"That may be the only thing they don't expect." Annja rolled her eyes. "Maybe they think they've got us all confused and unsure of ourselves."

Kessel grinned. "The only thing I'm sure of is that I'm going to do whatever it takes to get us the hell out of here."

25

Annja led Kessel up through the control room, pausing only to show him the banks of video monitors and the cables running all over. "I think this is one of the places they kept tabs on us."

Kessel frowned. "We really were like guinea pigs, weren't we?" He shook his head. "I don't like having my chain jerked without my consent."

"Neither do I," said Annja. "But at least this makes it somewhat easier in another way."

"What way is that?"

"Well, before you weren't sure how we should play up your role—whether you were still viable as Kessel the mute or not." She gestured at the video screens. "This pretty much answers that question for us, don't you think?"

She saw the realization hit Kessel. "If they've been watching, then they know I'm talking to you. So, it's safe to assume they're aware that I'm an undercover agent."

"Exactly."

Kessel grinned. "Good, I never liked playing the role of Greene's henchman, anyway. This will give him and me some really good quality time to catch up with each other. A little family reunion of sorts."

Annja frowned. Something about the way Kessel had said that had almost seemed gleeful. As if he was really looking forward to getting his hands on Greene. She shrugged. Tough to blame him for that sentiment. After all, she was feeling pretty much the same way about Fairclough.

And she couldn't wait to throw him around, old man or not. What he'd done here was unforgivable.

"We need to keep moving," she said then, suddenly aware of how exposed they were. If the ninja came back, he could cut them both down without expending much energy.

Annja didn't mind admitting that she was a bit confused why the ninja hadn't already finished her off. He could have taken me at any time, she thought as they walked out of the control room. And yet, he chose not to.

Nothing seemed to make much sense down in this place. But maybe once they got back to the real world, things would be different. Or at least apparent.

They continued to climb through more tunnels. Kessel grunted every so often behind her. Annja looked back. "You feeling okay?"

"As okay as you'd expect," Kessel said. "Just a little tough doing this climb right now with my head the way it is."

"Just think of each step as one foot closer to finding a real doctor."

Kessel nodded. "Oh, I am. Trust me on that one. It's just I didn't expect a little hike to take so much out of me. I'm used to hauling ass around mountains without breaking a sweat. And here we are walking a gentle incline and I'm heaving."

"You want to take a five-minute break?"

Kessel paused and she could see he was thinking it over. This was a test for him, she knew. Men like Kessel didn't like to think themselves weak, but he also knew that he had just undergone an invasive procedure and he had to take it easy or risk reinjuring himself.

"Five minutes might be good," he said finally.

Annja nodded and they hunkered down on opposite sides of the tunnel. She glanced around. "How far away from the surface do you think we are?"

"Not sure," he said. "I lost track of how deep we were. When we fell through the first room, we could have dropped several stories and not realized it. I don't know about you but my attention was on biting fish when I fell into the water."

"Mine, too. But we seem to have climbed back out of the abyss at least somewhat."

"I wish I knew—" Kessel rubbed his eyes "—where my end goal was, you know? Helps focus my brain on achieving it."

"Confusion and misdirection are a big part of this maze."

"No doubt," he agreed. "Whatever you did to this guy Fairclough, it must have been harsh to make him come up with something like this to torture you."

Annja sighed. "I honestly can't remember. When I laid eyes on Fairclough, I had no memory of seeing him before. I can't recall ever talking with him. And certainly I can't think of a thing I could have done to warrant this."

Kessel stared at her. "Well, unfortunately, it's not so much what you remember, or even if it's accurate, that counts. It's what Fairclough thinks you did to him. Or should I say, is convinced you did to him."

"And that's what sucks. I wish I knew if it was warranted or not."

"I'm guessing not."

She smiled. "Thanks. But I'm not so sure. There have been times in the past where I've had to dispense some intense justice."

"We've all been there, Annja." Kessel pointed a finger at her. "Don't forget who you're talking to here. I've been in more bloody battles than most people I know who are serving these days. Sometimes, the universe just opens its own alimentary canal and shits silly on you. In those cases, how are you supposed to react? With careful consideration? There's no time. You do what you're trained to do and try to get home safely. It's all any of us can do. We're human, after all. None of us is perfect."

Annja watched him for a moment and then smiled. "Thanks. I appreciate you saying that."

"Not trying to be a self-help guru or anything, just trying to make you see your situation objectively. The nature of the world these days is that it's full of evil and there are very few who answer the call to check evil's advance."

"You did."

Kessel shrugged. "It's what I do. I made that choice." He nodded at her. "But you? I don't know if you ever had a choice."

"What do you mean?"

"The sword," Kessel said. "How did you come by it?"

Annja looked down at the blade in her hand. It lay across her legs like it was taking a rest. "I think the sword chose me for some reason."

"Exactly. The sword chose you. And you were stuck with it." He leaned toward her across the tunnel. "Give it to me."

Annja frowned. "Excuse me?"

"The sword," he said with a grin. "I want you to give me the sword as a gift. Tell the sword I'm its new owner."

She shook her head. "I don't know if I can do that."

Kessel smiled. "Relax, Annja, I don't really want it. I just want to see what happens when you try to relieve yourself of that thing."

"What if it backfires?"

"And does what? Gets up and jumps around by itself, cutting us to shreds?" He laughed. "I doubt very much that's going to happen. Seriously. Now just try it and see."

Annja looked down at the sword again. She marveled at the length of its blade and how even in the dim light there was a luminescence about it. It truly was a marvel to behold.

"Annja."

She blinked. "Sorry." She closed her eyes and visualized herself giving Kessel the sword.

He will be your new owner, she thought to herself, trying to push the words into the sword. She felt a little silly, but did her best.

When she opened her eyes, the sword was still in her lap. Kessel was still leaning forward.

"Now give it to me."

Annja gripped the sword and then turned the hilt toward Kessel so he could grab it.

As soon as Kessel touched the hilt, there was a spark and a bang.

Then the sword vanished.

Panic seized Annja. Where did it go? She was relieved to see it hovering back where it always was in the otherwhere. She took it and the sword was back laying across her lap.

She smiled. "I think we just proved your theory."

"Sure as hell seems like it," he said. "Well, there's that settled now. So, hopefully, you know that you aren't entirely responsible for everything you do."

"So what—I get a free pass on things if I happen to be a complete bitch sometimes?"

Kessel shrugged. "Not really a free pass. If anything, I'd say you probably have to try even harder than the likes of us mere mortals do. That sword probably comes with its own set of rules and morals."

Annja nodded. "Lucky me."

"Would you give it away, if you could?"

Annja sighed. "Oh, hell, I don't know. I mean, there are times when I can't stand lugging this thing around anymore. It gets me into all sorts of trouble and then I have to fight my way back home." She smiled. "But there are also times when I'm damned grateful to have it. And on those days, I can't think what my life would be like without it."

Kessel let out a pained groan. "That sounds like just about every other relationship I've ever heard about. And here you thought you weren't ever going to get married."

Annja started to laugh. "You should do comedy," she said after a few moments.

He shook his head. “Nah, the thought of standing up on stage terrifies me. I could never do it.”

“You’re kidding me.”

“What?”

“A Navy SEAL and an FBI undercover agent and you can’t get up on stage to make people laugh? That’s ridiculous.”

“Why is it ridiculous?”

“Because your whole life has been about conquering your fears and overcoming obstacles. Hell, you get paid now to act in this role, right?”

“Well, yeah. But getting up in front of people, that’s scary stuff.”

“But you could do it. If you really wanted to.” She hefted the sword. “You’re not like me, Kessel. You’re not beholden to some ancient relic. You could do something completely different with your life and never look back.”

Kessel shook his head. “I’d always look back. I’ve left too many friends behind.”

“Poetic, too,” said Annja. “That could help your stage presence.”

Kessel grinned. “You planning this all out for me now?”

“Someone has to. I leave it up to you and it’ll never happen.”

“Maybe. Just don’t book me any appearances until I get my head back into shape.”

“Worried about your brain?”

“My brain?” Kessel shook his head. “Hell, no. I’m worried about looking like I just walked out of a lobotomy. I can’t go out there with half my head shaved and a hole in my skull. I’ve got my vanity, after all.”

Annja smiled. "I'll make sure you look good."

"Yeah?"

"Yeah."

Kessel stood. "Well, then, I guess I just found another reason to want to get home."

Annja pointed ahead of them. "The corridor keeps heading up. You think we'll find the entrance soon?"

"No idea," he replied. "But we've only got one choice, so I suggest we take it and don't stop until we start sucking in fresh, clean air."

"I like the way that sounds," Annja said.

26

Their excitement grew as they crested the slope and saw that it leveled out into a room with a hardwood floor. A first in the maze. Annja helped Kessel the last few steps and they looked back at how far they'd had to climb.

Kessel whistled. "I can't even figure out where we started. It's too dark to see the bottom from here."

"Got to be almost a quarter mile," Annja said. "At least."

Kessel turned and looked at the room they stood in. A single door faced them across the expanse of floor. "The exit. At last."

He strode across the floor and grabbed the doorknob even as Annja was shouting, "Stop!"

Kessel froze with his hand on the door.

Annja exhaled in a rush. "Sorry. Just a habit after so much crap in the maze—"

Kessel nodded. "We're not in the maze anymore, Annja. Now let's get out of here." He pulled the door open.

And as Annja stepped onto the floor, it shattered beneath her. For the briefest moment, she was frozen in space, screaming for Kessel to grab her hand.

To hold on.

To do anything.

But it was too late. Even as she saw Kessel lunge at her hand, Annja plummeted into darkness.

SHE HURTLED THROUGH the blackest tunnel she'd ever been in. It was worse than anything the maze had yet thrown at her. And to think, she'd been foolish enough to believe they could simply leave because the tunnels didn't look like those in the rest of the maze.

The realization stung. After all that buildup. After all that hope.

They were still in the maze.

Still a long way from escaping it.

And Annja was currently falling toward some inevitable conclusion. She had no idea how to prepare.

If I even draw the sword right now I'll impale myself, she thought. *It's just too risky.*

She kept her knees drawn up, trying to minimize the chances that she would break any bones.

Annja wanted to close her eyes and wake up back in Brooklyn. She wanted to find herself anywhere but in this maze, at the mercy of someone she didn't even recognize, didn't even know.

She wanted to be free.

But there was no way she was going to give Fairclough the satisfaction of breaking her.

She would have her own satisfaction when it came time to break him.

YOU IDIOT!

Kessel knelt by the gaping hole on his hands and knees. Seeing Annja plunge through the floor moments before had scared the crap out of him. How could he have been so stupid to open the door without checking it for a trip wire or some sort of booby trap?

Kessel shook his head. Annja was gone and Kessel couldn't even tell if she had vanished down another tunnel or what. Worse, with the condition his head was in, he couldn't take the chance of dropping behind her. If he even caught a glancing blow to his head now, he'd die.

He stood by the edge of the collapsed floor and stared into the pit for several minutes. But it was no use. Annja was gone, back down the rabbit hole, and Kessel had an open door behind him.

And only one way to go.

Through it.

He glanced back at the hole and frowned. I won't leave without you, Annja.

ANNJA COULD FEEL HER momentum slowing. Ahead of her, she could see light and, as she zipped onto a straight stretch of tunnel, she made a decision.

She brought the sword out and steeled herself for a sudden explosion of combat. Maybe they were waiting to kill her as soon as she came out of the tunnel.

I won't be such an easy mark, she thought. And she was feeling a heat pulsing throughout her veins now that she was determined not to crack. She'd played nice all along.

It was time to get mean.

KESSEL WALKED THROUGH the door and found himself facing a flight of steps. Looking up from the bottom, the steps numbered about twenty and ended at a single metal door.

Kessel frowned. The last time I opened a door the floor caved in. What would happen when he reached that door? Would the steps fall apart?

Kessel switched himself on and started checking the stair treads for any obvious signs that they'd been tampered with. He also looked for thin filament wires that might indicate the presence of explosives or something else that could ruin his day.

It took time, peering up at each step in succession, so he could make sure it was safe to proceed. And as he moved from stair to stair, sweat built up along his forehead, sliding down into his eyes. He'd forgotten how tense this kind of work could be. The potential existed for sudden mayhem at any moment.

And he could be killed if he lost focus for even one second.

And then Annja would truly be alone.

WHEN SHE CAME SPEEDING through the opening, Annja let out a war cry and leaped off the end of the tunnel, and came to her feet ready to slay an army of demons, if need be.

But she was in an empty room.

Lights overhead illuminated a single door. And since the only other exit was the tunnel, Annja started to move to the door.

But then she stopped.

No, this time we make sure there's truly no other way out of this place before I take the obvious. And so she spent the next thirty minutes prodding the walls trying to determine if there were any secret passages or other exits.

She found nothing.

Annja sighed as she walked to the door.

HE WAS CLOSE to the top.

Five stairs away, Kessel heard something on the other side of the door.

Movement.

Of course, he had no weapons at his disposal. Nothing but his body, which had been trained with the SEALs. But given his wound, unarmed combat wasn't exactly a good prescription for long life at the moment.

Still, if it came down to it, Kessel would fight to the death. He took a breath and continued checking the stairs, moving ever closer to the top.

And to the door that stood there.

IT WAS DARK WHEN Annja opened the door, standing to one side. There was no way she was going to frame it in case there was some booby trap or surprise attack waiting on the other side. So she positioned herself to one side of the doorjamb with a hand on the knob, slowly turning it until it clicked and opened back on the hinges. The door made no sound as it swung open, indicating that someone had oiled the hinges and kept them in good condition.

But what lay beyond it?

There was only one way to find out. Annja rose and, with her sword in her hands, walked toward the opening.

LAST STEP.

Kessel checked the tread and, as with the others before it, found nothing. He wiped the sweat from his face and then wiped his hands on his pants. The last time he'd had to check for stuff like this had been at an insurgent safe-house in Iraq.

But that had been a number of years ago. Since then, Kessel hadn't had to deal with trip wires and booby traps and improvised explosives or any of the other things that had killed lots of his friends.

Until today.

Until now.

He stood on the landing in front of the door.

This was the last thing he'd have to check over. And so he bent and got to work, running his hands over every inch of the frame.

IT WAS ANOTHER corridor.

Annja groaned, but then she heard a noise. Actually, a fair bit of noise. Were those voices? Were there people up ahead?

And if there were, what were they doing? If she'd been planning an ambush, she wouldn't be making noise when the target could hear it. That wouldn't be smart.

Maybe it's not an ambush, she thought.

She frowned. This whole damned thing has been one type of ambush or other. Even when she thought she was safe, it turned out to be just another trap.

Just another way to get her to go crazy.

I'm not falling for it again.

So she crept closer to the noise. Closer to what she hoped were some actual honest-to-goodness answers.

Instead of more questions.

THE DOOR WAS CLEAR.

Kessel finished checking and wiped his sweaty hands on his pants again. He'd gone over the door and the frame, peered through the keyhole and even felt around the underside of the jamb and the knob itself, trying to figure out if there was anything conceivably wrong with it.

When he was done, he was forced to conclude that the door was perfectly normal.

Which didn't make him feel good at all.

Nothing's been normal about this place from the moment Annja and I got put in here, he thought.

But there was little choice but to open the door. And that's what made him so upset. Fairclough had apparently designed this place to funnel people toward something. He'd removed their ability to choose their own destiny. He'd given them no choice at all. You either played the way he wanted you to play or else you stayed in the maze forever.

Well, I'm not staying in this dump any longer, thought Kessel.

I'm getting out.

He opened the door.

27

Annja drew closer to the light and the noise. She could clearly hear multiple voices in the room ahead. She couldn't make out what they were saying, but the tone of the conversation seemed light. Not dangerous.

Was it possible she had nothing to fear from going into the room ahead of her? Had she found some sort of safe zone?

Yeah, right, she thought. Fat chance of that happening. Everything to this point had been carefully calculated and plotted out by Fairclough. There was no way he'd ever let something like a safe zone find its way into his maze.

Annja kept her grip on her sword. *I won't trust anyone until I know for sure I'm not about to be stabbed in the back.*

And even then, she might not trust any of them completely.

"HELLO, KESSEL."

In front of him Greene aimed a silenced pistol directly at Kessel's chest. He had to remember that the charade was up; they'd had video cameras watching him talk to Annja. No sense prolonging the inevitable, he supposed.

"Greene, you're looking well."

The ecoterrorist looked incredibly smug. Kessel found the expression slightly nauseating. Or was that just his head injury?

"I'm glad to see you're not going to insult me by pretending to still be a mute."

Kessel shrugged. "What's the point? I know you guys had the maze wired for sight and sound. I'd only be fooling myself if I still played the part."

Greene nodded. "And now you and Annja have been separated again. How tragic for the both of you."

Kessel frowned. "Do you know where she is?"

The other man laughed. "Know where she is? Of course we do. We've known where you've been the entire time you went into the maze. There's nothing going on here right now that hasn't been planned for months, years even."

"You mind giving me a clue?"

Greene waved the pistol. "Come with me and we'll see if Fairclough feels like divulging anything or if he simply wants me to kill you right now."

"Oh, well, good," Kessel said. "At least that way I'll know what to wear to my funeral."

ANNJA SAW THE OUTLINE of a doorway more clearly now. The light coming from the room was bright. Yellow. And she smelled something.

Food.

Her mouth swam in its own juices as she detected the scent of roast chicken. It had been hours since she'd eaten and the stress was catching up with her. She'd been running on fumes. The thought of actually filling her stomach with food was almost too much to bear.

Annja could barely resist the urge to run into the room. But she held back, one last vestige of her discipline still intact despite the stress and exhaustion she'd had to deal with since being plucked out of Brooklyn earlier today.

Or was it yesterday?

Annja frowned. She no longer knew how long she'd been in the maze. A quick glance at the watch told her the thing had stopped working hours ago.

Or was it minutes ago?

Stupid watch.

She took another step closer to the room.

Another step closer to food.

GREENE KEPT KESSEL in front of him as they headed down a hallway lined with fluorescent bulbs overhead that flickered when they walked under them.

"What happened to your head, Kessel?"

"I got thrown into a wall by that thing you guys put down in the maze. What was it? A bigfoot or something?"

"Something," Greene said. "What's the matter? Did it get the better of you?"

"Temporarily."

"What's that mean?"

"It means it's dead," Kessel said. And he felt good saying that.

But if Greene was upset by the news, he didn't show it. He merely sniffed and told Kessel to keep walking. "We've got an appointment that I don't want to keep waiting. I think he's quite interested in talking to you about your work."

"My work?"

"Yes, you being a special agent with the FBI and all. He's quite keen on hearing about your exploits."

"My exploits," Kessel repeated. "Well, he ought to ask you about them, then. After all, I've been assigned to penetrate your organization and bring you down."

Greene laughed. "So much for that, then, eh?"

Kessel shrugged. "Day's not over just yet. Who knows? Halley's Comet could come crashing through this place and wipe us all out."

"But that would mean you'd be dead, too."

Kessel stopped, turned and looked at Greene. "As long as you're dead, I don't care about my own life."

Greene's smile spread across his face. "I do so love how superior you try to make yourself appear even in the face of defeat. That's something from your military career, isn't it?"

"Maybe."

"Well, we'll see how high and mighty you are when Fairclough asks me to serve you a dish of hot lead." Greene gestured with the pistol. "Now keep moving."

ANNJA BRACED HERSELF on the doorjamb and prepared to enter. Sounds continued on the other side of the doorway. The voices were lower now. But she still couldn't hear what they were talking about.

The smell of freshly cooked food was almost too much to bear. She gripped the sword and closed her eyes.

Please don't let this be a trick. Please let it be real. I just need something to eat.

She opened her eyes, took a breath and then steeled herself. On a count of three, Annja swiveled away from the door frame and entered the room.

WHEN KESSEL MADE his move, it caught Greene completely by surprise. Instead of turning and knocking the gun out of Greene's hand as the ecoterrorist might have suspected he would try, Kessel instead jumped straight up and punched his hand into one of the overhead fluorescent lights.

Shattered glass rained down on Greene's unprotected head, while Kessel landed and tucked himself into a ball, rolling as far away as he could.

The shattered bulb produced a chain reaction and the hall filled with the sound of exploding lightbulbs that shot down like a million tiny mercury-tipped spears. Greene looked up in horror and then screamed as a shard punctured the membrane of one of his eyes.

He dropped the pistol and ran past Kessel, screeching. He vanished into the darkness.

Kessel waited until the last of the bulbs had exploded and finished shattering their glass into the hallway before he got up and found the pistol.

The weight of the gun felt good in his hand. For the first time, he felt like maybe he'd just done something to tilt the odds in their favor.

He frowned. Well, at least, his favor for right now.

But he'd find Annja.

He would.

ANNJA LOOKED around.

The room was deserted. She frowned. Where was everyone? Where were those voices coming from?

She crossed the floor and saw the stereo speakers set up behind a table. The sounds came out of the speakers.

No.

She wheeled around, searching for the food that had teased her.

But the table was bare. And there was no other place the food could have been.

The smells, though, she wondered. Where were they coming from? Surely not the stereo speakers.

And then she saw the vent. It measured only about two feet by one foot but it was through this that the smell of food had been piped into the room.

Everything had been done to give the appearance that there were people eating in here.

But why?

More torture?

Or something more sinister?

KESSEL TOUCHED THE WOUND on his head and found that it didn't hurt any worse than before he'd made his move. Everything still seemed to be intact.

Good.

Kessel checked the slide on the pistol. He could tell even in the dark that he was holding a 9 mm suppressed Beretta. He popped the clip and checked the spring pressure. The weight of the clip and the resistance when he pressed on the top round told him he had enough rounds to make his point loud and clear.

He slid the clip back into the gun, racked the slide

and then put the safety on before adopting a low-ready stance.

Then Kessel started off after Greene.

Wherever he was, Kessel would find him.

ANNJA STARED at the empty table.

Okay, she felt like shouting, so what's the goddamned point of this? If Fairclough wanted to break her, he was very close to succeeding. But Annja also didn't want to give him the satisfaction of displaying her emotions.

So she clamped her jaw shut, aware that Fairclough might have cameras in the room watching her right at that very moment.

She looked at the table. The speakers.

The vent.

She frowned. The vent was obviously too small for her to crawl through. And she was willing to bet it wasn't that far away from the actual food she was smelling. That's what made it so incredibly tantalizing.

So especially painful.

Damn you, Fairclough, she thought. I don't know what I did that would make you want to do this to me, but I promise, when I get out of here and find you, I'm going to do something far worse than anything I've done so far.

And then it occurred to her.

There was no exit from this room.

There were no other doors.

She'd come down the tunnel and landed in the one place that then led her to this room. There were no secret passageways in the other room and now here she stood alone with a table, speakers and a vent.

How the hell was she going to get out of this?

KESSEL COULD HEAR Greene somewhere in the darkened corridor ahead of him—the ragged breathing from the intense pain Greene was no doubt feeling from the glass in his eyeball.

And Kessel, for the first time since he'd begun this operation, finally felt like he was the hunter.

He didn't envy Greene right now.

But he'd envy him even less when he caught up with him. Kessel glanced at the pistol in his hand.

And knew that using it on Greene was far too lenient a sentence.

Kessel lowered his stance and headed down the corridor. It was time to dispense some serious justice.

28

Kessel followed the sound of Greene's whimpering up the corridor. Although he couldn't see, Kessel was locked on his target. A few more minutes of trailing him and he had no doubt he'd be able to finish this for good.

Kessel grimaced at the thought of having such fine glass shards embedded in his own eye. He hadn't deliberately set out to do that to Greene, but the ecoterrorist had made the mistake of looking up.

Greene had taken the full brunt of the shattering bulbs right in his face.

Ouch. But then again, Greene had caused his own fair share of suffering. Maybe this was karma.

There had often been times when he felt as though the universe was using him for its own ends. When he'd come across the group of Taliban fighters that had just torched a girls' school in a remote town in Afghanistan, killing every single one of the eight-year-olds in the name of radical Islam. His heart beat faster as he remembered with striking clarity how he had been the instrument of their destruction, calling in a Predator air strike.

Greene was still scuffling up ahead. His breathing sounded more labored. He must have known Kessel was tailing him because the whimpers had quieted.

He'll try to get to safety and keep me down here, Kessel thought. I'll have to take him before he can reach the exit. Kessel increased his speed but not to the detriment of his stealth.

Kessel wanted Greene to feel what it was like to be hunted, to not have any control over his destiny.

He wanted to shout, "How does it feel, Greene?" into the darkness. Make Greene's fear palpable. But Kessel remained silent, focused on the task at hand.

As the corridor led him upward, it seemed as if the walls of the tunnel were starting to close in on him. He put out one hand and felt the cool stone. Everything seemed right.

And he could still hear Greene up ahead.

Was the man crying now?

Wasn't that always the way. So much for the false bravado, he thought. Greene was done.

And then Kessel picked up speed.

It was time to end this.

OKAY, ANNJA THOUGHT, I'm in a room with no exit.

A room with no apparent exit, she quickly corrected herself. Chances were good there was a way out. She felt sure that Fairclough still wasn't done with her yet—that he would funnel her into some other portion of his maze where she'd have to jump over a snake pit or something like that.

Or maybe he'd just keep tormenting her with this silliness until he saw her crack. *I'm not in the mood to fulfill this guy's fantasies. Not a damned chance.*

But she did want to get out of the room she was in. The smell of food was driving her nuts even if she was determined not to let it show on her face. She couldn't help walking close to the vent and inhaling the air. If she could have fed on smell alone, she'd be sated.

She took another breath. The room was twelve feet by twelve feet. Another perfect square in the heart of the maze. Well, she had no idea if this was the heart of the maze or not, but she had to think that after climbing up and almost out of the trap, and then finding herself right back down here, Fairclough must have wanted her close to the center by now. She felt sure that the guy had some sort of schedule Annja was adhering to whether she knew it or not.

Video cameras were probably tracking her as she paced the floor and tried to figure out how she was going to get out.

If she was supposed to get out at all.

She stopped. Was this where she was supposed to end up? Would this room serve as some sort of prison cell for Annja? Had she been sentenced to spend the rest of her life here? Well, without food or water, the rest of her life would be pretty short.

What gave Fairclough the right to sentence her to this place like a prisoner? What had she done that warranted such extreme action as this? Annja had always tried to defend good. The things she'd done in pursuit of justice weren't evil; they were necessary.

And yet she doubted Fairclough would ever understand that. In order to create something like this, his mind was most likely warped by fury.

And talking to him would do no good, either. Fairclough knew what he wanted and how to get it. Greene had brought her here to be a pawn in the bookseller's vengeance.

Annja's heart raced at the thought that Kessel was still out there. He was her one chance at salvation. If he was able to turn the tables on Fairclough and Greene, she might just have a shot at getting out.

But where was Kessel? Where was he and would he even know where to look for Annja? Plus, he was still wounded. She knew he'd have to take it easy. At this point, she wondered if it would be smarter for Kessel to save himself and get help before he tried to rescue her.

Annja swallowed. That meant he'd have to leave her behind.

She didn't like that thought at all.

KESSEL DREW CLOSER to Greene. Only a matter of twelve feet separated them now. Greene must have known he was there. The atmosphere in the hallway would have told him that someone was close. Kessel knew what it was like to have to fight in the dark and not see where your enemy was.

"Kessel?"

Kessel almost laughed at the sound of Greene's shaky voice. The man was terrified. There was nothing he could do but hope that Kessel would be mercifully quick in killing him.

But Kessel wasn't going to kill him—at least, not right away. First, he needed to know where Annja was.

He needed to know the layout of the maze so he could reach Annja and get her the hell out.

Then he would force Greene to take him to a phone where Kessel could call in the cavalry and get some medical attention, which he knew he badly needed. His head was much better than it had been, thanks to Annja, but he wasn't about to start kidding himself and pretend he didn't need some serious recuperation time.

But first he needed to make sure Annja was okay. It was the least he could do for her since she'd saved his life. What she'd done for him in the cavern had taken most of her courage. Kessel wondered if he would have been able to do the same thing.

He wasn't so sure.

But Annja had saved him. And now Greene was going to lead Kessel right to where he needed to go to help Annja.

Or else Kessel would put out his other eye.

ANNJA KEPT WALKING across the room. The floor was simple stone tile, but she saw no pattern or other indicator that stepping on one would produce poisoned darts as they had earlier on in the maze.

Annja shook her head. No, Fairclough was done with that stuff now. She felt pretty sure that, because she'd managed to reach this point, Fairclough would undoubtedly have something special to spring on her.

The question was: What would it be?

She'd already killed a Sasquatch and a pack of wild dogs. She'd dealt with the more maddening aspects of the maze and yet she still wasn't done. Fairclough wouldn't blow his greatest challenge on her until he was sure she was properly prepared to face it. That meant wearing her down and riling her up with annoyances like hunger, thirst and exhaustion.

Annja was all of those things.

But she was also angry.

And she was willing to bet that the fury slowly growing in her belly would be more than enough to thwart the annoyance factor. Once she was faced with Fairclough's ultimate challenge, she would strike hard and fast and without mercy.

Then she'd call him out. Give him the opportunity to gloat about her predicament. That didn't matter to Annja. All she needed was one shot at Fairclough and she'd take it.

And heaven help Fairclough when that happened.

KESSEL DREW CLOSE enough to reach out and touch Greene. He heard Greene yank himself away instinctively. And Kessel enjoyed knowing that Greene was so scared.

"I know you're there, Kessel."

Kessel swallowed and then touched Greene on his head. Greene yelped and fell back away from him. Perfect, thought Kessel, I can take him now. And then he moved in to grab his prey.

That's when he heard a different sound.

It was laughter.

Laughter?

Kessel froze. Then he brought the pistol up, flicking the safety off as he did so, ready to punch two rounds into Greene's brain.

But the gun was knocked away and, when it popped off, the bullet ricocheted off the walls before splintering away.

And the only thing Kessel heard next was Greene's voice very close to Kessel's ear.

"Gotcha."

ANNJA HEARD A NOISE through the vent. It sounded like a single pistol shot that had been suppressed by a silencer. Was it Kessel? Had he found a way to get to Fairclough? Had he found out where Greene was?

Annja bent close to the vent and strained to hear anything else. She thought she heard laughter.

She stood back up. "Are you having fun, Fairclough? Are you enjoying this little jaunt?"

For a moment, there was no response. And then through the same vent Annja had just been listening at, she heard Fairclough's voice come trickling through.

"I'm having a very enjoyable day, Annja Creed. Although I must say you are probably not enjoying yourself at all. Are you?"

"I've had better days," Annja said. "Why don't you come down here and we'll talk about it?"

"Oh, I shall. Very soon, in fact. But I'm afraid I've got a few more things to tend to first. In the meantime, I don't want you to get bored, so I've lined up a little distraction for you."

And then Annja heard the sound of crumbling or movement or something. But she soon figured it out.

The walls were starting to close in on her.

29

Kessel came awake blinking under a brilliant white light. He winced and then noticed that he couldn't move his arms or legs. He was strapped into what looked like a dentist's chair. He tried to flex against the leather wrist straps, but they were buckled tight. He wouldn't have much luck against them.

Damn.

A rolling cart stood near the chair. It held a series of tools laid out carefully on a sterilized tray. Kessel frowned at the sight of some of them. There were small saws, picks and several oddly shaped implements. He cringed at what they might be used for.

The door opened and Greene walked in. A white bandage covered one of his eyes. So, thought Kessel, he did take some glass, after all. He smirked at the memory of Greene shrieking.

Greene smiled at him. "Enjoying the fact that you put glass in my eye, you son of a bitch?"

"Definitely. After all the crap you've been involved with, it's nice to see a little justice dispensed in your direction."

"Spare me your soapbox, Fed," Greene snapped. "Your kind will never understand what drives people like me."

"When you kill innocent people? When you commit acts of terrorism? You deserve to die for that."

"Doesn't that run a little against your law enforcement code?" Greene asked. "I can't imagine your superiors would be thrilled knowing you'd just as soon shoot me as bring me in for the justice system to throw around between shrinks and prisons."

"At this point," Kessel said, "I'm more than willing to forsake my career to make sure you don't ever get a chance to hurt anyone else. You say you're all about saving the planet but you're not about peace. You're as dangerous as any suicide bomber."

Greene rubbed his chin thoughtfully. "Wow, you know, that's really fascinating. I so enjoy listening to you condemn me for killing people when you're proud of the kills you make in the name of justice. It's so much fun. So ironic. One man's enemy is another man's hero, after all."

"I think you're mixing up your sayings," Kessel replied. "But it doesn't matter. None of this does. You can do whatever you want. Just know this—when I get out of here, I'm coming for you."

"Your threats are tiresome." Greene yawned. "Now, I suppose I ought to bring in the good doctor and let him check you over. Make sure you're okay and whatnot."

Kessel narrowed his eyes. "Which doctor would that

be? Not that crackpot Jonas. I'd rather take my chances with infection."

"Now really, is that any way to treat a medical professional?" Greene opened the door and Jonas walked in wearing scrubs.

Jonas smiled at Kessel. "So nice to see you again. You've been keeping me busy today. I really had to do a number on Greene's eye there when he stumbled in. Fluorescent lightbulb glass is fragile stuff. I'm hopeful we got all of it out, but you never can tell. And, of course, that's made Greene rather unhappy with you."

"Fuck him," Kessel said. "And fuck you, too."

Jonas grinned. "I always enjoy a lively one when I'm working. It makes for such a thrill when I start probing."

Kessel flexed his wrists again but the cuffs held him tight. "Don't even think about it."

Jonas shrugged. "But you see, Kessel, your role in this is much greater than you imagine. And it's so convenient to have someone like you here to fulfill his mission. After all, that's what it's all about, isn't it? Leave no man behind and all that jazz?"

"What are you talking about?"

Greene leaned closer to Kessel. "I can't wait to see you squirm when the good doctor here starts sticking things in your head. It will be my turn to laugh as you reap what you've sown."

Jonas moved around behind him, picking up some of the tools on the tray at his side. "First things first," Jonas said, more to himself than Kessel. "I need to make sure that hole in your skull is okay. I mean, what use would you be if we didn't square that away? We can't have you dropping dead from infection or a quick blow to the skull. Not when you've got so much to do."

His face appeared in front of Kessel. He held a small implement that reminded Kessel of a handheld drill. "I'll make the opening a bit larger so I can smooth the ragged edges."

"Awesome," Greene said. "I've never seen anyone get their skull drilled. This should be interesting."

Jonas stepped away from Kessel. "I'm afraid we're a little short on painkillers and anesthesia around here. So you're going to feel what's about to occur. At least until you pass out from the pain."

Greene's smile was greasy. And Kessel hated him all the more for it. "Where's Fairclough?" he asked.

Greene shrugged. "Setting the stage for your friend Annja, I'd imagine. Lots to do, you know."

Jonas moved around the chair and started taking Kessel's vitals. "This is just standard practice, of course. I mean, it really doesn't matter how calm you are now. Once I start drilling into your head, your blood pressure is going to go through the roof, anyway." He whistled as he started pumping up the blood pressure cuff.

Kessel leaned closer to him. "Just so you know—I will find a way to kill you. It doesn't matter what you do to me. I won't stop until I break your fucking neck with my bare hands and watch the life leave your pathetic body."

Jonas blinked. "I think you'll find that a difficult promise to fulfill once I complete my work."

"Why?" Kessel asked. "I promise to make time for you once I kill Greene over there."

Jonas laughed. "Such a shame to have to do this to you. I actually like you a lot better now that you're talking." He shrugged. "But I guess that's the way it goes, eh?"

Greene looked at him. "Are we ready to start?"

Jonas nodded. "Yes, we are."

He moved behind Kessel.

And the hell began.

THE WALLS THAT SURROUNDED Annja moved slowly, inexorably closer.

Her one chance to avoid being squashed like a bug lay at the doorway, and so even as she recognized that the walls were closing in on her, Annja had already vaulted back toward it. She threw herself out of the room, into the hallway.

Speakers nearby blared to life. "Nice work, Annja. I can't say I'm surprised by your athleticism. I expected it. Counted on it, actually. It always helps when people do exactly what you expect them to do. It makes life so much easier."

"What's this all about, Fairclough?" Annja called. "You've got me captive here. So why not tell me why you're doing this?"

"Not yet," came Fairclough's reply. "It's more fun to keep you guessing. More hellish that way, don't you think?"

"Nothing compared to what I do to you once I get out of here."

"You're an optimist, of course," Fairclough said. "I respect that. However, I think you'll have to eventually admit that you're going to die here, Annja. And you're going to die alone where no one will ever find you again. You'll fade from memory and no one will know how you came to die."

Annja frowned. "In that case, I'll make sure I claw

my way back from the grave and drag you down to hell with me, you bastard."

"Yes, yes, I'm sure you will. In the meantime, you've got other things to concern yourself with, my dear."

That's when Annja heard the sound of barking.

Fairclough laughed. "We've been a little lax in feeding them, I'm afraid. I'd be willing to bet they'll eat pretty much anything they can get into their mouths."

Annja spun around in the corridor and went to meet the wild dogs.

KESSEL WAS SCREAMING.

In some remote part of his mind, he heard his own screams, felt the sweat that had long since soaked him through, and yet he was simultaneously detached from it.

Kessel's mind was invaded by the high-pitched sound of a drill that pierced his skull and drove into his brain matter. He screeched again, overwhelming the sound of the drill with his cries.

It went on for several minutes before Jonas mercifully finished drilling. Kessel would've slumped forward, but his head was lashed back with a restraining strap.

He retched and bile spilled out of his mouth. He heard Jonas telling him to calm down and breathe, that it would be over soon, but Kessel felt as if every nerve in his body had been doused in gasoline and set on fire.

What drove men like this to such cruelty?

Kessel's body bucked wildly as Jonas speared something into his brain. And then he shrieked again. Longer this time and even louder than before.

Hell had nothing on this.

THERE WERE ALMOST too many of them, Annja decided.

She'd already sent four of the scrawny but ferocious dogs to the next life with a series of slashes with her sword, but the dogs kept coming. How many did Fairclough have in here?

Their barking filled her head and she wanted to scream at them to shut up, to stop their incessant noise. But she had to keep fighting them. And they still kept coming in waves.

Blood splashed the hallway and Annja found herself covered in it as she swung back and forth, desperate.

Saving herself for Fairclough's final act, she realized.

She almost stopped and let the dogs take her. If anything, it would at least be a giant middle finger to Fairclough, that she hadn't allowed him to fulfill his dream of torturing her to death.

But Annja kept going for one reason: Kessel.

If she could live through this, then they could both escape.

The barking continued and Annja realized that Fairclough was piping in more noise than there actually were dogs. Its effect served two purposes: it riled the dogs and it nearly drove Annja insane.

But still she fought on.

SOMEWHERE OUTSIDE of himself, Kessel heard the noises stop. He was drenched. And then he picked up the sound of voices that sounded as if they'd been melted together into some syrupy mixture. Almost as if he was underwater listening to an exchange between Jonas and Greene.

But he strained to make the words out clearly.

"Is it done?"

Kessel heard Jonas laugh. "It's done. At last."

"Are you sure it will work?"

"I'm not sure of anything. But it will be lots of fun seeing what happens next, won't it?"

He was about to be released, he suspected, very much unlike the man who had first sat down in Jonas's chair.

But what he was, he had no idea.

ANNJA SQUATTED AMID the corpses and heaved.

She tried to flush oxygen back into her lungs but they felt like a fiery bellows. Sweat flowed like a river down her back, soaking through her shirt and mixing with the blood and gore of the dogs.

Such senseless death, she thought. Such mindless violence.

The dogs weren't to blame. They were driven by a need for food. By the cruelty of Fairclough.

Annja looked around at the husks that surrounded her. She fought back the regret and sadness that threatened to overwhelm her.

I'll see to it that he pays, she whispered to the dogs she'd been forced to kill.

Even if it kills me.

I promise.

30

Several hundred yards from where Annja squatted in the tunnel, Greene and Jonas entered the maze's real control room, followed by the hulking form of the man called Kessel. At a bank of computers and video screens, Fairclough turned when they entered.

"Is he ready?" He directed the question at Jonas, who was still eyeing Kessel as if he were some creature that had just lumbered out of the grave.

"It's untested," the doctor said. "We ought to have done an early experiment prior to using this one."

"There was no time," Fairclough snapped. "This hinged on finding someone she would form a relationship with who I could then use to destroy her."

Greene sighed. "Why don't you just let us kill her and be done with it? Hell of a lot faster that way."

Fairclough looked at him with contempt. "You don't have the capacity to appreciate what it is I'm doing here, so do me a favor and please shut your mouth unless I directly ask for your input, all right?"

Greene snapped his mouth shut and shrugged at Jonas. "I guess he knows best."

"I do know best," Fairclough said. "Your organization benefits because of me. Without my money, you'd just be a bunch of hoodlums with no means to ever support your cause."

Greene frowned. "We were doing pretty well before you came along."

Fairclough laughed. "You're joking, right? That protest you staged at the G8 summit? That was pathetic. You had no vision until you met me and learned what you could be with the right resources."

"But if that's true, then why are we wasting time on this diversion? Shouldn't we be out fulfilling the grand plan?"

Fairclough pointed at a video screen that revealed Annja through night vision. "What we ought to be doing is right here, right now. What we ought to be doing is destroying the woman who caused me heartache. Once we've finished with her, then we can continue our environmental work. But until she is rendered impotent, she will still be a threat to us."

Greene studied Annja. "She didn't seem like much of a threat yesterday when we picked her up."

"That's because you took advantage of her huge sense of compassion. You're no match for her physically. None of us are."

"So, again, why not just shoot her?"

"I don't think she can be killed that way."

Jonas waggled his eyebrows. "You think she's immortal?"

"I think she's remarkably strong," Fairclough explained. "And that strength comes not just from a physical place but also from a spiritual place. And that means she's that much harder to kill."

"Never met anyone who couldn't be taken down with a dozen bullets in their skull," Greene said. "Why don't you let us try it and find out?"

Fairclough shook his head. "No. The stage has been set for Annja Creed's demise and I shall now enjoy putting it into motion at long last."

Greene shrugged. "What'd this chick do to you, anyway? She steal your Bible and kick your dog?"

Fairclough's expression was stony. "It's not for you to understand. All I ask is for you to carry out your role."

Greene nodded. "Fair enough. Tell us when and we'll be there."

Fairclough consulted his watch. "Give me about twenty minutes and then release that thing into the maze."

Jonas nudged Kessel. "Let's go."

Fairclough watched them leave the control room and then turned back to the video screen. Idiots, he thought. They would never understand how great the thrill of vengeance was. She must be made to understand that her actions resulted in these consequences.

Surely Annja Creed was close to realizing that.

And if she wasn't, then in a few short minutes, Fairclough would gladly tell her.

Right before he watched her die.

ANNJA HUDDLED in the corridor, alert for any change in her environment. The darkness had lightened somewhat and she could make out vague shapes in the distance. Back the way she'd come down the slippery tunnel.

Her entire journey through this damned maze had been choreographed from start to finish. At every point, she'd been controlled.

Annja frowned. This had all been leading to a final showdown she felt certain was coming soon.

Otherwise, Fairclough wouldn't have broken his silence. He was gloating. Trying to psyche her out.

He loved this.

Annja glanced around. Was he watching her right now? The darkness didn't matter. He could have night vision scopes on his cameras that could easily pick her out. He could be basking in her uncertainty, carefully choosing just the right moment to spring the final part of this mad play on her.

Annja shook her head. This has to end. And not the way Fairclough wanted it to.

The way Annja decided.

She got to her feet. Looked back down the corridor toward the slide that had ejected her into this portion of the maze.

She smiled.

Then Annja Creed did the unpredictable for the first time since she'd been here.

FAIRCLOUGH SAW ANNJA move and sat up. What was she doing? She had nowhere to go. And yet she was on the move. Fairclough had thought he'd driven her to the brink of madness. She should have been immobilized by fear and stress—and geography—at this point.

She was heading back down the corridor. Fairclough frowned. Perhaps she was desperate to find a way out so she was going back to the slide to see if she could get out that way? He smirked. That was a dead end. The slide had been coated with an advanced Teflon polymer that made climbing it impossible. It defied friction.

Still, Fairclough watched as she made her way to the slide. She ran her hands on the surface and realized that climbing it was impossible.

But she didn't seem upset.

Instead, to Fairclough's horror, she stabbed her sword—that damned sword—into the slide and used it to pull herself up.

Fairclough's eyes ballooned and he jabbed the radio that connected him with Greene and Jonas. "Release him!"

"Are you sure?" Greene sounded hesitant.

"Dammit, just do it! Release him now!"

"Okay."

Fairclough leaned closer to the screens. If she got too much of a head start, Kessel would never reach her in time.

And that wouldn't be good at all.

"I'M GETTING TIRED of this old clown," Greene said in the corridor as he and Jonas positioned Kessel.

Jonas shrugged. "So, what do you want to do? Kill him and be done with it? We'd lose out on all his money and then we'd be back to spraying graffiti instead of making an impact."

Greene sighed. "There are lots of people out there with a ton of money they wouldn't mind spending on a couple of guys like us. Guys with a plan."

"Yeah, but would they buy into our goals?" Jonas

turned Kessel around and faced him toward a doorway. "He's ready."

Greene sighed. "You're probably right. But I don't like how he talks to us as if we don't know anything. He came to us, remember?"

"Come on, let's do this."

Greene jabbed the door release. As it slid open, Jonas reached up to the back of Kessel's head and pushed a small button attached to a transmitter at the base of his brain. As it blinked, Kessel shifted. Then he lumbered forward into the maze.

Greene chuckled. "Annja, meet Fairclough's monster."

Then he closed the door behind Kessel.

ANNJA STABBED HER SWORD into the slide again and again, slowly making her way higher up the slide. The coating on the slide was almost impossible to get purchase on, but by using her sword and bracing herself on the sides, she could eke out small distances.

She was already sweating like a pig, but who cared? She was covered in blood and gore from slaughtering the dogs. A little sweat didn't bother her any.

Beneath her, Annja heard a noise like a door opening. So, now it's begun, she thought.

But what would Fairclough throw at her? she wondered. Some creature she hadn't yet met?

She thought briefly about Kessel. Was he still out there ready to swoop in and save her? Or was he dead already?

She couldn't kid herself. With Kessel's injury the way it was, a simple knock of his head on the roof of the tunnel could have done him in. And if he'd run into Greene or any of his thugs, then the chances were greater that he was already dead than still alive.

Best not to focus on what might be. Better to focus on what she was sure of.

And Annja was sure Fairclough hadn't expected her to do this.

FAIRCLOUGH DIDN'T ACKNOWLEDGE Greene and Jonas as they reentered the control room. Greene cleared his throat. "It's done."

Fairclough nodded. "Excellent. Then all that remains is for the man to carry out his programmed orders and destroy Annja." He glanced at Jonas. "Does the transmitter work?"

"Checked it myself," said Jonas. "Light came on and started blinking. That means it's good to go."

"Excellent," Fairclough said. "In that case, let's activate his orders." He leaned forward and pressed another button on the console. Fairclough cleared his throat and spoke into the microphone. "Kill the woman known as Annja Creed. Reply if you understand your directives."

From the speakers on the wall came the disembodied sound of Kessel's voice. "I understand."

Fairclough switched off the microphone. "This is what I've been waiting for. To witness her destruction."

Greene and Jonas looked at each other. If Fairclough was happy when this was all over, then he'd be a lot more generous with their funding.

It all came down to money, thought Greene. If they had the cash, they could continue to bring peace to the environment. By destroying humanity. And he supposed that made putting up with Fairclough and his various eccentricities worth it.

But only just.

Fairclough pointed at the screen. “There he is!”

31

She heard him before she actually saw him.

On the edges of her awareness, Annja heard his lumbering shuffle into the room while she was busy climbing the slide. In the dim light, she caught the massive hulk of a man. But she was already twenty feet up and had no intention of stopping.

Instead of paying him any attention, Annja turned, pried out her sword and then stabbed it in farther up. Then she wedged her feet on the sides and maneuvered herself higher.

Which is the moment the speakers from somewhere overhead clicked on and squealed for a moment before she heard breathing through a microphone.

"You've no doubt ascertained that I would be sending something special at you before this was all over," Fairclough said.

Annja was breathing too hard to answer. The strain

of pulling herself up the slide was exhausting her faster than she'd expected it would.

"Not feeling conversational? How rude." Fairclough laughed, and it set Annja's teeth on edge. She pulled harder.

"The problem I ran into was figuring out what would work best against you. I've had plenty of time to study you, find out about you—including that magnificent sword in your possession—and try to determine your weak point, if any."

So, he'd known about the sword before she'd had to use it in the maze. Fine. Maybe her demonstrated prowess with it would make him hesitate—slip up—when she finally brought the sword against him.

"And what I came up with was interesting. You are very much your own woman. You like doing what you do, even though you're lonely."

Great, Fairclough was the embodiment of every pushy mother out there. Something she'd never had the pleasure of knowing as an orphan. "You'll be asking for grandkids next," she murmured through gritted teeth.

"Your strength is obviously your greatest asset—your reflexes are without peer—and your cunning is something to be admired, as well."

Annja yanked the sword out and then plunged it in higher up. The shearing sound of the blade cutting through metal echoed across the room.

"You are most vulnerable when your friends are at risk."

She stopped. Frowned. Well, so were a lot of people. But it was true. Annja valued her friendships. Loyalty. It drove her to do what she could for people.

But I don't see that as a weakness, she thought. Just

because other people bought and sold their loyalty like two-bit crack whores didn't mean she had to, as well.

"So, of course, I needed to find a friend I could… exploit."

Exploit? What the hell did that mean? Annja wedged herself against the sides of the slide and eked her way higher. Somewhere below her, she heard the sound of breathing. Labored breathing.

Annja peered into the shadows. What was down there? What had Fairclough done now?

Fairclough's voice continued to drone on. Clearly, Annja thought, he enjoyed the sound of it.

"…but we couldn't find someone who matched what we were looking for. After all, we had plans for them. They needed to be your equal in certain respects. Someone who would challenge you, so to speak."

A shadow below the slide shifted. And Annja saw new movement as the man down there stepped out into the dim light.

"Imagine my delight when I noticed that you were actually developing a bond with your fellow maze traveler. It was almost too much to dare hope for, and yet here it was, happening right in front of my eyes."

Annja squinted. Was that some sort of metallic glint? She frowned and cleared her throat. "Kessel?"

"Kessel," Fairclough agreed overhead. "Or rather, it was Kessel. I'm afraid we had to do a bit of work on him to ensure that he'd be more, shall we say, compliant. He was quite the stubborn candidate, but I believe we've gotten past his stalwart inhibitions."

Annja felt something brush against the slide, sending vibrations up and into her body. She tensed, holding on to the sword.

"Kessel?" she repeated.

Fairclough's laughter fairly bubbled out of the speakers. "I wouldn't expect him to respond the way he might once have. Jonas has made a few alterations to his personality."

Annja almost slipped. They'd gotten to Kessel. But how? In the dim light she saw something blinking. Red. A light? It seemed to be at the base of his skull. What the hell was that?

"And now, I think it's time for a demonstration. Kessel, can you hear me?"

Annja heard a voice answer from somewhere far below her. "I hear you."

"Annja is on the slide to your right. Destroy the slide, and when she falls to the floor, kill her."

"I hear and comply."

Annja's heartbeat raced. They'd been friends—possibly a little something more—and now, he was going to kill her.

Or Annja would have to kill him to save herself.

The dilemma was immediate and uncompromising. If she didn't kill him, he would kill her. And judging by what Fairclough had said and what Annja herself had seen, she didn't think it would be possible to reach Kessel. No way to appeal to him.

They'd turned him into a machine. One that bled, she imagined, but a machine nonetheless.

Annja felt the slide shudder as Kessel crashed into it below. If she'd been any lower, the impact might have jarred her loose.

Annja tried to figure out how much farther she'd have to travel before she found a place to rest out of Kessel's reach.

The realization hit her hard: too far. The slide curved about twenty feet farther on before leveling out. It was also stronger up there, bolted to the sides of the wall with what looked like industrial-grade screws.

But until she reached that point, the slide was a trap.

Kessel crashed into it again and the shuddering impact sent waves of vibrations up the metal and into Annja's body. She gripped her sword and pressed her feet into the sides.

It was like mountain climbing, where she'd had to brace herself by leaning out away from the rock face, instead of hugging it. Annja took a breath and grimaced. Whatever it took to hold on, she would do it.

Falling would be a death sentence for her. And she didn't want to have to kill Kessel. There might be a way to help him.

"What do you think, Annja? Is this the way you thought you would some day be killed? At the hands of someone you might have grown to love in time?"

Annja took another breath as Kessel once again slammed his body into the bottom of the slide. She tensed and then relaxed as Kessel moved away with a dull groan. Had he injured himself?

That might buy her some time. Annja turned her attention back to climbing. Twenty feet wasn't that far, was it? She pulled the sword out, plunged it in higher, then brought her feet up. It was slow progress. She gained maybe two feet as she repeated the movement.

And she had to hold on each time Kessel attacked the slide.

Annja froze. Was that the sound of metal rattling?

Crap. Something was coming apart.

She'd have to work doubly fast now. Annja watched as

Kessel bounced off the slide again and then she immediately climbed toward the next section, which wouldn't be affected by Kessel's demolishing the lower part.

Annja glanced up. Fifteen feet.

It might as well have been three miles.

But she kept climbing. And each time Kessel slammed the slide, she felt it give a little bit more. Annja glanced down at the flickering red light. Kessel was probably receiving his commands through some sort of transmitter. What would happen if Annja broke that off? Would he be free from Fairclough's influence?

Or would breaking the antenna off injure Kessel or even kill him?

"You won't escape, Annja," Fairclough repeated. "I've got contingency plans in place to accommodate your cunning."

If Annja could have flipped him the bird, she would have. But she was too busy.

Kessel's attacks on the slide increased. Fairclough must have sent him another command.

Pieces of the slide started to come away from the wall.

Ten feet.

"You're not playing nicely, Annja." Fairclough sounded vaguely annoyed. "You're forcing me to do things I don't want to do."

Good. Bring it on.

Somewhere high above her, she heard something but couldn't quite place the sound. It grew in intensity, however, and Annja realized what it was almost too late. She barely had time to duck her head as she held on for dear life.

A torrent of water crashed down on her. If she'd had

her face up, it would have dislodged her. But her instincts had saved her once again. And by keeping her head down, she was able to withstand the flood.

Kessel didn't sound so lucky. She heard him fall over and moan on the floor below her.

That would buy her some time.

Annja shook her head like a dog and then continued her climb. She had to reach the next section.

"Go faster, Kessel."

Fairclough's command had an immediate effect. Kessel got to his feet quickly and then drove himself into the slide over and over again. Annja had to cling to the slide while he did that, hoping that she could hold on.

Finally, Kessel had to take a break or risk injuring himself too much. Annja knew Fairclough wanted Kessel and Annja to square off in combat. So that meant he couldn't waste Kessel.

Annja started climbing again. She got to eight feet before she heard Fairclough's voice again.

"You're starting to try my patience, Annja."

And then Annja heard something else far above. More water? she wondered. More like the rattling of what sounded like stones.

Six feet remained between her and the second section of the slide.

Kessel crashed into the slide from below and Annja nearly lost her grip on her sword. As it was, she swung out on one side and had to swing back to get her loose hand on the sword again.

This was becoming too precarious.

The rattling suddenly grew deafening and Annja risked a glance up, before ducking her head back down as the stones rained down on her. She set her jaw and clenched her teeth as her head took the brunt of rocks and sand. The sharp, jagged edges bit into her skin. She let out a roar as the rocks rolled over her and onto Kessel far below.

"Did you enjoy that, Annja?"

Annja gritted her teeth and spat out the dust. She yanked the sword out and plunged it in higher.

And then she wedged her feet, repeating the process once more.

There.

Annja swung herself onto the next section of the slide just as Kessel tore the lower portion free from the wall.

Annja glanced down at the slide as it swung free. She leaned back and breathed a sigh of relief. If she'd been still on that, she would have fallen.

But the slide was connected to where Annja sat. And she could still feel Kessel's attacks.

I've got just the answer, she thought. And with the sword, she hacked the lower part away. It swung clear, and hurtled toward Kessel.

Annja watched it crumple as it fell.

For the moment, she was safe.

32

Fairclough's face was mere inches from the video monitors. "Where the hell did she go?"

Greene was enjoying the fact that Fairclough was growing increasingly agitated. "Maybe she fell with the wreckage of the slide."

Fairclough shook his head. "No, I would've seen her fall." He wheeled around. "How is it she was able to hang on to something? How did she not fall?"

Greene shrugged. "How would I know? You're the one that's devoted so much time to studying her. Is she capable of defying gravity with that sword of hers?"

Fairclough's eyes narrowed. "Don't mock me, Greene. You don't know anything about that accursed blade. You have no idea the horrible things she's done with it."

"You're right," Greene said. "I don't. But she's out there somewhere, because she didn't fall and Kessel wasn't able to knock her down. That means she's presumably farther up the slide than you thought. Can she get out of there if she climbs high enough?"

Fairclough was silent for a moment. "It's possible, I suppose. But she'd have to climb a long way up and it would be tough going for her. Not that she seems to have let that stop her so far."

"She is quite resilient," Greene said. "But we can get her if you tell us where to look."

Fairclough nodded. "Take Kessel up to the third level entry point. You'll find an access hatch that leads to the slide. If you hurry, you can set up an ambush that she won't see coming."

Greene peered at the monitors. "Is Kessel still where you left him?"

"Yes." Fairclough pointed. "Use the secret door in this wall here. Follow the corridor back from where you initially put him into the maze and you'll see a light. There's a door release hidden behind it."

Greene nodded. "All right. We'll get him and set up the ambush."

Fairclough listened to him leave with Jonas and sat staring at the monitors. With a sigh of disgust, he spun around in his chair and closed his eyes. This should have been a simple thing to do. She's just one woman, after all. Why is it proving so difficult to exact his revenge?

He steepled his fingers and thought things through. If Greene and Jonas got Kessel into position, then everything would work out fine. They could bring her back down to where Fairclough could watch them battle it out.

He grinned. Annja the protector of the innocent being forced to kill her new friend or die. It was marvelous.

And he knew she'd choose her own life over that of Kessel's.

Fairclough considered the idea that Annja could escape and then dismissed it. She was boxed in.

And besides, if she did find a way to elude Greene and Kessel, there was always Fairclough's mercenary. He'd been ordered to only engage her enough so that she continued to lose herself in the maze. But things were different now.

Fairclough keyed a microphone on another console. "Kozumi, can you hear me?"

After a pause Fairclough heard the man's heavily accented voice. "I am here."

"The girl has eluded my attempts to kill her."

"You should have let me do it when I had the chance."

Fairclough frowned. What was with his hired help? "Yes, well, you're now authorized to kill her if you find her wandering the maze. Understand?"

"I understand."

"I'd prefer it if you did it in front of the cameras, but if that can't be managed, then kill her and be done with it."

"Very well."

Fairclough turned off the microphone and closed his eyes again. She might be off the radar right now, but she couldn't elude him for long. And when she was found again, that would be the end of Annja Creed.

GREENE AND JONAS opened the secret door and waited. After a moment, they saw Kessel standing there, eyes unfocused. Ready to accept any order they gave him.

Greene waved. "Come with us."

Kessel shifted and then lumbered over to them.

Greene watched and was fascinated by the thing's jerky movements. And to think he used to be so quick on his feet. Now it was like watching a baby try to remember to put one foot in front of the other foot.

Incredible.

He glanced at Jonas. "You did a pretty amazing job rendering him obedient."

Jonas shrugged. "The cerebral cortex. And he was already suffering from a traumatic brain injury, so that made things a little easier."

Kessel appeared in the doorway, blocking most of the dim light behind him. Greene looked over his shoulder and saw the remnants of the lower portion of the slide. It looked as if someone had cut a part of the metal and he could also see where Annja had been stabbing her blade into the slide itself.

Greene shook his head. "Enemy or not. That's an impressive woman. I don't know many people who could climb a slide without falling."

Jonas nodded. "I wouldn't want to face her, that's for sure."

Greene patted Kessel on his arm. "With luck, we won't have to. Our big monster here will do the dirty work for us."

Jonas nodded. "Okay, monster, let's go."

Together, they all walked out.

THIRTY FEET ABOVE, Annja, crouched on the edge of the second portion of the slide, had heard every word they'd said. So Kessel was gone. And she was now free to ruin Fairclough's plans for her death.

Annja looked at the floor far below. Thirty feet was a long way to drop, she thought. Add to that the fact that the floor was littered with scrap metal. Even if she landed lightly, she'd still have to roll in order to compensate for the inertia she'd be generating.

But how could she roll safely with all of that jagged metal? She'd impale herself on the edges.

She needed another way down.

FAIRCLOUGH WATCHED as Greene and Jonas led Kessel along another corridor. The two ecoterrorists annoyed him. They were such fools.

Bah, it didn't matter. Once they had outlived their usefulness, Fairclough would have Kessel dispose of them. And barring that, Fairclough would have Kozumi kill them.

When you had money, there wasn't much you couldn't buy. And life was among the cheapest commodities on the market these days.

Greene led Kessel down another corridor while Jonas brought up the rear. Fairclough rubbed his chin. Still, the doctor was useful. When Fairclough had mentioned what he wanted to do, Jonas hadn't balked. If anything, he'd seemed excited about tinkering with someone's brain.

Perhaps he could still find a place for him. If he killed Greene in front of him, Jonas might be very willing to stay on with Fairclough and continue his work.

It might be an option, Fairclough thought. Of course, if Jonas considered running, then he'd have to be killed.

But he could cross that bridge if they came to it.

GREENE WALKED KESSEL down the corridor. "You ever wonder what drives that old coot up there?"

Jonas shrugged. "We've got our agenda and he's got

his. For right now, this meeting of the minds works. We both get to fulfill our goals."

Greene nodded. "Yeah, but what if there comes a point when we don't see eye to eye? What then?"

"We could always kill him."

Greene chewed his lip. "Before we do that, we'd need him to sign over his assets to us. That way, we could still have the funding to carry out our plans for protecting our world."

"That shouldn't be difficult," Jonas said. "After all, he is a weak old man. What could he possibly do to us?"

"I don't know. I wouldn't underestimate him, though. He didn't get to be old by being stupid. He's been living this role as an antique book dealer for years apparently and no one ever caught on. That's got to count for something, right?"

"Only if you let it," Jonas said. "My opinion. We get his cash and then dump his body somewhere. No sense keeping him around."

Greene stopped and patted Kessel. "We could even use our monster here to force him to sign."

Jonas smiled. "That's almost poetic justice."

ANNJA FELT HER GRIP slipping, but as she dangled from the bra strap, which was attached to the belt she'd pulled off, she waited until the Lycra/spandex blend stretched out to its full length. She glanced down and saw she was still more than twenty feet above the floor.

She wasn't going to get any closer. And she wasn't at all sure her makeshift rope would stay anchored to the metal she'd attached it to.

It was now or never.

Annja took a deep breath and closed her eyes. In her

mind's eye, she visualized dropping lightly to the floor below, then letting her knees and ankles absorb the force of impact as she rolled quickly, then came up to her feet unscathed. Avoiding the metal debris.

When she opened her eyes, she was finally ready.

Here goes nothing, she thought.

She let go.

Air rushed past her and then she was already crashing to the ground, sinking, squatting and rolling as she breathed out hard. A piece of metal bit into her exposed back, but she dismissed it. She could worry about pain later.

Annja got to her feet and yanked the small shard out. It hadn't gone deep, but it had drawn blood.

Annja tossed it aside. Then she walked to the wall nearby and pressed. It gave a little.

But it was locked.

Annja ran her hand over the edges until she found the small space. There. The lock.

Annja drew out her sword and stabbed it through the opening. There was the briefest resistance and then the lock popped off and the hidden door swung open.

Annja was out of the maze.

33

Greene and Jonas reached the entry point to the slide. Greene looked in and then ducked back. "So, what, we put Kessel in and let him maneuver his way down? How's that going to work?"

Jonas frowned. "If it's a stupid idea, then so be it. We didn't come up with it. Who cares?"

Greene shook his head. "We put Kessel on that slide, all he's going to do is slide down and crash into Annja. It's a waste of an asset."

"So call him."

Greene reached into his pocket and pulled out the walkie-talkie. "Fairclough, this is Greene."

"What is it?" came the terse reply.

"We're at the entry point. But you want us to put Kessel on the slide? We don't know if that's such a good idea."

"Is that what I told you to do?" Fairclough asked. "No. I told you to position Kessel by the entry point and then, when Annja managed to climb up there, he could kill her. I never said anything about putting Kessel on the slide. That wouldn't make any sense at all, now would it?"

Greene rolled his eyes at Jonas. "No. No, it wouldn't."

"I'm so glad we agree," Fairclough said. "Now leave Kessel there and come back to the control room. I have something else for you to do."

Greene switched the radio off and turned to Jonas. "I'm feeling less and less like an equal partner in this thing."

"He's certainly not treating us like equals."

"No," Greene said as he glanced at Kessel. "No, he's not. It might be time to rectify that situation."

ANNJA WORKED HER WAY down the corridor. Unlike those in the maze, this one was finished and had dim lights every few feet running along the upper part of the walls. Here and there, she could see light fixtures that she supposed concealed hidden access points to the maze.

The longer she walked, the more impressed she was with the depth and scale of Fairclough's operation. Fairclough had very obviously invested and planned this whole layout very carefully. Arrows pointed to coded room numbers and one large red arrow said *CR* in front of it, which Annja assumed meant Control Room. There were speakers and monitors at various points along the way, but in these corridors there didn't seem to be much surveillance.

He probably never expected to have an intruder in this part of the labyrinth. Annja smiled. It will be great fun surprising him, she thought.

All she had to do was keep working toward Fairclough. And the handy red arrows gave her the ability to do just that. If she could keep quiet and stay out of the way of video cameras, there was no reason to think she couldn't get to him and stop him.

Annja kept moving.

"HE'LL BE PLENTY SURPRISED when we show up with Kessel," Greene chuckled as they moved back toward the control room.

"But what's the plan?" Jonas asked. "You're just going to storm in there and demand he treat us like partners? He's too consumed right now with the idea of killing Annja. You really think he's going to be open to discussion?"

"If he's not," Greene said, "then I'll have Kessel deal with him."

"You can't kill him yet," Jonas reminded Greene. "We don't have his money. We kill him now and we'll be flat broke. I don't know about you, but I didn't like that lifestyle all that much."

Greene smiled. "I'm not going to kill him…yet. All I want is to show Fairclough that we have Kessel under our control. Not his. And if I need Kessel to lean on the old man to bring him around to our way of thinking, then I'll do it. A few broken bones shouldn't keep Fairclough from being able to adjust his will so that we benefit, you know?"

Jonas nodded. "All right."

Greene eyed him. "You're on board with this, right?"

Jonas shrugged. "Why wouldn't I be?"

"Just checking. I'd hate to lose your friendship over this. That would be a shame." He turned up the corridor.

Behind him, Jonas frowned. He didn't like the way

Greene had said that. And as they walked, Jonas pulled out a small transmitter, made a few adjustments and then put it back in his pocket.

ANNJA APPROACHED an intersection.

She slowed and squatted in the shadows nearby. Her heart was beating faster and she needed a moment to calm herself down. She was dangerously close to dehydrating. Her tongue felt thick and mossy. She'd also stopped sweating. And she had a vague sense of nausea. She needed water, and soon; otherwise, she wasn't going to be much good to anyone—let alone herself.

She glanced up and down the corridor and then spotted a small door with a graphic on it. A toilet.

A bathroom meant water.

Taking another quick glance up and down the hallway, she checked for any surveillance cameras, but saw nothing unusual. That didn't mean they weren't there. Fairclough had hidden them well in the maze.

But she had to take the chance. She needed water desperately.

And so she rose and quickly crossed the hall to the bathroom. She turned the doorknob and went inside.

WHAT WAS TAKING those two so long? Fairclough checked numerous camera angles before he finally found them down one of the hallways. With Kessel. Those idiots! He leaned closer and saw that Greene and Jonas were both engaged in an animated discussion.

Fairclough was under no illusion—these two were rabid opportunists. If they saw a chance to tilt things in their favor, they'd do it. And if that meant Fairclough was in the way, he didn't doubt that they'd take steps to eliminate him. He assumed that was why they were dragging Kessel back to the control room.

Fairclough quickly pulled up the video tape of that particular hallway and wound it back to try to understand what had triggered them to leave the ambush. Something caught his eye and he stopped the tape and hit Play. Interesting. The doctor—Jonas—pulled out a transmitter behind Greene's back and pushed several buttons on it. A code? He rewound the footage and zoomed in, watching Jonas punch the number in several times until Fairclough had committed the code to memory.

So his partners were about to make a power grab. Fairclough sighed. This wasn't going according to plan at all. And worst of all, Annja Creed wasn't even to blame for it.

But Fairclough had contingency plans in place. And after watching Greene and Jonas talk among themselves, Fairclough decided it was time to put one of those plans into motion.

He keyed a microphone again. "Kozumi-san, are you there?"

There was a brief pause, then, "I am here."

"Would you return to the control room as soon as possible? I need you here, I think."

"Is there a problem?"

"Not yet." Fairclough smiled. "But there may be one shortly. And I think it would be best if you were here to deal with it."

ANNJA RAN THE FAUCET slowly so the rush of water couldn't be heard outside the bathroom. Then she ducked her head under the stream and gulped water down until she couldn't stand it any longer. She lifted her head and swallowed a few more times.

Already, she could feel her body responding to the water. Her limbs felt more pliable. She felt less sluggish. And the nausea was gone, too.

While dehydration could take you down quickly, rehydrating also took surprisingly little time. Annja continued to swallow more water and then burped slightly as she raced to put herself back in fighting shape.

Maybe twenty minutes, she thought, to get her fluid levels back up.

And be ready for whatever Fairclough wanted to throw at her.

GREENE, JONAS AND KESSEL all trudged down the corridor. As they passed the bathroom, Jonas stopped Greene. "I need to take a leak."

Greene frowned. "You're joking, right?"

"I haven't gone in a long time. My bladder's about to burst."

Greene rolled his eyes. "Man, tie a knot in it, okay? What the hell, we've got to take this to Fairclough right now before he gets wind of what we're up to. There's no time to take a bathroom break."

"I'm not going to be comfortable," Jonas said.

"Fuck comfort," said Greene. "We're going to the control room now. Pee your pants for all I care, but we have to settle this thing."

Jonas sighed. "Fine. Whatever."

They kept moving.

ON THE OTHER SIDE of the door, her ear pressed against it, Annja waited until she couldn't hear anything else before allowing herself to exhale. She'd caught the sound of footsteps and pulled the sword out. She would have been ready if Jonas had come through the door. But knowing they had Kessel with them concerned her. She had hoped that he would be elsewhere in the maze. That way, she could take care of business and hopefully figure out how to break their control over him.

But Kessel was with them.

And that meant Annja would have to deal with him.

She took several more gulps of water. She felt as keen as a knife edge. Thank God for the water, she thought. If she'd had to go into combat without it, she wouldn't have stood a chance.

With the three men in front of her, they'd lead her straight to the control room. Annja crept out of the bathroom just in time to see Greene, Jonas and Kessel disappear around a corner.

Annja followed. Once she got to the control room, there'd be a lot of bodies to deal with. But she'd cope.

And then she could settle with Fairclough once and for all.

BEHIND HER, ANNJA NEVER noticed the shadow detach itself from the wall and follow her. It, too, was headed for the control room.

And the impending storm.

34

Annja watched as Greene led Kessel and Jonas into the control room. From her position by the corner, she could see everything clearly. Voices were somewhat subdued but she could tell that Greene was very excited in his speech and hand motions. For his part, Fairclough looked remarkably unperturbed. Annja noticed the condescension in his expression and wondered how Greene would respond to being talked to as if he was a child.

Having interacted with Greene and noticed that he had a fairly large ego, Annja guessed this wasn't going to end well. But if they were going to turn on one another, then that would make her job easier.

She settled in to wait and watch the fireworks. If there were going to be any.

"YOU REALIZE, OF COURSE, that you're going to ruin my plans if you insist on this silliness."

Greene eyed Fairclough. "The fact of the matter, Reggie, is that you've been treating us like servants. Do this, do that. We came into this with an understanding. As equals."

Fairclough's eyes narrowed. "Did you now? Is that what you thought it was? That the power share was fifty-fifty? How intriguing. You see, from my perspective, I recruited you to help me put something into motion. The power structure was fairly clear from my vantage point. I am in command of this project. Not you, not him. Not anyone."

Bastard, Greene thought. I should just kill him now. But he could feel Jonas's eyes on him, sending him a silent message. Jonas was right, of course. They needed Fairclough's money. But once they had that, then Greene was going to drill holes in the old man's head.

"Your organization was little more than a band of ruffians who threw their lot in with you because you have a certain degree of charisma," Fairclough continued. "And a violent streak that is apparently so appealing to today's youth. That's about it."

Greene frowned. "You're underestimating us. The FBI thought enough of what we'd done to put one of their guys undercover with us to take us down." He thumbed over his shoulder at Kessel. "Here's the proof."

Fairclough shrugged. "So what? So the government decided to put someone under in your little club. Big deal. Hardly worth their time, if you ask me, but then again, why should that be surprising? The government can't find its own ass without a road map, a GPS and a Congressional oversight committee. You got lucky."

Greene shook his head. "This is exactly what we're talking about. You minimize our contributions to this project and everything we've done. And frankly, I'm tired of your bullshit."

"Are you? And just what would you propose to do about it? Divorce me? Maybe force me to give you money so you can continue your charade elsewhere? Is that it?"

Greene leveled a look at the old man. "The thought had occurred to me."

"Well, it's a wonder something did, given all the other junk you've got rattling through that tiny brain of yours." Fairclough leaned back in his chair. "However, you should both know that it's not easy to get at my money. As I've aged, you see, I've known I might prove a tempting target for someone intent on stealing what I've worked hard to attain."

"Yeah, right." Greene sniffed. "Inheriting your money is such a tough struggle to go through. Please."

"Regardless of how you think I acquired my wealth, there's little chance of you ever getting it. Unless I decide you've proven yourselves worthy."

"And what the hell does that mean?"

"It means if you keep playing along with my project here, you just might be on the receiving end of some of that money. But you won't see a cent otherwise."

ANNJA WANTED TO whistle. As their voices had grown louder, she was amazed to hear everything that Greene and Fairclough had said to each other. Jonas, for his part, had remained silent. Probably trying to figure out whose team to play for. He struck her as the smarter of the two environmental extremists.

Was Greene's organization smaller than she had thought? According to Fairclough, it was just a gang with nothing else to do. And yet, some of their exploits seemed well organized.

Most likely Fairclough was ripping Greene down for his own benefit. I'd do the same thing if I was in his position, Annja thought. The only thing was, you had to be careful with that strategy. Push Greene too far and he was liable to snap.

And judging from the man's body language, he was pretty damned close to doing just that.

FAIRCLOUGH REGARDED Greene, who stood in front of him jabbering about respect and being treated as equals. Ridiculous. Fairclough had put this together. Why would he recognize Greene for something he hadn't had much of a hand in?

Fairclough glanced at the wall clock. Kozumi should have been back by now. What was keeping him? Fairclough wasn't in a position to take on three men by himself.

But with Kozumi by his side, he could rein Greene in and refocus him on the matter at hand: killing Annja Creed.

Where was he?

BEHIND ANNJA, a shadow shifted and Kozumi peered out from his hiding spot. His keen eyes zeroed in on Annja's back and then beyond her into the control room. Clearly, the old man had angered the people who supposedly worked for him. Kozumi frowned in disgust. Loyalty was an unknown concept these days. Honor, too. All anyone cared about was the power of the dollar.

True, Kozumi was a mercenary, and a highly paid

one at that. But by taking a client's money, he gave his loyalty for as long as the contract was in place.

Few could turn it on and off like Kozumi could, but that's one more thing that made him indispensable to a variety of powerful clients all over the world.

Fairclough needed him.

But the woman was in the way.

Fairclough had said she was now a viable target, so why not start with her and then work his way into the control room? Once the woman was gone, Kozumi could do as the old man wished.

Noiselessly, he rose from the shadow that had concealed him.

ANNJA SHIFTED.

She felt the air around her move—and rolled without thinking, coming to her feet, her sword out in front of her as the Asian man materialized out of the dim corridor. His katana streaked in and would have decapitated Annja with a single strike.

Except she was feeling much better after the water she'd drunk and she leaned back out of range of the strike. The Asian squinted at her as he redirected his next attack, coming in with a horizontal slash to her neck.

Annja flicked her sword up and into the blade, deflecting it, then she dropped and cut at his legs. He leaped into the air and came down some distance away.

Both of them took the second to catch their breath. The suddenness of combat had been startling. Who the hell was this guy? He moved like some of the ninja she'd once trained with in Japan. And yet, his movement was also different, and conventional enough to make her think he probably wasn't a ninja at all. Just a highly skilled fighter.

Still, something about him seemed familiar. His facial features? She couldn't quite place it.

But then there was no time to ponder it, because he came flying at her again and the fight was back on.

FAIRCLOUGH FELT A WAVE of relief as the noise erupted in the corridor. He pointed. "There, you see? There she is!" Once Kozumi was finished with Annja, Fairclough would have him take care of Greene. Enough was enough. Fairclough didn't like the young man's impudence.

Then Fairclough would ask Jonas to stay on as his new second. It was an easy choice for the doctor to make with his partner-in-crime lying dead in a pool of blood in front of him.

Fairclough smiled.

All he had to do was wait for Kozumi to kill Annja Creed.

ANNJA DUCKED as the katana flashed overhead. From the squat, she shot out one leg to kick the Asian in his left knee. Her kick connected and she heard him grunt as he reeled back and away.

Annja rose, intent on finishing this. She had no idea if Greene and Jonas were maneuvering into position behind her, but every second she kept her back to the control room, the less secure she felt.

The Asian limped backward and Annja used that to drive in, cutting down from above again and again. The force of her charge drove the man back more and more until he hit the wall. He twisted out of range as Annja's sword came down to strike him in two.

The sound of their breathing filled the air. Both of them were winded, but Annja, driven by the fury of having been caged in the maze for so long, fought harder for her survival than the Asian did for his paycheck.

And when she cut at him again, the discrepancy showed.

As he brought his katana up to ward off her attack, Annja feinted another way, cutting past his head before suddenly dropping straight down and slashing horizontally across his midsection.

For the briefest moment, she heard nothing. But then an abrupt wet gasp filled the corridor as Annja's blade cut deep into the Asian's bowels. Annja rose as he fell, his katana sliding from his grasp toward the blood-slick floor.

It was done.

"LOOKS LIKE YOUR ninja-for-hire didn't fare so well, old man," Greene said with a grin on his face. "That lady looks plenty pissed off."

Fairclough struggled to keep his composure. "Well, don't just stand there. Get Kessel into the fray. Annja will be as anxious to kill you as any one of us. But she won't want to kill Kessel, so send him out, Jonas!"

Greene nodded at Jonas. And then Fairclough watched as Jonas flicked a switch on his remote and Kessel wandered out into the corridor to meet Annja Creed.

35

Annja turned as she heard the noise behind her.

Kessel.

He came lumbering out of the control room, reaching for Annja, as if to embrace her. Except Annja knew it would be a deadly embrace. One she would never emerge from alive.

She had to think quickly. Was she going to kill Kessel? No way. But how in the world was she going to handle him when he seemed hell-bent on killing her? How could she reach him? Break through the influence Fairclough had over him?

Annja put her sword away. If it was in her hands, she might be tempted to use it. Without it, she'd have to rely on speed and agility to outwit Kessel.

Kessel's movement suddenly became a lot more fluid. And when he launched a roundhouse kick at Annja's right side, she was caught unawares. Kessel's shin slammed into Annja's rib cage and she grunted through gritted teeth as it felt like some of her ribs broke under the force of the impact.

Dammit, that hurt. Annja grabbed at her side and jumped away, forcing herself to keep breathing. That was the most important thing right now. If she seized up, she'd have no energy.

Kessel circled her like a shark, but his eyes were still vacant. He was running on remote control and Annja caught glimpses of the red light at the base of his skull.

He feinted and came down on her with a lunging punch that Annja just barely avoided. She drove an elbow into his midsection as he went past her and she heard him grunt.

His breathing seemed more labored. And his speed had slowed considerably now that Annja had managed to score a hit.

She moved around him and he mirrored her perfectly. If there had been life in his eyes, he would have seemed like a giant jungle cat. But the vacancy only made Annja hate Fairclough all the more for what he'd done.

She wanted to reach out to Kessel. She wanted to pull him in and tell him it was going to be okay. But she wasn't sure it would be. Sooner or later, she was going to have to take him down. And Annja wasn't positive how she was going to do that without hurting him. Or possibly even killing him.

He came at her again. This time with a straight kick aimed at her midsection. As Annja evaded it on the outside, Kessel suddenly dropped the leg and planted a hook into Annja's left side. If there'd been more power to it, Kessel would have broken ribs on that side for sure. But Annja twisted as the hook came in and the force was somewhat nullified.

Still, the punch hurt. And Annja drew herself back and away. If she could grapple with Kessel and get him into a hold, maybe she could rip that antenna off.

But what if it killed him?

It might just be a chance she'd have to take. The only other choice was to actually kill Kessel.

Because Annja was pretty sure he wasn't going to stop.

At least, not until Annja was dead.

"HE'S REMARKABLY AGILE for someone not under his own control," Fairclough said. "That was quite a hit."

Jonas smiled. "The technology uses the person's own skill to their advantage."

"And how did you come up with this?"

Jonas shrugged. "I had plenty of time to experiment when I was working in Southeast Asia. Lots of patients, too. All I had to do was convince them that they needed brain surgery and they were more than eager to participate."

"Remarkable." Behind him, Fairclough was eyeing a drawer across the room. Inside there, he knew he'd find a pistol with a full clip ready to fire.

Something told him he was going to need it to convince Greene that his personal plans were insignificant compared to Fairclough's.

ANNJA BACKPEDALED AWAY from Kessel as he advanced on her again. He was breathing hard and there was sweat on his brow. Annja stared into his eyes and thought she saw something there, some sort of glimmer of the man he used to be.

Did he realize he was trying to kill her? Was he trying to fight the command? Was there a way he could overcome the instructions he was being given? Could Annja interrupt the transmissions?

But just as she thought she might have a chance to get through to him, Kessel's eyes clouded and he threw a series of kicks at Annja, backing her up toward where Kozumi's body lay in a widening pool.

Annja managed not to retch at the grim stench of death. She took a breath and forced herself to accept the stink invading her nostrils.

Kessel drove in again, his feet slipping in the blood. He nearly went down. Annja jumped over him as he skidded to a stop, getting herself closer to the control room.

The answer was there, she thought. If she could get into the control room and rip that transmitter away from Jonas, she might have a chance to reach Kessel.

But Kessel got to his feet quickly, his hands now stained with Kozumi's entrails. He rushed at Annja and she was forced to duck away. Even as she did so, her ribs howled in protest and Kessel dropped an elbow on her back, slamming her into the floor.

She rolled and came to her feet, panting, trying to relieve the pain in her side. It was no use; Kessel was driving her back too hard and she was going to have a hellish time trying to reach the control room without him getting to her first.

Annja drew her sword.

FAIRCLOUGH'S EYES LIT up as he saw the appearance of Annja's blade. "This is it! This is the moment that will ruin her—the moment where she has to kill a friend to save herself." He rubbed his hands together. "Fantastic!"

Greene eyed him. "You're already celebrating? You think that's wise?"

Fairclough waved him off. "You know, I've had just about enough of you. Allow me this small pleasure. It's the very least she deserves."

Greene looked at him and then shook his head. But Fairclough was too excited to care.

ANNJA CIRCLED Kessel.

She didn't want to have to do this, but the giant man in front of her was leaving her no alternative. With each attack, Kessel was hurting her more and more. Annja would reach a point soon where she would be incapacitated by one of his strikes. And at that moment, Kessel would kill her.

I can't let that happen, she thought.

She circled him, and he watched her through squinted eyes. Was he still trying to regain control of himself?

But in the next moment, he drove in despite the presence of Annja's sword and attempted to backhand her across the jaw. If he'd connected, Annja would have gone down for the count. He was aiming at the precise spot where she'd been nailed earlier.

But as he came close, Annja used the flat of her blade to smack Kessel in the face. The force broke his nose and blood poured out.

Annja saw his vision cloud and she used the opportunity to evade another one of his kicks.

I can't keep this up, she thought. He's too strong for me. And I can't break through to him. I can't do anything.

She steeled herself for what she had to do.

What she must do.

FAIRCLOUGH RECOGNIZED the look on Annja's face. "There it is," he said quietly. "She'll do it now."

Greene stared at the monitor. "How can you be so sure?"

"I know her limits. She's been taken to them and beyond through the course of the maze. There are lines even she has to cross. Things even she has to do." Fairclough smiled. "And I've so enjoyed inflicting such pain upon her."

"Well, then, I suppose this is the proudest moment of your life?"

Fairclough looked at him. "Not even close. Once this is done, we'll all sit down and discuss my plans for the future and what your roles will be. And I can assure you, it will blow your mind."

ANNJA WAITED UNTIL she felt Kessel was committing himself to an attack. She could hear him breathing harder, trying to get more air into his lungs and his muscles for the effort it would take.

And then he came at her harder than he ever had so far. His kicks and punches rained down on her and Annja did her best to avoid each of them. She backed up, circled and dove twice out of the way. But with each attack, he grew closer to landing the decisive strike that would finish her.

Annja dove a final time and came up, her sword in front of her.

"I'm so sorry, Kessel."

And then he launched himself at her in a flying tackle meant to take Annja off her feet and slam her into the ground.

If Annja had been there.

Instead, she leaped over him as he flew at her and cut down, her blade swinging freely.

God help me, she prayed.

And God help Kessel.

IN THE CONTROL ROOM, everything went silent as they watched Annja jump into the air. Kessel's body passed underneath her.

And then Annja's sword came down like a final judgment.

And Fairclough held his breath.

ANNJA'S SWORD SLICED the antenna off the back of Kessel's skull, sending the little piece of metal skittering across the floor into the excrement and blood. She heard a faint hiss and then the red light went dark.

Kessel slumped over.

Annja ran to him and rolled him over, still on guard in case she hadn't severed the connection.

"Kessel?"

His eyes blinked and then opened. There was something there.

"Annja."

She smiled and sobbed at the same time. "I'm here. I'm so sorry I had to do it. I tried to avoid it, but—"

He grabbed her hand. "You did the right thing. Thank you."

Then his eyes closed.

And Annja Creed felt her world shatter.

36

"Bring her to me."

Fairclough's words were hushed and tinged with excitement. Greene was genuinely disturbed for the first time since he'd known Fairclough. He nodded at Jonas and, together, they left the control room.

Annja Creed sat in the blood-slick hallway, cradling Kessel's head in her lap. She wept quietly. Greene, despite himself, felt a twinge of compassion for her. He might have condoned violence to support his aims for saving the world, but even he thought that Fairclough might have taken this a bit too far.

He glanced at Jonas, who only shrugged. What could they do now?

Greene got his arms under Annja, aware that her sword was gone. At least they didn't have to contend with that right now. With Jonas's help, he got her to her feet.

She didn't fight them. She now seemed as vacant as

Kessel had been when Jonas got done tinkering with his brain. Without a word, Annja let them lead her to the control room.

Behind them, the body of Kessel lay still.

"I'M PLEASED TO SEE you again at last, Annja."

If she showed any sign of hearing him, it wasn't evident. Greene and Jonas stood on either side of her, ready to tackle her if she exploded into action. But Annja's body was slumped forward, as if someone had let the air out of a balloon and was left holding the limp rubber itself.

She was destroyed.

Fairclough swiveled his chair around. "I've been waiting for this day for a long time."

"I don't really care what you have to say," Annja said finally. "You've finished what you meant to accomplish. Congratulations."

Fairclough stopped spinning. "You think this is finished? Oh, I'm not done with you."

Annja looked up at him, her eyes bloated red. "I don't care what you do to me."

"Good," Fairclough said. "Then you won't mind if I have Jonas over there take you into the examination room and perform a similar operation on you as we did to your friend Kessel. Would you?"

Annja's answer was so flat and monotone that Greene wondered if she'd already been lobotomized. "No."

Fairclough clapped his hands. "Excellent." He gestured to Jonas. "Can you be ready to perform the operation, say, in about ten minutes?"

Jonas looked stunned. "I wasn't aware I'd be doing two operations. I'm not really outfitted for it."

Fairclough waved his hands. “I took the liberty of making sure we had enough supplies on hand. You’ll find everything you need in the examination room.”

Jonas raised his eyebrows. “Are you sure?”

Fairclough nodded. “Absolutely. I’ll have Greene bring her down in a few minutes. Once you set the proper mood and all.”

Jonas grinned. “Okay.”

Greene watched him go and then turned to Fairclough. “What would you like me to do?”

Fairclough smiled. “I’ve got quite the idea for you, Greene. I’ve been giving this a lot of thought. And I think what would work best for all of us is if you would be so good as to die.”

Fairclough raised the silenced pistol he’d stored in the control room and shot Greene twice through the head.

Annja, standing beside Greene, didn’t even wince as the two bullets smacked into his forehead and exited the back of his skull, taking a large amount of his gray matter with them.

The smell of cordite hung in the air and Fairclough blew across the smoking barrel. “Now, that’s much better. Don’t you think, Annja?”

Annja looked down at Greene’s body. The stench of death was rapidly becoming too much for her to stand. “It’s whatever you think it is.”

Fairclough laughed. “Maybe I don’t even need Jonas to perform that operation on you, do I?”

Annja stared straight ahead with a blank expression.

Fairclough frowned. This wasn’t as much fun as he’d thought it would be. He would have preferred to have a defiant Annja Creed standing before him instead of the zombie that faced him now. Still, he had at least accomplished what he'd set out to do: reduce Annja Creed to nothing.

JONAS WONDERED WHERE Greene was with Annja. He shrugged. Probably helping Fairclough with something related to the woman. No matter, Fairclough was right—there were plenty of supplies here to perform the operation.

The thought of poking around another brain actually made him almost giddy. Things had gone so well with Kessel, he couldn't wait to see if he could improve his technique when he operated on Annja.

Maybe tweak the transmitter a little to improve reaction time?

Anything was possible, Jonas thought. As long as Fairclough liked what he was getting out of the deal, Jonas saw no reason not to stay around for a while.

He just hoped Greene felt the same way.

FAIRCLOUGH WALKED OUT of the control room and eyed Kessel's body as he passed it. The transmitter had indeed been broken. He could see where the antenna lay in the coagulated blood.

Beyond Kessel was the body of Kozumi. Fairclough held up a handkerchief to his nose and winced.

"A shame she was able to kill you," said Fairclough to the corpse. "But I thank you for your service." He reached down and patted Kozumi's shoulder in a brief display of affection.

The Japanese mercenary had been loyal.

And that was considerably more than Greene had been able to muster.

Fairclough knew that was the risk one took when dealing with the younger generation.

But whatever. He had Annja Creed and he had Jonas.

And that would be enough. For now.

Fairclough rose. He'd have to make arrangements for the man's body to be shipped back to Japan, of course. It was the least he could do for the loyalty he'd shown. And he'd also send some money back to Kozumi's family. Kozumi had known the risks associated with his profession, of course, but that didn't mean his family had. A severance package was the only proper thing to do.

Fairclough made that mental note and then walked back toward the control room.

Annja still stood exactly where he'd left her. She was now his to do what he wanted.

"Annja, can you hear me?"

"Yes."

Fairclough nodded. "I want you to come with me. Do you understand? It's time you were seen by the doctor."

"All right," she said.

This was even easier than he'd expected. He wondered what sort of fun he could have once Jonas was done working on her.

"Follow me."

Fairclough walked out of the control room and Annja followed him. Down the corridor, Fairclough turned left and headed toward the medical examination room. Annja trailed a few paces behind.

Together, they exited the bloodstained corridor.

But in their wake, something stirred on the floor.

KESSEL GROGGILY LIFTED himself off the floor and stretched to his full height. Looking around at the scene, he quickly surmised what had happened.

And then with a more normal gait, he took off down the corridor after Annja and Fairclough.

Kessel, the man, had returned.

37

Fairclough led Annja down the hallway. He glanced back at her. “Are you still with me, Annja? Still feeling all melancholy?”

Annja looked through him. He didn’t matter anymore. She’d been giving him all sorts of credit throughout her ordeal in the maze—what was he up to; what was he trying to accomplish? And she realized that was wrong. Showing Fairclough respect had been more than he deserved.

So Annja stopped caring about him.

Fairclough didn’t like the fact that she didn’t answer him. He stopped and leaned closer to her. “I asked you a question.”

“Did you?”

Fairclough leaned back. “Didn’t you hear me?”

Annja shrugged. “I’m not sure if I did. What did you ask me again? I might have been thinking about something else.”

"I asked if you were still melancholy." Fairclough's eyes narrowed as he repeated himself.

Annja took a breath and blew it out. "I'm not really sure. What I do know is that you don't matter all that much to me any longer."

"And what the hell is that supposed to mean?" Fairclough's face reddened. "I'm in control of this situation."

"Okay," said Annja. "You're in control. Congratulations. I don't really care, however."

"You ought to care," said Fairclough. "I've been hunting you for years now."

Annja shrugged. "Well, I probably did something that hurt you a lot. And for that, I'm sorry. But it doesn't mean I don't deserve whatever it is you're about to do."

"You…what?" Fairclough grabbed her by the neck. "What the hell is the matter with you, woman?"

"I told you," said Annja. "I don't much care about what happens to me anymore."

"That's the most ridiculous thing I've ever heard."

"Is it?"

Fairclough nodded. "You ought to be cowering in fear of what I'm about to do to you. The payback I'm about to collect for what you did to my family. It's a horrible ending for you, Annja. And you ought to be scared."

"I've seen lots of things in my life. But I learned that by fearing them, I've actually been empowering them. I don't know if I'm going to do that again. Evil is going to be evil no matter what I do, so why give it any extra power or respect? That doesn't make sense."

"But you will respect me!" Fairclough yelled.

Annja only shook her head. "I don't know that I will. I'm sorry, but I think I've already given you more respect than you deserve."

"You've given me nothing of what you owe me, Annja Creed." Fairclough was almost spitting now as his face continued to grow more red. "You killed my brother and ruined the only family I had."

"I killed your brother?"

"Yes."

Annja considered this. She'd killed many people since the sword had come into her life. And to think, she once thought that having the sword would help her protect people. But she'd spilled more blood than she'd saved lives.

Annja bowed her head. "I'm sorry for your loss. Truly, I am. I realize that I can't bring him back, but I feel bad that you suffered that loss by my hand."

Fairclough was silent for a moment. "Where is your sword now?"

Annja shrugged. "Where it goes when I don't have it out."

"Can you get it?"

Annja paused and then nodded. "Of course."

"In that case, I want you to give it to me."

Annja looked at him. "I don't think so."

Fairclough frowned. "If you were genuinely sorry, then you'd be willing to part with it."

Annja shook her head. "It's not that I don't want to. It's just that I don't think it's possible for me to give the sword to someone else. I tried earlier, in your maze. As soon as I handed it to Kessel, the sword vanished."

"Did you really want to be rid of it then?"

Annja considered that. "Well, no, I guess not. I thought I might need it to fight my way out of your maze."

"And what about now?" Fairclough's voice was quiet. "Do you still want it so badly?"

"I don't want it at all," Annja said. "I've given my life to the service of it and it failed to protect a person I cared about. So what's the use any longer?"

"Perhaps it would be better if you did let it go. You might even get your life back, eh?"

She nodded.

"Then do it, Annja. If you truly no longer want it, give it to me now. You'd like that, wouldn't you?"

"Yes, I would."

"Then give me your sword."

BEHIND THEM FARTHER down the corridor, Kessel crouched near the wall. He'd overheard the conversation and his mind was racing. What had happened to him? And why was Annja just letting herself be led around by Fairclough like this?

He'd already seen the two bodies near the control room. Greene was dead—that was good news—and the Asian man had been disemboweled, presumably by Annja's sword.

The last thing Kessel could remember was Jonas standing behind him when he'd been strapped into the dentist's chair.

And then he winced as the memories of the agony came flooding back. My God, the pain!

Kessel's heart started pounding and he had to take several deep breaths to calm himself. There'd be time to sort out Jonas for what he'd done.

But right now, he had to help Annja.

She didn't seem to understand what Fairclough was

asking her to do. Hand over her sword? It wouldn't work, right?

And what if it did? What if she was actually able to give it to Fairclough? That would make the old man virtually indestructible. There'd be no telling what sort of evil he could spread.

Kessel got to his feet.

He had to stop Annja from giving it to him.

"If you give me your sword, I promise that I will forgive you, Annja Creed," Fairclough said. "I'll forgive you for killing my brother and destroying my family."

Annja looked up at him. "You will?"

Fairclough nodded. "You have my word of honor on it. Despite what you may think of me, I am a man of honor. And if I give you my word, then you don't need to question it."

Annja bowed her head.

She saw the sword in the otherwhere.

And reached out for it.

Kessel stumbled on. His legs still seemed to be awkward, as if he'd forgotten how to move. It was a bizarre feeling to look at the hallway ahead of him and know he needed to walk down it—he could see himself doing it—but then his body just didn't respond as well as it used to.

That damned doctor had done something to him that had fouled him up and good. Kessel cursed. Maybe the effects were only temporary. Maybe with each step his body and brain were learning how to work together again.

Maybe.

Kessel refused to let it slow him down. He pushed off from the wall and kept himself moving forward.

He had to help Annja.

ANNJA HELD THE SWORD in her hands and it glowed in the corridor. She could see the desire in Fairclough's eyes as it lit up his face. He wanted the blade.

Badly.

"It's incredible," he breathed. "Is it heavy?"

Annja shrugged. "It weighs about what you'd expect. But I don't find it so tiring to swing it around."

"Amazing. And it's really the sword that once belonged to Joan of Arc?"

"From what we've been able to figure out, yes," she said. "She was obviously an incredible warrior. Far better than I'll ever be."

Fairclough shook his head. "Don't belittle yourself, Annja. It's unbecoming for someone with your skill. There's humility and then there's just foolishness. You are every bit the warrior she was. In some respects, I'd imagine you are far superior to her."

"It doesn't matter any longer. I'm done fighting. I'm tired. And I don't feel like I've made a difference. Look at what I did to you. If I hadn't killed your brother, would you even have done any of this? No. So, because of my actions against your brother, I'm directly responsible for the deaths of a lot of innocent people." She paused. "I can't live with that anymore."

Fairclough took a breath. "Then are you ready to give up the sword, Annja? Are you truly ready?"

"Yes," Annja said. "I am."

"Then do it."

As Kessel watched in disbelief, Annja held her sword up and then closed her eyes. For a brief second, there was nothing, and then she lowered the sword in front of her face, turned it around and handed it over hilt first to Fairclough.

As he wrapped his hands around it, a sharp crackle of electricity punctured the hallway. Kessel winced, expecting the sword to vanish as it had when Annja had tried to give it to him.

Except the sword didn't disappear.

Fairclough stood in the hallway holding Annja's blade.

My God, Kessel thought, she's done it.

Annja Creed had given away her sword.

38

Fairclough stood still, not even daring to draw a breath. His eyes gleamed with excitement and his hands would have shaken if not for the fact that he now held the sword of Annja Creed.

He still couldn't believe it. He hadn't expected it to be so easy to convince her to part with it. And then so easy to get the sword.

The blade gleamed as he held it in front of his face. The gray glow that had illuminated part of the hallway seemed brighter now and less gray. Fairclough found that interesting. Perhaps it really was time for Annja to separate herself from it. Perhaps the gray glow meant that her energy with the sword was waning.

And now that it had a new owner, things were already different.

Amazing.

Annja stood there watching him intently. But there was no regret on her face. None whatsoever. If anything, she looked relieved. After a moment, she asked him quietly, "Are you happy now?"

Fairclough nodded. "I am." He looked at her. "And I meant what I said. I have forgiven you, Annja."

"Thank you."

"No," said Fairclough. "Thank *you.* You don't know how long I've waited for this moment. And there were times I didn't dare dream that it might even be possible. I'm quite amazed that I stand before you now holding your very sword."

"But you do."

"Yes," he said. "I do. And I won't ever part with it. Unlike you, I will cherish this gift that is now part of me."

Annja nodded. "Use it in good spirit and conscience. It deserves to be used well."

Fairclough glared at her. "Are you telling me how to use what is mine?"

"I'm telling you the sword is yours and I hope that it's put to good use. That's all."

"Of course you are." He smiled. "Let's go."

"Where?"

Fairclough grinned. "To the doctor's office, of course. He's expecting us."

"I thought you told me you'd forgive me if I gave you the sword." Annja's brow furrowed. "But you're still going to make him do that…thing?"

Fairclough shushed her. "Don't be upset, my dear. I did forgive you. But that doesn't mean your crimes are excused. It means you've admitted your guilt and culpability in the murders that you committed. And I can't let those go unpunished."

Fairclough laughed long and loud, a shrill nasal

sound that echoed off the walls of the hallway and made the man behind them wince.

IT WAS DONE.

Kessel had frozen in place when he realized that Fairclough now had Annja's sword. How was Kessel going to rescue Annja now? He stood no chance against that sword, not in his present condition.

Fairclough would cut him down without any effort at all.

How could she do it? He wanted to scream at her that she shouldn't give it to him, but his voice failed him and what should have been a shout came out as a croak instead.

It was as if he hadn't said anything at all.

And look at the result, he thought with a frown. Fairclough had control of the sword and was still going to kill Annja.

Enraged, Kessel had to take several breaths to calm himself down. Like all warriors, Kessel knew that rage had very limited uses. Too much emotion meant that he would lose control and be at the mercy of his opponents.

But rage tempered to acute anger could be a useful tool. And so Kessel began a series of biofeedback exercises he'd learned on the Teams.

And when he was ready, Kessel moved again.

FAIRCLOUGH LED ANNJA toward the examination room. Outside the door, he let her go in first. The bright white luminescent interior showed that Jonas had settled in well. He'd moved the chair into position and was dressed in scrubs with a mask over his face.

He looked up as they entered. "Where's Greene?"

"Fairclough shot him," Annja said.

"What?"

"It gets worse. He's got my sword now."

Fairclough stepped out from behind Annja and held the sword aloft. "What do you think, Jonas? Rather a compelling picture, isn't it? And no offense, Annja, but I rather think the sword looks better in my hands than it ever did in yours."

"How could you kill Greene?" Jonas asked. "We had an agreement. We were supposed to be partners!"

Fairclough kept staring at the sword. "You know, Doctor, Greene really ought to have been more careful about voicing his concerns. He knew I had this place wired for video and sound and yet he felt safe to talk about betraying me. I know you both had that conversation."

Jonas backed up. "I never agreed. I only went along because Greene was mentally unstable."

Annja sniffed. "And you're a beacon of rational thought, huh?"

Jonas ignored her. "Seriously, Fairclough, I never intended to stab you in the back. I even made some adjustments to Kessel in case Greene got carried away and suspected me of not backing him."

Fairclough smiled. "And that is why you are still alive, my good doctor. I saw the adjustments you made to Kessel. Not that it helped all that much, since Annja still killed him. But I appreciate your professed loyalty."

"Well, it's just that you'd been good to us—what with the money and resources and stuff like that."

Fairclough's smile grew. "It's nice to be appreciated."

"I'm still ready to play for your team."

"I know," Fairclough said. "Which is why I need you

to go ahead and carry out your brain control on Annja here. And I need it done immediately."

Jonas nodded. "All right, I'll get an IV line into her so I can anesthetize her and get started."

"No anesthesia," Fairclough said.

Jonas looked at him. "Are you kidding? The pain almost killed the big FBI agent. Surely it will hurt her that much more."

"And that would be tragic." Fairclough eyed Annja. "But she gets no anesthesia. I want her awake and able to feel every twinge of pain and agony as you destroy her brain and turn her into my slave."

KESSEL HAD DRAWN almost level to the medical examination room. He felt slightly woozy and he figured that was from the extreme duress his body had been under for the past day or so, not to mention the cerebral edema and then Jonas poking around in his skull. That'd be enough to put anyone else on a slab, he thought with a grin.

But not him.

Kessel pushed off the wall next to him and moved closer to the doorway. He saw Jonas readying things as Fairclough forced Annja into the chair.

The chair.

The same chair Kessel had sat in right before Jonas had turned him into a zombie.

Kessel felt the pull of the rage he'd kept controlled. Giving in would be so easy, but the result would be undisciplined chaos. He needed focused vengeance.

And for Annja's sake, Kessel had to make sure he didn't put her in more danger or make a bad situation even worse.

But when he got his hands on Jonas, all bets were off the table.

JONAS STRAPPED ANNJA into the chair, tightening the wrist straps as much as he could without cutting off her circulation. He glanced at her. "Sorry I have to tie these so tight, but I'm afraid the pain is going to make you want to tear your arms off. And I can't afford to have you do that, or else I might accidentally turn you into a vegetable."

Annja eyed him. "Yeah, that would be the last thing we'd want to happen, wouldn't it?"

Jonas shrugged. "This isn't my fault. I'm just doing as ordered."

Annja almost laughed. "I love people who use that defense. You know, the crazy thing about life is that you can always stop what you're doing and choose to take a stand for what's right. It's not rocket science. The problem is, people are lazy and it's easier not to care. It's easier not to rock the boat or risk conflict."

Jonas frowned. "Hey, you gave up your sword. What does that say about you and your so-called fight for the powers of good?"

Annja ignored him. "The problem with being lazy is that, sooner or later, if you've never stood up for anyone else, when evil comes knocking on your door, no one will be there to have your back." She smiled. "And you'll get squashed."

Jonas backed away. "Lady, I only want to stay alive."

"What sort of life is it when you spend it hiding in fear and insecurity? Better to be dead having taken a stand for what's right than laid down for evil."

"Hypocrisy."

Jonas looked at Fairclough, who was still admiring the sword in his hands. "She's ready."

Fairclough seemed almost not to hear him, but then he nodded. "In that case, begin."

KESSEL TOOK THREE deep breaths, then pushed off from the wall opposite the examination room entrance and launched himself through the doorway.

Jonas saw him first and his eyes went wide as Kessel barreled into him. Together they crashed back into a tray of surgical implements, knocking it over and spilling the tools everywhere.

Jonas screamed as Kessel came up astride his chest and rained down half a dozen punches on the doctor. "You did this to me," Kessel said through gritted teeth. "And now I aim to repay you for your service."

Jonas brought his hands up to ward off the attacks, but Kessel was too strong and too committed. He saw one of the scalpels out of the corner of his eye, lying on the floor.

With one hand holding Jonas down, Kessel reached for it.

Then he brought it up over Jonas's right eyeball. "I'm going to cut you into very, very small pieces now, Doctor."

Jonas shrieked and waved his head from side to side. Kessel punched him in the jaw and Jonas stopped moving, dazed as he was from the blow. Kessel leaned over him.

And brought the scalpel down toward the soft, gelatinous eyeball.

"Stop!"

Kessel jerked around.

Fairclough held the sword—Annja's sword—high over Annja's head.

Kessel froze.

Fairclough nodded. “That’s right. Just stop moving. You even blink and I’ll chop her head right off.”

Kessel waited.

“Throw the scalpel away.”

Kessel eyed the surgical tool and then tossed it across the room. “There.”

Fairclough smiled. “See? That wasn’t so difficult. There’s no reason we can’t all get along with one another.”

Kessel shook his head. “I’m going to kill you. Right after I finish dealing with Dr. Jekyll here.”

Fairclough frowned. “You’ll do no such thing. If you even move, I’ll kill the woman.”

“Do it,” Annja said, speaking for the first time. “You’re better off just killing me now and getting it over with.”

Fairclough looked at her for a moment. “You know what? I think you just might be right, Annja.”

Then he leaned back, raised the sword even higher and brought it screaming down at Annja’s head.

39

For a moment, the sword seemed suspended in space. Kessel watched in horror as it then shot down faster than he'd ever seen anything move. And there was nothing he could do to stop it.

One final image burned itself into his memory as he watched. It was the image of Annja, looking…serene.

And then all hell broke loose.

The sword exploded in light and then vanished, leaving Annja completely unharmed.

Fairclough's reaction was immediate. He started screaming and howling. His sword was gone.

Kessel almost missed the act of Jonas grabbing another scalpel and driving it toward his head. But his instincts saved him and, as the scalpel came up, Kessel twisted, evading the strike.

He leaned down and drove an elbow into Jonas's sternum, down and into his heart. Kessel heard the pop as the xyphoid process bone shattered and then punctured the wall of the heart.

Jonas jerked once and a small bubble of blood popped out of his mouth and dribbled down the side of his face. Kessel leaned back and then grabbed Jonas's head and jerked it to the side. The neck vertebrae shattered.

"Just to be sure," he said quietly.

He climbed off Jonas and looked at Annja, who was still sitting very calmly in the chair. "Took you long enough to get here," she said.

Kessel almost did a double take. "You knew I was alive?"

Annja raised her hands to draw his attention to her predicament. "I could tell you were still breathing. But it was shallow. I have to admit I was concerned that maybe I'd made a mistake."

Kessel looked around.

"Fairclough's gone. I think he's probably going to be running for some time to come." She looked down at the cuffs holding her to the chair. "You mind getting me out of here?"

Kessel fidgeted with the cuffs until they came loose. Annja stepped out of the chair and hugged him close. "Thank you. For coming for me."

Kessel looked at her. "As if you wouldn't have done the same thing for me. Hell, you *did* do the same thing for me. You saved my life."

"I might have killed you."

Kessel nodded. "But you didn't. You had faith. You tried to make sure I still had a shot at living. And you gave me that second chance I needed."

Annja smiled. "So, we're even now? No debts? No bizarre obligations that I'll have to collect on or give up?"

Kessel nodded. "We're cool."

Annja looked over his shoulder at Jonas's corpse lying on the ground. "Imagine if he'd used his skill for good."

Kessel shook his head. "Guys like that can't even fathom being good. That's why I might have gone a little overboard with him."

"I don't think anyone would call it unjustified given what you went through."

Kessel took a deep breath. "Yeah, well, I just wanted to make sure there was no way he could rise from the dead, you know?"

"Unlike you."

"Resurrection's a bitch. What can I say?"

Annja turned and walked across the room. "We should leave. I don't think we can do anymore down here, and frankly, I'd like to see the sun."

Kessel held up a hand. "Hang on a second."

Annja stopped. "What is it?"

"How come you gave him the sword? I mean, earlier you tried to give it to me and it didn't work. So how come you gave it to him freely like that? You looked shattered. I really thought you were gone."

"The fact that I couldn't give you the sword earlier in the maze was actually what helped me defeat Fairclough. I had to do something so completely unexpected in order to have any hope of getting out of this place."

"Sorry," Kessel said, "might be the knock on my head or that I'm more tired than I've been in a very long time. But I don't follow your line of reasoning."

Annja leaned against the counter. "This maze, every aspect of it, was set up—designed—to take advantage of our actions and our human nature. Fairclough knew that if we were faced with certain obstacles and challenges, we'd respond predictably. He was able to dictate every step we took. And as our frustration mounted, we would be depressed, tired and on the verge of giving up."

"Yeah, I was pretty devastated."

"Exactly," Annja said. "And that's what he wanted. Not so much you, but he wanted to break me. Only then would he be able to get what he really wanted."

"You."

Annja rolled her right shoulder to loosen it. "I was prize B. What Fairclough really wanted was the sword."

"How do you know?"

"I wasn't sure until I offered it to him. Or rather, I let him lead the conversation where the offer could come up."

"You manipulated him, in other words."

"It was the only way I could turn the tables on him. Starting back in the maze, I had to do something that went against everything Fairclough had set up. I had to do something that none of his research could have predicted. So I climbed the slide, that impossible Teflon-coated slide that was like defying gravity. Fairclough never expected that—he never thought someone would even attempt it, so that was his weak point."

"And you exploited that."

"Yes."

"But then—"

"When I had to fight you, I could see that you'd been altered. I didn't know how, just that you weren't under your own control. A red light kept blinking at the base of your skull, so I knew there had to be something to that."

"Big risk," he pointed out.

"Huge," Annja agreed. "But it was the only thing I had to go on. And like you said, I needed a lot of faith."

"Okay, so you took me down and severed the connection. Weren't you scared you'd hurt me?"

"Terrified. But as soon as I could feel you breathing, I knew you were still alive, albeit unconscious. In that moment, I had another opportunity to turn things on Fairclough."

"So you pretended to give up."

"Yes."

"And then when things really fell apart, you offered the sword to Fairclough."

Annja smiled. "Of course, he told me some sob story about me killing his brother, but I don't know if that's accurate or not. What I think is that Fairclough heard about me and started tracking me down. The rumor that some mystical sword existed is enough that people would want to get their hands on it any way they could."

Kessel gestured around them. "But to go to these lengths? You really think this was for the sword?"

"Honestly, I want to say yes," Annja said. "But who can really tell?"

"Fairclough could."

Annja smiled. "I don't think he'll stop running for a while," she repeated. "Especially now that he doesn't have the sword anymore."

"Speaking of which," Kessel said, "I'd love to know how you pulled that one off. That was some trick if ever I saw one."

Annja shook her head. "It wasn't a trick. Fairclough really did have the sword in his possession."

"You're kidding."

"Nope." Annja sighed. "When I was unable to give

it to you earlier on, I had to wonder why I hadn't been successful. I couldn't really figure it out, but then Fairclough of all people clarified things for me."

"He did?"

"Believe it or not," Annja said. "He told me that the reason I hadn't been successful in giving it to you was because deep down I still knew I needed it. There was still evil to battle here in the maze. And I couldn't do it without the sword."

"But you still had to battle Fairclough," Kessel said. "So how could you give it up right then and there?"

"Because," Annja said patiently. "I knew at that point that I had something even more powerful than the sword to defeat Fairclough."

"And what was that?"

"Faith."

"Faith." Kessel shook his head. "That's going pretty damned far on such a little thing."

"Is it?" Annja stretched her hands overhead, enjoying the pull on her muscles. "I think you're right. Faith is such a little thing that most people take it for granted in their daily lives. They get to it when they get to it. Marginalized."

Kessel eyed her. "You turning religious on me now, Annja?"

"My point is this. Since most people marginalize their faith—in God, the universe, Mother Nature—they are never really prepared to have it tested. And when those tests come, most people fail them."

"You've never had a crisis of faith, then? I find that hard to believe," he said.

Annja laughed. "My entire life has been a crisis of faith. From the time I was a little girl, I've always wanted to know what the deal was with all the bullshit in my life. Why me? What did I do to warrant all this? Was I an evil person in a former life and this is my punishment? What?"

"So what did you do?"

She shrugged. "I never stopped believing in the power of good."

"That's it?"

"There you go again. Don't minimize it. Because if anything, it's bigger than everything we know."

"It certainly was this time."

"Every time," Annja said. "No matter how down we might get, no matter how depressed or overwhelmed we feel, if we simply accept that the universe is a balance, then we know that it will correct itself. And if we can help it correct itself, then we owe it to the universe to do just that."

"You're an amazing woman," Kessel said.

"No, I'm really not. I'm just trying to figure out life. Sometimes I feel like I might have an idea what it's all about, but then something else happens and it ruins all my theories."

"Then why bother trying to understand it?"

"Because that's what I'm supposed to be doing. That's what my purpose in this life is."

"Not to battle evil? I think some might disagree with you on that one."

"Battling evil comes with the territory. You can't quest for the purpose of life without encountering evil attempting to manipulate things to its own end. Anyone questing for answers will always run into evil. It's unavoidable."

"Which explains why so few people ever do search for the truth."

"Exactly. I've just been lucky enough to find some answers along the way."

Kessel grabbed her in his arms. "I like to think that maybe I've been pretty lucky this time out."

Annja kissed him. "You think?"

"I do."

Kessel was just about to kiss her again when the walls of the examination room started to shake and crumple and a series of explosions went off.

Annja pulled away from Kessel. "It's caving in—we've got to get out of here!"

40

They ran up the corridor beyond the examination room. Green arrows pointed the way and Annja was relieved that Fairclough had at least had the good sense to show people how to exit.

Kessel was moving slowly, however—the result of his body still not firing on all cylinders. Annja yanked him along through the corridors and implored him to move faster.

"Come on, we've got to get the hell out!"

Kessel frowned and kept moving himself forward, but his nerve impulses didn't seem to be reaching his brain or else his brain wasn't passing the command down to his legs. Either way, he was slowing things down. "Go without me or you'll never make it, Annja."

She shook her head. "Don't be an idiot. I'm not leaving you behind. We just have to get back up to the outside before Fairclough seals us in this giant tomb."

Kessel nodded and they kept moving.

As they ran, the walls shuddered when more explosions went off. Clouds of dust and debris choked the air and they had to cover their faces with their clothing to breathe properly.

But even still, Annja and Kessel were both choking and coughing as they tripped along the corridor.

"He must have planted explosives," Kessel shouted over the din of more crumbling walls.

"How do you know?"

Kessel's face was grim. "I'm pretty well acquainted with how explosives work, Annja. And these are set charges to bring this place down."

"How much time do we have?"

"Probably not enough."

They reached a stairwell and Annja pushed through the door to get to the stairs. In here, the air was less dusty and they could take a breath again.

Annja looked up and groaned.

Kessel frowned as he followed her gaze. "About how many flights of stairs would you say that looks like?"

"More than I feel like climbing," she replied. "But we either climb them or we die down here."

"I really admire how succinctly you put everything." Kessel mounted the stairs and Annja followed him. "Let's go."

They started climbing, and with each stair, they could hear more explosions echoing off the walls. Behind them, the stairwell started filling with flames and smoke.

Kessel pointed skyward. "If we can't get up there fast, we'll die of smoke inhalation."

Annja squeezed his hand. "We're not quitting!"

Annja's lungs burned and her legs felt like lead. Kessel seemed to be dragging and she was forced to pull him along. He moved slowly and she saw that his head injury had started to bleed, as well.

They had to reach the surface!

At one point, Annja tripped and fell forward, bruising her knee on the tread in front of her. She grunted and then Kessel was there, helping her to her feet.

"Now we're both hobbled," he said with a sooty grin. "Come on—let's get out of here."

Together they made it through the first few flights, but even as they approached the halfway point, Annja knew that it was a long shot. After all of this, to come so far and be so close…

She pictured the sword to see if it was in the otherwhere. She hadn't even had a chance to check to see if it was back.

But it was. And its glow was much less gray than it had been before. Annja smiled. It was almost like seeing an old friend come back to town.

She felt a new rush of adrenaline flood her bloodstream. She raced ahead.

At the next landing, he pulled her to a stop. "My legs are shot. I'm slowing you down."

"I'm not stopping. You can either get your ass in gear or else I can carry you."

Kessel looked at her. "Carry me?"

She leaned over and got Kessel onto her shoulders in a fireman's carry. "You owe me big for this one, Navy SEAL." And then she started back up the stairs, powering her legs to keep churning despite the weight of Kessel's body.

They cleared another two flights before Kessel prodded her. "Put me down, I can walk it from here."

"You sure?"

"No, but I'm not going to put you out any more."

Annja set him down. "Don't make me have to do that again. We go together or not at all. And frankly, I still need to have a few words with our host."

Kessel nodded. As they reached the next flight, they heard a shriek of metal and the lower portion of the staircase came away from the wall, and fell back into the flames licking their way up from the bottom.

Kessel needed no further encouragement and grabbed Annja. "Come on, let's hurry!"

Annja's lungs were on fire. As the smoke drifted skyward, it raced past them, and clouded the entire stairwell.

"I can't see!" she called.

Kessel forced her to stoop over so they could try to stay under the smoke. But since the smoke was creeping up from below them, they couldn't get low enough. Annja was coughing. Kessel hacked and spat out a foul-colored mucus.

They reached the second-last flight of stairs. Kessel pumped Annja's hand. "We're almost there. Almost home free!"

But she had fallen back against the stairway wall, nearly passed out.

In the next moment she felt herself being lifted and carried up more steps. Was Kessel carrying her toward the open air? She couldn't think anymore. She couldn't breathe.

She focused on the sword. In her mind's eye, she was using the sword to cut through the smoke ahead of Kessel. As the smoke threatened to cut off their path,

Annja swiped at it and cleared it away so Kessel could rush through.

She felt Kessel trip or fall forward and then there was a split second of uncertainty. Were they still trapped in the stairwell? Were they outside? Or had they fallen right back down the stairs into the flames that threatened to burn them alive.

When a cool breeze blew across her face, Annja opened her eyes and saw that Kessel had cleared the staircase and they were indeed outside.

It was dark.

Night?

Annja had no idea what time it might be. She rolled onto her back and gasped the fresh air. Kessel lay next to her, heaving and hacking his lungs free of the smoke.

"Annja."

She took another breath and coughed. "Yes."

"We did it."

Annja allowed herself a smile. "Thanks to you."

"And you." Kessel retched twice before he wiped his mouth and crawled over to Annja. For the longest time, they just lay there and held each other.

DAWN BROKE OVER Fairclough's property. A delicate red-orange sky spilled along the line of oaks that stretched toward the horizon and the Berkshire Mountains in the distance.

Annja shivered in the fall early-morning air and turned over. She blanched. She stunk to high heavens like smoke and about a dozen other nasty things.

You need a shower.

Maybe a dozen.

Kessel lay nearby, breathing deeply and resting quietly. Annja crawled over to him and nudged him awake. "How are you feeling?"

"Like someone used the inside of my mouth and lungs to line a camel tent," he said. "But I'm alive."

"We're both alive," she replied. "And we've got each other to thank for that." She punched him on the arm. "So, thanks."

"I get a punch on the arm for saving your life?" Kessel shrugged. "Something's wrong when you don't even get a kiss from the princess you save from the dragon. Sheesh."

"Tell you what, Mr. Charming, when you get a shower and a shave, I'll get you that kiss."

"Sounds like a fair trade." Kessel rolled over and got to his feet.

Annja watched him as he moved. And there seemed to be something more certain about his steps. "How are you feeling today?"

Kessel looked at her. "You know, actually pretty good. I think my legs are coming back online. Would have been nice if they'd been working better when I was fleeing that massive inferno, but you know, I'll take what I can get."

"Speaking of which." Annja rose and walked back toward the stairwell entryway, a small shed that looked like something you'd normally find on any large property.

But when she reached out to touch the door handle, she jerked her hand back. "Hot."

"The whole place has probably melted," Kessel said. "No sense going back down there, anyway."

"I'm surprised there isn't a fire department on scene,"

Annja said. "You'd think someone would have noticed this fire."

Kessel shook his head. "Not at night. And it was all underground. About the only thing that would have been visible would be the smoke, and since the darkness would have concealed that, no one might even know this happened."

"Except for us."

"Us," he agreed.

"So what happens now?"

Kessel shrugged. "I go call the FBI and get them out here pronto. And then once I turn this over to them, I'm going to get a room and a shower somewhere close by. Apparently, I stink to high heaven."

"You do indeed," she said. "You think there's any chance the Bureau will comp me a room at that same hotel where you're planning on getting a room?"

"I'm not sure. Their standards are pretty high and whatnot. I don't know if the bean counters will cough up another room. Budget cuts and all that jazz."

Annja eyed him. "So what you're saying is if I want a shower, I'll have to suck it up and share a room with some hulking behemoth?"

"It's a distinct possibility," Kessel said. "I mean, I hate telling you that, but it's probably the reality of the situation."

"I think you're using your power to influence the outcome of this situation."

"Are you claiming I'm abusing my position?"

Annja smiled. "Well, you're not abusing any position

just yet. But if you clean up real good, you might just a chance to try out a few of them."

Kessel grinned. "You know, that's about the best thing I've heard in a really long time."

Epilogue

The hot water running over her body felt like someone was slowly dragging the finest silks of Persia over her skin. As Annja soaped, rinsed and relathered, she could scarcely believe that a few hours earlier she'd been trapped in that hellish prison underground.

Now, in this bed-and-breakfast in western Massachusetts, Annja was finally halfway to feeling human again. She and Kessel had flipped for the shower and Kessel had won. He'd gone first and shaved the rest of his hair off his scalp. It wasn't normally a look Annja thought she'd go for, but seeing his gleaming dome under the fresh bandages later when he'd dressed, she had to admit he looked good.

Damned good. Amazing, really, considering everything he'd been through.

It had taken the FBI several hours to mobilize forces from the Boston, Worcester and even the Albany offices. By the time they arrived, the day was half-gone and Annja and Kessel were nearly starving to death.

The FBI had immediately gotten Kessel medical attention and he'd been patched up on-site by a mobile medical facility that they normally only rolled out in times of mass casualty incidents. When he'd emerged from the medical truck, Kessel already looked about a hundred percent better than he had earlier. Still far from perfect, but the onsite doctor hadn't insisted on Kessel going to a hospital.

The question now was whether he was going to be able to go back to work with the Bureau or not. The doctors would still need time to determine if he had any lasting effects from the brain surgery he'd undergone. And then there were some concerns about his mental state, as well, given that he'd been subjected to such trauma.

Kessel had characteristically written off the PTSD concerns. "You know, I went on some really bad missions in Afghanistan. On one of them, we lost half the team. We got hunted and shot at for days while we waited for choppers to scream in and grab us. And after all of that, they subjected us to these interviews with the psychologist. You know what? The shrink scored higher as mentally troubled than we did."

After his shower, Kessel had even felt rejuvenated enough to go find a place for them to eat. "Town like this has got to have a cute little bistro where we can enjoy a good bottle of wine and a meal together."

Annja had relished being alone in the shower, feeling the spray of hot water and the joy of perfumed soaps. It went a long way toward helping her accept what she'd been subjected to in the maze.

She rinsed a final time and then grabbed the fluffy terry-cloth towel hanging on the rack, wrapped it around herself and then stepped out onto the thick bathroom rug. The bed-and-breakfast wasn't large, but it was luxurious. And all of it paid for by the Bureau. Kessel's handler had given him his credit card and told him to go wild.

Annja thought that was the least they could do for Kessel after everything he'd endured throughout the course of his two-year assignment.

There was no way to recover the bodies left behind in the maze, however. Short of excavating the entire facility, they would have to stay where they were. Most likely, they'd been incinerated, anyway. As one of the agents said, with the heat as strong as it was, everything would have melted and fell in on itself.

Annja shrugged. No longer her concern.

Her more immediate concern was what to wear tonight to dinner. She'd asked the B and B owner if she had an outfit she might borrow to change into after her shower. Annja planned to go shopping in town for something of her own to wear. To her surprise, the owner had outfitted Annja with a cashmere turtleneck in heather gray, a pair of black slacks and a pair of black heels.

Simple, but elegant.

Annja slid into the new bra and panties that one of the female FBI agents had gotten for her. They weren't her usual style, but the white lace looked good on her. And while Annja wasn't a huge fan of boy shorts, she had to admit they were comfortable enough.

As soon as she pulled on the rest of her clothes, she checked herself over in the mirror.

"Not bad, Creed," she said quietly. And the chances were high Kessel would feel the same way.

It was virtually guaranteed, she thought. Kessel would love the outfit.

Annja sat on the bed and allowed her eyes to close for a moment. Just to lay there without any concerns whatsoever, it was heavenly.

But she had to be ready. Annja groaned and rolled off the bed. She wondered if maybe Kessel could be convinced to have dinner here instead. And then afterward, they could pass out and sleep for about a hundred years.

Yes, that would work.

In the bathroom, Annja switched on the blow dryer. As she blew her hair dry, the heat relaxed her even more.

Was that the door?

She switched off the dryer. "Kessel?"

No answer.

Annja frowned. And turned toward the door. A man stood there pointing a pistol at her. Even with a wig on, Annja could tell it was Fairclough.

"You don't know when to quit, do you?"

Fairclough eyed her. "You betrayed me."

"And when did I ever swear loyalty to you? Never. So I can't really have betrayed you, Fairclough. I let you think you were calling all the shots. Just like you'd been doing the entire time I was trapped in that damned maze of yours."

Fairclough shook his head. "I should have killed you when I had the chance."

"But you didn't. And look what that mistake cost you. Pretty much everything, near as I can figure it."

"Shut up!" Fairclough pulled the hammer back on

the pistol. "Look at you standing there. As if you don't have a care in the world."

"Well, actually, I don't. Except maybe for the fact that there's a gun pointed at my chest."

"And I intend to use it," Fairclough said. "To kill you for what you've done to me and my family."

Annja shook her head. "You know, I've been meaning to ask you about that. Want to know what I think? That we never did meet before. That you never really were around me or that I ever killed your brother. I think you were after the sword the entire time. That maybe you heard about the sword and decided that it might just be the key to giving you incredible power or granting you immortality or something like that. Do you really believe that if you kill me you can finally wield the sword?"

For a moment, Fairclough didn't say anything. Then he smiled. "Well, perhaps you'll never find out what the truth is, Annja. Because it will be too late when you're dead."

Behind Fairclough the door opened and Kessel walked in. Immediately realizing what was happening, he dove and tackled Fairclough.

"Kessel, no!" she yelled. "Your head!"

The pistol dropped to the floor. Annja went for it, but Fairclough kicked it away from her. Kessel got him on the ground and then drove three punches into the old man's face, shattering his nose.

But Fairclough wasn't done. He pulled out a knife and slashed it across Kessel's belly, drawing blood. Kessel fell off him, clutching at his stomach.

And then Fairclough dove for the pistol. His hand

wrapped around it and he came up, already aiming at Kessel's head.

"Fairclough!"

He turned and was immediately flung backward by the sword Annja had thrown at him. It plunged into Fairclough's chest and pinned him to the opposite wall.

Annja stood there heaving as Fairclough looked down at the blade jutting out of his chest and died.

"You wanted the sword so badly," Annja said. "Now you've got it."

Kessel got to his feet.

Annja rushed over. "Are you all right?"

Kessel nodded. "Cut wasn't deep, but it hurts."

"I meant your head."

He just smiled and shrugged, then looked around. "I think we're going to need a new room, huh?"

THE MANSION WAS palatial by even the most demanding standards. Indeed, had its owner been forthcoming and open, monarchs and presidents might have enjoyed the hospitality within it. But the mansion was more like a secluded fortress.

Roux paced the floor expectantly. His phone hadn't rung in more than twenty-four hours and the person who should have been calling him had failed to miss his most recent check-in time.

His butler entered the drawing room, passing by the elaborate jewel-encrusted artifacts that Roux had spent much of his elongated existence collecting and hoarding. "Sir?"

Roux turned. He liked the irony of a Frenchman keeping an English butler. "What is it?"

"A telephone call, sir."

"From Fairclough?"

"I'm afraid not, sir. Will you take it in here or outside?"

Roux frowned. "In here." He walked to the massive oak desk in one corner near the fireplace and sat in the well-worn leather chair. He leaned back and waited. The phone buzzed quietly and he picked it up.

"Yes?"

"It's Garin."

Roux's frown deepened. "And what the devil do you want?"

"I just thought you'd be interested in a little information that I came across."

"And what's that?"

"Seems like there was a rather massive fire at an underground facility in Massachusetts yesterday. Some sort of maze that imploded on itself. But that's not the most unusual thing. Want to know what is?"

Roux gripped the receiver tighter. "Yes."

"Seems the man who owned it—man by the name of Fairclough—turned up dead yesterday afternoon at a small bed-and-breakfast a few miles away from this inferno. Can you imagine? I mean, what are the chances of that happening?"

"I don't follow you, Garin. If you've got a point to make, I wish you would do so. I'm quite busy here."

"Busy waiting for a phone call that you're never going to get," Garin said. "Imagine how Annja would feel if she knew about your connection to Fairclough? I think she'd be upset, don't you?"

"She need never know about it," Roux snapped.

"You still want it, don't you?"

Roux said nothing.

"After all this time, you still want that sword," Garin continued. "Even though it's hers, you want it. And this man Fairclough was supposed to find a way to get it for you, wasn't he?'

Roux could feel his anger rising. "You really shouldn't make accusations you can't prove."

"You're right," Garin said. "I can't prove it. But I don't really need to, either. Do I? Because a few words in Annja's ear will be all it takes for her to figure out exactly who was behind this. I don't imagine she'll be all that thrilled with you once she hears of it."

Roux smirked. "You're not intimidating me, Garin. You have skeletons of your own. And plenty I could quid-pro-quo you with. So, while I appreciate you calling to gloat over your assumptions, I really must bid you adieu."

"Before you do," Garin cut in. "Just don't forget what I've said. Bye now."

The phone went dead in Roux's hand. Sitting in his chair, he turned and stared out the window that overlooked his grounds.

And for a long time, he just sat there.

Planning.

* * * * *

The Don Pendleton's Executioner®
NUCLEAR STORM

Ecoterrorists plan a deadly strike.

An ecoterrorist group in Yellowstone National Park has a plan to save the planet. The group has set in motion a plot to kill millions in seconds and leave the rest of the human race on the verge of extinction. Nothing and no one will throw them off course—but Mack Bolan isn't your average outdoorsman.

Available February wherever books are sold.

www.readgoldeagle.blogspot.com

GEX399

TAKE 'EM FREE

2 action-packed novels plus a mystery bonus

NO RISK

NO OBLIGATION TO BUY

SPECIAL LIMITED-TIME OFFER

Mail to: The Reader Service

IN U.S.A.: P.O. Box 1867, Buffalo, NY 14240-1867

IN CANADA: P.O. Box 609, Fort Erie, Ontario L2A 5X3

YEAH! Rush me 2 FREE Gold Eagle® novels and my FREE mystery bonus (bonus is worth about $5). If I don't cancel, I will receive 6 hot-off-the-press novels every other month. Bill me at the low price of just $31.94 for each shipment.* That's a savings of at least 24% off the combined cover prices and there is NO extra charge for shipping and handling! There is no minimum number of books I must buy. I can always cancel at any time simply by returning a shipment at your cost or by returning any shipping statement marked "cancel." Even if I never buy another book, the 2 free books and mystery bonus are mine to keep forever.

166/366 ADN FEJF

Name (PLEASE PRINT)

Address Apt. #

City State/Prov. Zip/Postal Code

Signature (if under 18, parent or guardian must sign)

Not valid to current subscribers of Gold Eagle books.

Want to try two free books from another series?

Call 1-800-873-8635 or visit www.ReaderService.com.

* Terms and prices subject to change without notice. Prices do not include applicable taxes. Sales tax applicable in N.Y. Canadian residents will be charged applicable taxes. Offer not valid in Quebec. This offer is limited to one order per household. All orders subject to credit approval. Credit or debit balances in a customer's account(s) may be offset by any other outstanding balance owed by or to the customer. Please allow 4 to 6 weeks for delivery. Offer available while quantities last.

Your Privacy—The Reader Service is committed to protecting your privacy. Our Privacy Policy is available online at www.ReaderService.com or upon request from the Reader Service.

We make a portion of our mailing list available to reputable third parties that offer products we believe may interest you. If you prefer that we not exchange your name with third parties, or if you wish to clarify or modify your communication preferences, please visit us at www.ReaderService.com/consumerschoice or write to us at Reader Service Preference Service, P.O. Box 9062, Buffalo, NY 14269. Include your complete name and address.

GE11B

Don Pendleton's Mack Bolan®

Decision Point

Stolen technology puts a ticking time bomb in terrorist hands.

The Liberation Tigers of Tamil Eelam are on the move again. The death of a uniquely positioned software engineer tips to something big in the works. Mack Bolan follows the crime trail to Singapore where the Tigers and their calculating leader give Bolan a fight for his life.

Available March wherever books are sold.

Or order your copy now by sending your name, address, zip or postal code, along with a check or money order (please do not send cash) for $6.99 for each book ordered ($7.99 in Canada), plus 75¢ postage and handling ($1.00 in Canada), payable to Gold Eagle Books, to:

In the U.S.
Gold Eagle Books
3010 Walden Avenue
P.O. Box 9077
Buffalo, NY 14269-9077

In Canada
Gold Eagle Books
P.O. Box 636
Fort Erie, Ontario
L2A 5X3

Please specify book title with your order.
Canadian residents add applicable federal and provincial taxes.

www.readgoldeagle.blogspot.com

GSB148